THE HEALER'S SECRET

HELEN PRYKE

ALSO BY HELEN PRYKE

Suspense
The Lost Girls (Maggie Turner Book #1)
Right Beside You (Maggie Turner Book #2)

ॐ

Historical Fiction

Walls of Silence

ॐ

Children's Books

(under the pen name Julia E. Clements)

Dreamland (also available as audiobook)
Unicorns, Mermaids, and Magical Tales
Adventure in Malasorte Castle
The Last of the Guardians (a short story)
Autumn Sky (a short story)

For my mum, who always encouraged me to write.
No longer with us but never forgotten.

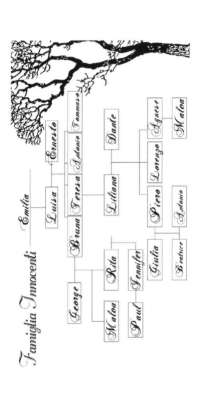

Famiglia Innocenti

Emilia

Luisa — Ernesto

George — Bruna — Teresa — Antonio — Tommaso

Matea
Paul — Rita
Jennifer

Liliana — Dante

Giulia — Piero — Lorenzo — Agnese

Beatrice — Antonio — Matea

TUSCANY, APRIL 1349

The world was dark and still, the birds and insects asleep, resting in the final moments before dawn, when they would fill the air once more with their chaotic sounds and incessant movement. Agnes slipped quietly out of the cottage, taking care not to wake the rest of the household.

She made her way down through the garden, the dew on the grass soaking her thin slippers, sending cold chills up her feet. She pulled her cape tighter, and opened the gate to the fenced-off piece of ground that was her own private space. Stepping inside, she breathed in the rich aroma of freshly dug earth. She'd planted the last herbs the day before, and now her garden was complete.

When Agnes had proudly shown it to her husband, she'd enjoyed seeing the look of amazement on his face as he'd gazed upon the work she'd done. From the beginning, he'd insisted she get the gardeners to do everything, telling her it wasn't work for a noble woman. She'd let them plant the hedge and the large fruit trees, but she hadn't trusted anyone else with her precious herbs.

'What on earth?' he'd cried out as an insect flew near them, its wings vibrating with a low hum.

'It's only a dragonfly,' she'd replied, laughing. 'It's full of them here. Look.'

He'd stared in wonder as he saw the insects on every plant and bush, their brightly coloured bodies shining like jewels in the sun.

'I'm going to call this place the Dragonfly Grove. What do you think?' Agnes had chewed her nail as she waited for his answer, needing his benediction.

'I think it's perfect,' he'd replied, putting an arm around her.

She'd looked down at the baby in her arms, held in a sling across her body so that she was free to move. 'Now she's sleeping,' she said softly. 'Not like last night.'

'She's got a right pair of lungs, hasn't she?' Riccardo had grumbled, rubbing a hand across his face. 'Thank goodness we don't live up at the main house, my parents would have thrown us out.'

Agnes smiled at the memory, glad her daughter had passed a quieter night and they'd all managed to get some sleep. She moved quickly through the garden, having no need of light as she walked among the plants and picked the ingredients she required. She murmured an apology each time before she removed the leaves, caressing the plant before going on to the next one.

Back at the cottage, Agnes stirred up the ashes in the grate so she could start boiling the leaves. Young Matteo's wound was serious, and she needed to prepare the herbs for his poultice. They had brought the boy to her a few days earlier, a deep cut in his leg. She'd cleaned it and stitched him up while he told her how the scythe he'd been using had slipped out of his grip and embedded itself in his flesh, so deeply that he'd thought for a moment they'd have to amputate his leg. She'd laughed and reassured him that as long as she was looking after him, there'd be no need for that.

The leaves simmering gently in a pot, she went down the corridor to the pantry. She lit a candle and held it in front of her, proud of what she had achieved in so little time – the shelves were full of earthenware jars and glass bottles containing chopped, dried herbs, ready-made salves, and every type of lotion she might need for every ailment she could think of.

I'll have to write down the recipes, she suddenly thought. *So I don't forget them, so I can make notes of what works and what doesn't, the right amounts…*

She was rudely awakened from her thoughts by a loud banging at the back door. She grabbed the candle and hurried to the kitchen. One of the servants had already opened the door to their visitor, an old man with a worried look on his weathered face. He jumped as she entered the room, startled.

The knocking woke up everyone else. Riccardo was in his usual place at the kitchen table, while Olivia the scullery maid sat on a wooden stool beside the fireplace, yawning widely as she tossed sticks onto the fire. A couple of other servants stood in the corridor, nudging each other and whispering. Agnes remained standing, waiting for the old man in front of them to speak. She heard her daughter's faint wails coming from upstairs, and hoped he would tell them whatever he had to say before she started bawling.

He cleared his throat, twisting his cap nervously in his hands. She recognised him as one of the gardeners; Giacomo, if she remembered rightly.

'Please, tell us why you've come,' she said gently.

'It's, ahem… well, Matteo.' He stopped.

'Yes?' She tried to keep calm, knowing that any sign of impatience would make him clam up immediately.

'He-he… oh, to hell with it!' The old man looked mortified at his slip of the tongue in front of the lady of the house. 'He died this morning, just half an hour ago, ma'am.'

She clasped her hands to her chest and swayed as her legs threatened to give way. 'No,' she whispered. 'No, it's not possible.'

Riccardo reached her in two strides and took hold of her outstretched hands, clasping them in his. 'These hands can heal, Agnes, but they can't do miracles,' he told her, understanding her turmoil. 'You can't defeat death.'

She squeezed her eyes shut, tears escaping from beneath her lashes. She fell against his chest, sobbing uncontrollably, scenes of death and destruction flashing before her, the sickly stench of rotting carcasses filling her senses. She was vaguely aware of her daughter's cries in the distance, but all she could hear were her husband's words echoing around her head: *You can't defeat death, Agnes, you can't defeat death.*

JENNIFER

1

Hurtling through the sky towards Italy, England's grey shores far behind me, I wondered how on earth I'd got myself into this situation. Wedged between two other passengers, I thought for the thousandth time about how pathetic my life was. The well-built man to my right was fast asleep, snoring softly with his head against the window, his enormous beard and wild, matted hair blocking my view. The woman on the other side had taken a book out of her handbag as soon as she'd sat down and buried her nose in it straight away, making it patently obvious that any conversation was out of the question.

I reclined my seat, pretending not to hear the muted comment from the annoyed person behind me, and tried to ignore the ever-increasing pressure on my bladder. I glanced over at my neighbour, and instantly cast aside any idea of attempting to push my way past her in the two-inch gap between her knees and the seat in front, imagining her librarian-style tutting and fierce stare. My own book was in the overhead locker; I hadn't been as prepared as Antisocial Bookworm.

Bearded Guy's snoring grew louder, competing with the rumble of the plane's engines. I desperately wished I had some earplugs or the nerve to dig him in the side with my elbow. I glanced at my phone and saw there was at least another half hour to go. The usual irritation started to build up in me, so I concentrated on my breathing to calm down. Closing my eyes, I focused on each breath, in, out, in, out, until the moment passed and I was in control once more.

Mum had managed to convince me that this break in Italy was exactly what I needed. After losing my husband and my job, and all the other problems I'd been through, we'd talked for hours before coming up with a solution. I frowned, remembering that fateful day only a month and a half earlier.

We were sitting in the kitchen. Mum had her hands clasped together, twisting her fingers together as if unsure how to begin. 'I've had an idea, Jen. It's a bit drastic, but it might work.' I raised my eyebrows. 'You remember Grandma Luisa?'

'Of course.' I had heard all about Grandma Luisa, my maternal great-grandmother, while I was growing up. Her countryside cottage was nestled in the mountains of Gallicano, Tuscany. Mum had visited her when she was little, and often told me how much she'd loved picking the fresh vegetables for their lunch, or helping her work in the garden. Grandma Luisa lived off the land; she grew the food she needed and kept a few chickens and goats for eggs, milk and meat. Mum said it had been fun staying there for a short holiday in the summer, but she'd often wondered how Luisa coped in the winter without any central heating and only an outdoor toilet. It seemed I was about to find out.

'Well, after she died a couple of years ago, I inherited her cottage.'

'Really? You never told me.' I felt irritated at being left out yet again.

'I did, but you probably don't remember.'

'Harsh,' I muttered.

'Anyway, after the funeral I got a call from the lawyer's office about the reading of the will. She only had the cottage and the land, but apparently she wanted to leave it to me and not the rest of the family. I asked them to send me some photos. It's a bit more run-down now, and it needs some work, but in my opinion, it's liveable. What do you think?'

'I-I don't understand. You want me to go to Italy?'

'Why not? You'd be away from everything, a complete break, just you and the countryside. It could be what you need.'

'Why not? Maybe because I wouldn't have a clue how to get there, where to buy food or how to get on with the locals. And it doesn't even have a bathroom.' I could feel the panic building in me.

'It's been revamped since I went there, it's probably got an indoor bathroom by now,' Mum said calmly.

'But you're not certain,' I grumbled. She ignored me.

'You already speak Italian. Granted it's a bit rusty, but you'll soon pick it up again. We can print out some maps so you know how to get there, and see where the nearest shops are. And anyway, there are some aunts, uncles and cousins who live in the village, they'll help you. I think it will be character-building.'

'Character-building my–' I slammed my fist on the table and stood up. 'I'm not going, and that's final. What the hell am I going to do in Italy, in a place I've never been before, surrounded by people I don't even know? What good is that going to do me?' I leaned on the table, panting heavily, my throat sore from the yelling. I was overwhelmed by the emotions running through me, fear making me tremble.

'Sit down.' Mum's tone was cold, and I knew I was making her angry. I was past caring. I remained where I was, glaring defiantly at her.

'I'm not going to force you, neither am I going to shout at you. I haven't got the energy anymore for that. You've lost your job, your husband's given up on you, and the drink's taken what little dignity you had left.' I opened my mouth to reply but she interrupted me. 'Do you really think you can sort your life out here? With all this temptation everywhere? I think you've proved already that you can't.' She took a deep breath. 'As I see it, you've got two choices. You can use this opportunity to turn your life around, with something new to focus on that might take your mind off your problems. Or you can wait until something catastrophic happens and I have to pick up the pieces. Again. Except maybe this time there won't be anything left to pick up, you'll have gone too far.'

'Oh, stop being a drama queen,' I yelled. 'You always think the worst, you never trust me to do the right thing. You want me to go to Italy just so you can get rid of me. Don't you? You can't cope anymore, so now I have to go.' I stopped when I saw the look on her face.

'You stupid girl.' There were two red blotches on her cheeks, and her voice shook with emotion. I looked at her then, and saw how tired she was. Her eyes had new creases at the corners, and her hair had streaks of grey. Shocked more by her appearance than her words, I remained silent. 'You think I enjoy worrying about you? Wondering if you're going to come home or whether I'll get a phone call from the police. Of course I don't want to send you away. I want to keep you here, so I can look after you and make sure you're all right. But I can't do that, can I? I can't keep you a prisoner in this house, and every time you go out, you're one step away from destroying yourself. Think about it, Jen. Go to Italy, where you'll be far from everything that reminds you of the past. It could be a clean start. Time to think, grieve, and then find the strength to carry on. Who knows, maybe you won't want to come back.'

I laughed bitterly. 'Yeah right, I can see myself wanting to spend the rest of my life in a run-down cottage that's full of damp and mould, and *probably* having to go out in the garden in the middle of the night if I need to pee. Does the toilet even flush? Do you remember if it flushes?' I sat down heavily, my legs suddenly wobbly as I realised the enormity of the decision I had to make.

Mum laughed. 'Yes, it flushes. Stop being so dramatic, Jen. Try it. If you hate it, you can come back home again whenever you want. If you like it, stay as long as you like. There's no time limit. I put some money away for you after your dad died, now's probably the right time to use it.'

'But what if I relapse?'

'You won't. You're going to get through this, Jen, and Great-grandmother Luisa's cottage is the place to do it. My mum said there was magic there, and even though she left when she was twenty-one to marry your granddad and come to England, she always felt its pull. That's why she taught me to speak Italian, and she encouraged me to do the same with you. She told me so many stories of that cottage, stories that you'd laugh at today, but I always believed them, and I still do. When I went back there a couple of years ago, I felt... something. I can't explain what it is, but it seems to me it's centred around the cottage. Go, see if you can feel it too or if it's only your old mother's imagination.'

'All right, I'll go, to keep you happy. But I might be back sooner than you think,' I warned.

'I'll be waiting.' Mum smiled.

'Magic, humph,' I muttered.

Snoring Bearded Guy gave a sudden loud snort that jolted me out of my memories and brought me back to the present. He gave a little shrug and settled back to sleep, unperturbed. I wriggled in my seat, trying to get some feeling back in my legs, and thought anxiously about what awaited me. After much anguish, soul-searching, and more than a few tantrums, I'd agreed that Mum had come up with the best solution and that a holiday in Italy was exactly what I needed. I'd brushed up on my Italian so that I'd be able to say more than '*ciao*', and Mum and I had checked out the area on the internet, printed out detailed maps, and planned my journey meticulously. Back in England I'd felt ready for the great adventure ahead of me. Now, I wasn't so sure.

2

As the plane came in to land at the Pisa Galileo Galilei International airport, I was feeling even less sure of myself. I had to get a taxi from the airport to Gallicano, a journey of about forty-five miles, and wasn't looking forward to being stuck in a car with a talkative Italian who probably reeked of garlic.

I sauntered out of the air-conditioned airport into the bright May sunshine of Tuscany, a far cry from the rainy, wind-swept UK I'd left behind. I took off my heavy coat and rested it on top of my suitcases, then stood still, soaking up the Italian atmosphere. A car horn suddenly blasted behind me, making me jump. I turned and saw a taxi driver leaning out of the window.

'You need taxi?' he called, pointing at himself. 'I take you!'

Suitcases safely stored in the boot, I got into the back of the taxi and settled myself down for the long journey. As I'd feared, the driver was determined to talk, but at least he didn't stink of garlic.

'*Parlo italiano*,' I told him, hoping that I'd be able to under-stand him.

'No, no, I want speak English, I speak all time with tourists, my English good, no?'

I grimaced and gave in gracefully. Mum had told me that Italians were very friendly people, but never took no for an answer. 'Yes, it's very good. So how long have you been driving a taxi then?'

As we drove along the busy roads, he kept up a constant stream of chatter. It helped distract me from the industrial landscape I could see outside of factories, warehouses, and scrap metal yards with the crumpled, rusting carcasses of once-mighty machines. Huge white gashes scarred the mountainsides from all the quarrying for marble, ruining the panorama. It was depressingly disappointing, after everything I'd heard about Tuscany and seen from Mum's photos.

'In my thirty years as *tassista*, I must have took, hmm, let's see now, maybe thousands of passengers.' He suddenly beeped the horn and let forth a stream of angry words in Italian as someone pulled out in front of him. Making himself comfortable again, he continued. 'I like tourists, they nice people, much better than these damn Italians.' He turned and grinned at me. I nodded back, wishing he'd keep his eyes on the road.

'Sometimes I take famous people.' He paused, obviously waiting for a comment from me.

'Really?' I faked enthusiasm. 'Like who?'

'You know Berlusconi? He was the Italian prime minister.'

'*Berlusconi?*' I asked incredulously. 'He's been in this taxi?'

'Well, not exactly Berlusconi, but his brother, who is also very famous here in Italy. We had long talk, very interesting. Of course, this was before the scandals.' He shook his head and gave that typical Italian shrug of disappointment. 'Otherwise, imagine what I could have found out!'

'Yes, what a pity,' I remarked. 'Is the Tuscan countryside like this everywhere? I thought it would be prettier, somehow.'

He glanced out of his window. 'Here is industrial area, where they make marble. Soon we arrive to the proper mountains, you will like them a lot.' He leaned over and opened the glove compartment. The car wobbled slightly, and I tightened my grip on the armrest, praying to all the gods that we would arrive at the cottage unscathed.

He took out a piece of wood and passed it back to me over his shoulder. I saw it had a painting on it of a mountain scene in winter, with a small house in the background and an elderly man walking towards it.

'That's pretty,' I said. It was; it had been painted by a talented artist, each flake of snow painstakingly dabbed on to create an incredibly realistic effect.

'I painted it,' the driver said, with a hint of pride in his voice.

'*You* did this?'

'Yes, I am also painter, when I get the time. I started when I was young, and still like to do it when I can. This one I did last winter. It is good, no?'

'It's very good.' I was amused at his lack of modesty, but had to admit that he was right, he was a talented artist. I leaned forward and tapped the piece of wood on his shoulder. 'Here.'

'No, no, is for you.'

'For me? No, I can't accept this,' I replied, panicking that he was about to fleece me for the painting.

'No, please, I like to give it to you. I often give my paintings to the passengers. Only the nice ones, of course.' He looked in the rear-view mirror at me and winked.

'I can't accept this, I haven't got much money, only enough for the journey,' I blurted.

He looked hurt. 'I no want your money, is a gift.'

'Oh.' I'd offended him. 'I-I'm sorry, I didn't mean to–'

'Is okay,' he interrupted. 'My wife tell me I am too good, but I don't care, I like to be nice to people, make them happy. I hope, with these gifts, to make their day better.'

I felt worse than ever. I coughed to hide my embarrassment. 'Well, if you insist, I'd love to have it. I'm sorry if I upset you.'

'Everything is good, we friends as before.'

I turned it over in my hands. There was a name and date on the back. 'Umberto Bini. Is that you?'

'The one and only.'

'Tell me how you started painting.' I made myself more comfortable and looked out of the window at the changing scenery as he told me his life story. The industrial valley gave way to the first big mountains, and I finally started to relax and enjoy the view. The Tuscan countryside was stunningly beautiful in spring, with the deep greens of the tree-covered slopes contrasting vividly with brilliant blue sky and white clouds. There were tiny villages nestled on the slopes, half-hidden by the thick vegetation around them. Every now and then I saw a church perched right on the top of a rocky spur, a mind-blowing feat of gravity-defying skill. Even more so when I considered it had probably been built hundreds of years earlier.

Umberto commented on the towns we passed and places of interest I might like to visit as we drove along the winding roads through the mountains.

'Close to Gallicano there is the Grotta del Vento. Large caves, very exciting to see. The locals used them as a fridge to store their food until only few decades ago. You should visit, is definitely worth a look.'

'Okay, thanks, I will. How far is it now?' Adrenalin flooded through me at the thought of what I'd find once I got there.

'Oh, about five minutes. Few more curves, then we go through the town, the house is on other side, by itself.'

'You know my grandmother's cottage?'

'No, I look on GPS, it tell me. See?' He indicated the screen in the middle of the dashboard, with the arrival flag already visible.

The closer we got, the happier I felt. I'd made it. I'd travelled all the way from England to the heart of Tuscany, and managed to arrive in the middle of nowhere. I couldn't wait to let Mum know.

We passed through a picturesque town full of traditional houses and more modern apartment buildings, then followed a small country lane up a steep slope. After a few minutes, the taxi stopped in front of a pair of huge white gates. The setting sun shone through the metal bars, casting their elongated shadows across the gravel. There was no sign of the cottage, or any people.

'This must be it. The GPS says we are arrived.' Umberto turned and smiled at me. 'Remember your painting.'

Staring mutely at the imposing entrance, I held the picture up to show him I still had it, then slowly got out of the car, my legs aching at having been still for so long.

After taking his business card and saying a brief goodbye, I stood in front of the gates, my luggage on the ground beside me. I lifted my hand to wave but he was already gone, leaving behind a cloud of dust. I sighed and turned back to the gates. A curved gravel driveway overgrown with weeds led, I presumed, up to the cottage, which was hidden from view by a thick clump of trees.

The lock was rusty and it took me several attempts to unlock the gates. After a few pushes on the handle, the right one swung open, squeaking as it scraped over the gravel. I collected my luggage, took a few steps inside, then put everything down to lock it again.

'I see Grandma Luisa didn't believe in automatic gates,' I grumbled. The travelling was catching up with me, and I was exhausted. My earlier adrenalin rush had given way to sudden lethargy. I couldn't wait to get inside the house and relax. As I lugged my bags around the curve in the driveway, the cottage came into view.

'What the–?' I said, dismayed. The stone exterior of the cottage was covered in ivy, and thick, wild bushes grew right up to the walls. Most of the shutters were open, hanging half off their hinges. The windows were grimy and one had a hole in it, as if someone had thrown a brick through it. I slowly walked up to the door. As I touched the handle, the door swung open with a long creak. *This is the moment I should run*, I told myself. *There's probably an axe murderer waiting inside for you, Jen, so run!*

Instead I took a deep breath and entered the cottage. And wished I hadn't. My lungs filled with a rancid, musty smell that literally took my breath away. I ran outside, coughing furiously. I grabbed Umberto's business card from my pocket, tempted to phone him and ask him to come and take me back to the airport. I could get the next flight to the UK and be home by the morning. Then I thought of Mum having to start worrying about me once more, and how I would hurt her for the umpteenth time. Deep down, I knew she was right. If I returned to England, I'd set out on a path of self-destruction, and I wasn't sure if I would get through it this time. Scared as I was, I had to face this head-on, prove to myself that I could do it.

Pulling up my T-shirt, I covered my mouth and went back indoors. I dumped my bags inside the door and looked around, briefly taking in the kitchen and living room, then I spotted the stairs. I was too tired to think about cooking or cleaning. I grabbed my overnight bag, leaving the rest of the luggage where it was, and stumbled upstairs, thinking only of finding a bed and going to sleep. Everything else could wait until the morning.

I almost sobbed with relief when I opened the first door and found a bathroom. Mum had been right, at least I wouldn't have to use an outside loo. There were three bedrooms, and I chose the smallest one for myself – not out of respect for my great-grandmother, but because it seemed to be the least dusty. I took some clean sheets out of my bag and made up the bed. Then I sent a quick message to Mum to let her know I'd arrived safely, before finally collapsing into oblivion.

3

When I awoke early the next morning, I couldn't remember where I was for a moment. Then it all came flooding back to me as I looked down and saw my footprints clearly visible in the dust on the floor. Thoughts flew through my mind as I fought the urge to start scrubbing right away, and I clenched my fists tightly, willing myself to ignore the grime everywhere. There were more important things to be done first.

I got out of bed, gingerly standing on tiptoes while I dressed, trying to keep my feet inside the slightly cleaner footprints until I managed to get my shoes on. Finally ready, I took a deep breath and went out on to the landing.

I walked from room to room, opening the windows, the fresh mountain breeze blowing through the cottage and removing some of the musty smell. The sun was strong enough to penetrate the dirt-smeared windows; it streamed into the cottage, chasing away the shadows, making it seem a bit more welcoming. I checked out the upstairs rooms again since I'd had only a cursory look the night before. There were two decent-sized rooms with double beds, and the smaller one I'd slept in, with a single bed. Apart from everything needing a thorough clean, the rooms seemed in good condition, with only a few damp patches on the walls. The bathroom was small but functional, with a bath/shower, toilet, sink and bidet, although the flowery tiles were a bit overpowering. I'd discovered the previous night there was running water and I couldn't wait to unpack my bags, grab some clean clothes and a towel, and jump in the shower.

I was curious to see what the rest of the cottage was like. The stairs led directly down to the living room, with a sofa and a couple of comfortable armchairs in front of a fireplace, a tall sideboard with an old-fashioned TV on top of it, and a bookcase full of books. I made a mental note to have a look through it later. It was a dark room, full of dark furniture, the only light filtering through the glass panel in the top half of the back door. I imagined it in the winter, with the fireplace lit, a family sitting in front of it in the warm, cosy atmosphere.

The kitchen was on the opposite side of the room. In modern terms it would be called open-plan, but it formed an integral part of the living room, as if it were impossible to divide the two areas. The cupboards looked like they'd been there for a long time, the doors made of solid walnut, their rich brown colour adding character to the place. I ran my finger through a thick layer of dust on the worktop, flinching at the cold surface. It seemed to be made of marble, as far as I could tell. The ceramic sink sat underneath a window that looked out on to the front, a grey moth-eaten net curtain preventing anyone from seeing either in or out.

Just off the living area, a long corridor led down to the front door. A tall, solitary cabinet stood soldier-straight against the wall, shadowy objects stacked behind its dusty glass-fronted top half, wooden doors perhaps hiding secret treasures at the bottom. I decided to leave it and carry on exploring. Another door opened into a room without any windows. I flicked the light switch, but nothing happened. I took my phone out of my pocket and turned on its torch, shining it around the room. The walls were covered in wooden shelves holding glass jars of every size and shape, some full of unidentifiable items, others empty. Some of the shelves had hooks screwed into the edges, dried bunches of flowers or herbs hanging suspended from them. I reached out and touched one. It was so brittle it crumbled under my fingers, and the sweet smell of lavender filled the air. I looked around me, enthralled by the room, wondering why it was there.

Closing the door, I went back into the kitchen, suddenly desperate for a coffee. Mum and I always drank espresso coffee at home in the mornings, and I'd brought a couple of packets with me; we couldn't abide the watery granulated stuff, and neither of us managed to function very well until we'd had at least two. I opened the cupboards until I found the Italian coffee percolator and filled it with water, letting the tap run until the water turned from a rusty brown to its usual transparent colour. There was a black wood-burning stove in the corner, and a more modern cooker next to it. I didn't have a clue how to use the stove, so I ignored it.

After some searching, I found the gas valve and turned it, grunting as it resisted at first, then finally gave way. Holding my breath, I tried to turn on one of the gas rings. There was silence, not even the quiet tick, tick, tick of the igniter.

I waited a few minutes for the gas to fill the pipes and the ring to burst into flame, before realising that if there was no electricity, there'd be no gas either. I cursed out loud and emptied the water from the percolator, grimacing as I saw a couple of tiny black beetles lying in the sink, their legs kicking feebly. I suddenly felt grateful for small blessings!

Disappointed, I grabbed a bottle of water and some cookies from my suitcase and carried my meagre breakfast out into the garden, taking in the view as I munched on the biscuits. There was a patio area outside the back door, covered with a trellis and what looked like a grapevine. The rest of the garden was a blanket of weeds, with a few trees and some broken-down wooden frames that might have been chicken coops or rabbit hutches. There was a ramshackle garage to the left which didn't seem too sturdy. The garden was so big that I could hardly see the bottom of it, although I could make out some sort of hedged area further down. I sighed and brushed some crumbs off my fingers. The garden would have to wait, the cottage was my main priority. I felt exhausted at the mere idea of tackling the grime.

I sat on the back doorstep, my hair gently ruffled by the breeze, and thought about everything that had gone wrong with my life.

I'd got back from yet another night out at the pub, giggling as I tripped up the stairs, shushing myself like a drunk from a comedy sketch and stumbling along the landing, which I hardly recognised in my state. When I found my husband in our bed with another woman, my whole world fell apart in a few seconds. I quietly closed the bedroom door, praying they hadn't seen me, and instead of confronting them, I sneaked out of the house as if I was the guilty party. I somehow made my way to my mum's house, where I knew I would be in for endless cups of coffee and long, tearful conversations.

'We've gone over this a thousand times, Jen. You know why this happened, don't you?' Mum asked once again, after she'd listened to me cry my heart out for a whole week. We were sitting at the kitchen table, a box of tissues in front of me and a bottle of wine next to it.

'Because he's a lying, cheating bastard?' I muttered, pouring yet another, rather full, glass of white wine.

'Not only,' she said quietly.

'What do you mean, "not only"? What other reason could there be?' I took a long swig, almost gagging on the slightly chemical taste at the back of my throat.

Mum pointed at my wine glass. 'That.'

'What, this glass?' I giggled, confused.

'No, Jenny, the fact that you've emptied it in ten seconds flat, and it's your third, and it's only nine in the morning.' She folded her arms and leaned back in her chair.

'Don't call me Jenny, you know I hate it,' I snapped, jumping to my feet. 'So a girl can't have a drink now, not even when her husband cheats on her?'

'Sit down, Jennifer Blakely,' Mum said sternly.

I sat.

'He phoned me yesterday.'

I glared at her. 'You didn't tell me.'

'Just like you didn't tell me he'd moved out. When did that happen?'

I decided to ignore the question, mainly because I couldn't remember. 'You're taking his side now?' I'd make her feel guilty, for once.

Mum sighed. 'I'm not taking anyone's side. He told me your drinking is out of hand, that you were getting through at least two bottles every evening, from the moment you got in from work to when you went to bed. He even found you passed out sometimes on the sofa the morning after. That's why he left you.'

'So.' I hesitated. 'I like to drink.'

'Jen, liking a drink is having a glass during dinner and maybe another later on to wind down. Not two bottles a day. Have you looked at yourself lately?'

I scowled mutinously at her.

'Your skin is blotchy and your face is puffy. And your hands shake if you don't have a glass of wine as soon as you get indoors. I don't know how you manage all day long at work.'

I blushed.

'Jen!'

'It's nothing, Mum, only a glass or two at lunchtime. Everyone does it, we all go to the pub for lunch.'

She gave me 'the look', the one that needed no words.

'Don't, Mum,' I mumbled. I plucked a tissue from the box and pulled nervously at it, tearing small pieces off and rolling them between my fingers before letting them fall to the table. My hands shook as I swept the tissue balls into a pile, shaping them into a square, while I avoided looking at Mum.

We were getting dangerously close to the forbidden subject, the reason why I'd started drinking, and the reason why my marriage had fallen apart. We'd become experts at skirting the issue of my miscarriages, and I didn't want to talk to her about it. Not yet.

She came around to my side of the table and gave me a big hug. 'Ever since your dad died,' she said, her eyes tearing up, 'you're all I've got left. I need you as much as you need me. It's time you stop drinking and start living, sweetie.' She wiped away the tears with the crumpled tissue she'd been clenching in her fist the whole time.

I knew she was right. Something had to change. Soon.

4

For the next week, I tried my best to stay away from alcohol. I really did. Mum insisted I stay with her, I was in no fit state to go back home. She hunted out her bottles of wine and Christmas brandy, tucked away in various cupboards for when visitors arrived as she didn't drink much. We held a ritual cleansing, and my hands shook as I poured the precious liquid down the sink.

For a few days after we purged the house of every drop of wine, Mum and I spent the evenings together, cooking dinner, chatting about our day and watching TV until it was time for bed. It was a somewhat peaceful coexistence. But on the fourth day, I bought a bottle of wine. Every day, on my way home from work, I had to pass the shop at the top of the road. I'd been a regular customer when I was younger, popping in for a bar of chocolate or a packet of sweets. I knew they had a small selection of alcohol, and that knowledge kept niggling at the back of my mind, until I couldn't bear it any longer. I crossed the threshold of the shop, trying not to think of Mum, or my husband Paul and our failed marriage, which had mainly been due to my drinking. I hid the bottle of wine at the bottom of my handbag, and when I arrived home I immediately put it at the back of my wardrobe for later. Oh, I so looked forward to that first sip!

Every evening after that day, I said goodnight to Mum like a dutiful daughter, went to bed at ten, sober, and by half past I was a drunken wreck. I didn't even taste the sweetness of the grapes, I didn't care. All I knew was that I became a guzzler, once again. One bottle became two, two became three. Then I decided to try vodka, as it was getting too difficult to hide the bottles. I quickly found out that one bottle of vodka was the equivalent of three or four bottles of wine, and much easier to carry home in my handbag. I only had to get through the evening and hide my shaking hands as my thoughts kept going to the hidden bottle upstairs, as if it were a lover. My eyes followed the endless ticking movement of the clock.

The television was mere noise and flickering images at the edge of my vision that had no meaning. I laughed when I heard the canned laughter, gasped when I heard Mum gasp, even managed to make comments on some of the storylines, but all the time I was listening to the call of that bottle upstairs. The last half hour before bedtime was the worst; time slowed down almost to a stop, the clock hand taking an hour to mark off every minute.

Mum had her suspicions. She kept begging me to admit I had a problem, until I lost my patience.

'Remember we poured every last drop of alcohol down the sink two weeks ago, Mum?' I barely waited for her to reply. 'So everything's sorted, isn't it?'

She reminded me constantly that I'd lost my husband and my home, and that she was worried about me. She complained about the weight she was losing from the stress. But still I carried on with my secret drinking. It seemed that nothing could stop me from self-destructing, I felt that I could handle anything. However, there was one issue Mum couldn't nag me about since she didn't know; my work was suffering too.

One day I was called into the HR office.

'Hi, Jennifer,' bright, cheery Rebecca chirped as I sat down. Her painted fingernails flew over the keyboard as she brought up my employee data on the computer.

'Morning, Rebecca,' I replied, not half as bright and cheerily. My head was thumping and I felt like I was going to be sick at any moment. I had finished off the last few swigs of vodka this morning rather than have breakfast, and was regretting it. Note to self: no more vodka on an empty stomach. No. Not a good idea.

Rebecca was chattering away about something, but I couldn't focus. She looked like some kind of canary, all bright colours and non-stop cheeping.

'Wh-what?' I said, as she stopped and looked at me expectantly.

'Oh dear, Jennifer, you don't look very well, you know.' She peered at me over the top of her glasses. 'I hope you haven't got that stomach bug that's going around.'

'I don't feel too good, to be honest,' I said. 'I'm sorry, I didn't really catch what you were saying.'

'I'll try not to take too long.' She tapped her fingers on the desktop, reading the file on her computer screen. 'I've got a report here from Mr Pennington.'

Mr Pennington was head of my department and a right pain in the backside. He'd had it in for me ever since I started working at the company two years before, and now it seemed he'd found the perfect excuse to get me into trouble.

'He says that on three occasions in the last month you've come back from lunch drunk, and tiddly on numerous other occasions. He also says that the quality of your work is much lower than it used to be, and he has to proofread any letters you type as they're often full of mistakes.'

'What? How dare he?'

'He's not the only one. We've had complaints from various members of your department about your lunchtime drinking and the quality of your work, or lack of it.'

'I don't understand. Who on earth–?'

'Jennifer, I have to issue you with an official warning,' Rebecca said, suddenly much less chirpy. 'The next time you come back from lunch even the tiniest bit tiddly, I'm afraid you'll be asked to leave the company.'

'I'll be fired, you mean,' I said bitterly. 'You do know that the men have a few pints every lunchtime, don't you? Even dear old Mr Pennington.'

'Yes, I know. It's acceptable if their work doesn't suffer in any way.'

I frowned. 'So it's one rule for them and another for us women, is that right?'

Rebecca pursed her lips. 'Jennifer, try to understand. We turn a blind eye to anyone, *anyone*, drinking at lunchtime as long as they are able to work as normal. From these complaints, it would appear that your drinking is impairing you from working in the afternoons.'

I glared at her. I could feel the vodka burning in my empty stomach, and the thumping in my head was an incessant drumbeat that was getting louder by the second. I swallowed hard to stop myself from being sick on chirpy Rebecca's office carpet.

'I need a coffee,' I mumbled.

'All right, off you go now.' Rebecca picked up a pen and scribbled something on a notepad. 'And remember what I said. This is your last chance.'

. . .

Two cups of coffee and some biscuits later, I was feeling more human. And very upset. *How dare they treat me like this*, I fumed. *It's so unfair.* I sat at my desk that morning, the anger building as I went over and over my telling-off from Rebecca. By lunchtime I was ready for the pub, more than ready.

I staggered back into the office at three, my breath stinking of vodka, singing 'I Want to Know What Love Is' at the top of my voice. Or at least, the words I could remember of it. At ten past three I was being shown out of the building, hugging my handbag to my chest, still singing.

'Goodbye, dear friends, Romans, and countrymen,' I yelled, bowing towards the shocked faces at the windows. 'I hope I never see you bastards again!'

Somehow I made it home. Mum didn't say anything, she just gave me a glass of water and put me to bed. I woke up several times during the night and she was always there, on a chair next to my bed, watching me. I might have been sick a few times too; I vaguely noticed her wiping my hair from my sweaty face and cleaning my mouth, but I was too weak to care.

When I finally managed to drag myself out of bed the next day, Mum was waiting downstairs in the kitchen. 'Want a coffee?'

I nodded, unable to speak for the moment. She banged around the kitchen, opening cupboards and shutting them more forcefully than was necessary, slammed two cups on the counter-top, and shoved the lid back on the metal coffee canister with an echoing clang. Each sound made me wince, as if she had hit me over the head with a hammer. The bubbling of the water in the kettle was similar to the thundering cascade of Niagara Falls, and the click as it turned off rang out clear as a gunshot. I glanced at Mum with a pained expression when she passed me a mug and sat down opposite me without a word.

I took a sip, and the hot, steaming liquid managed to revive me. I started to feel more human and quickly drained the cup.

'Want anything to eat?'

'N-no thanks.' I noticed my hands were shaking and hid them in my lap, under the table. 'This is fine.'

'We need to talk, Jen.' She leaned towards me, looking concerned.

'Not now, Mum. I don't know if you've noticed, but I feel like shit. I'm a thirty-one-year-old divorcee with no job and no future. Do you really have to dig the knife in right now?'

'What better time?'

I groaned. 'Okay, get the lecture over and done with. Then leave me alone.'

'You've become a horrible, obnoxious person, Jen. I can see why Paul left you.'

'He didn't leave me, he cheated on me.'

'That's not what he told me. He said he told you to stop drinking or he'd walk out. You decided to carry on drinking.'

'So why did I find him in our bed with another woman, if he'd left me?' I smirked at her, self-righteous indignation flowing through me. 'What was he still doing in the house?'

'He wasn't in your house.'

'What?'

'He was in his new place. You stole his keys when he popped back to pick up his things, and then you let yourself in to his new house.'

'No, that's not right, it can't be,' I exclaimed. 'He was in our bed, in our house.' I stopped, suddenly unsure. Everything was a blur. He hadn't yet left me, had he? I couldn't remember the exact date he'd moved out, since every day ran into the next. I no longer had any conception of time. I tried to focus on certain memories, but they fluttered through my head, running away from me. I tried to remember the scene, something that would tell me I was right, anything, the curtains, the bedspread, the carpet...

'Oh my God,' I moaned, holding my head between my hands. 'The carpet on the stairs. Red. It was red, like blood. Oh no.' I started sobbing and Mum was there, holding me, until the anxiety attack had passed.

'I went to his house, didn't I?' I whispered, shaking violently.

'Yes, sweetie, you did.'

'How could I have been so stupid?'

'The drink, it's the alcohol,' she said, stroking my hair. 'You become another person when you drink. You get out of control, nasty. You have to stop, Jen, it's the only way.'

'How? How do I do that, Mum?'

'I don't know. We'll think of something. But you have to stop pretending and lying, you're only hurting yourself.'

Mum had been right. It had taken a harsh wake-up call to make me realise I had to change my life. I thought I'd hit rock bottom when I lost my job, but things got worse, much worse, afterwards. However, it was too beautiful a morning to dwell on that. Determined to leave my memories in the past where they belonged, I stood, my bottom numb after sitting so long on the step, and decided I would walk to the village and get a coffee. Or two. Before I started thinking about... I stopped there, otherwise the thought would become an obsession, not leaving me in peace until I succumbed to its siren call, and continued to make a mental list of things to do. I had to see about getting the utilities switched back on, get started on cleaning up the cottage, and organise someone to come and sort out the garden. It was going to be a long day.

5

I grabbed my handbag and keys, and went out the front door. A short path led to a small entrance gate, which I'd missed the evening before in my tired state. The front of the cottage was much closer to the road; the drive curved around from the huge metal gates in a long winding shape, finishing up at the back door. If the taxi driver had gone a bit further ahead, we would have noticed the other entrance. The garden at the front was planted with rose bushes, I could see small buds already forming on the thorny branches. I hoped they were the perfumed kind and would fill the cottage with their sweet aroma.

I took a pleasant walk down to the village, along the quiet country road lined with trees that were so overgrown it was like walking through a tunnel. It was early, and there was no noise of traffic, just the occasional dog barking and the flapping of wings when a bird suddenly flew away as I approached. The cool breeze was pleasant on my skin, and I breathed in deeply, relishing the clean mountain air filling my lungs.

Gallicano was as pretty as I remembered it from the day before, passing through in the taxi. It was a typical Italian village, with houses made out of local stone and wooden shutters at the windows. All around the main piazza were small shops and bars with tables and chairs out on the pavement. There were apartments above the shops where people lived; it appeared that not a metre of space was wasted in Italy. Baskets of flowers hung off the balconies, giving everything a very Mediterranean look.

I stopped at the first bar I found, passing by a row of elderly gentlemen sitting on chairs along the wall, who were gesticulating and shouting so loudly that it seemed a fight would break out at any moment. Then they all burst out laughing, slapping each other on the shoulders. Bemused, I went in and ordered myself an espresso, sighing deeply as the caffeine entered my bloodstream.

Next on my list was stocking up on food and cleaning supplies, so I went into the grocery store next door. Ignoring the shelves of wine and liquor, I filled my shopping basket with boxes of pasta, cartons of milk, various pasta sauces and cleaning materials, then approached the counter. *Now's the time to try out my Italian*, I thought nervously. I took a deep breath and...

'Excuse me, do you need some help?' said a very British voice in perfect English. I turned, irritated, ready to snap that I was more than capable of doing it myself. My voice failed as I saw the man standing behind me. Tall, dark and handsome is how they usually describe the hero in a romance novel, and it described him perfectly. I added relaxed, casually dressed, with almond-brown eyes and sexy stubble for a slightly more accurate description of him.

'Ah, oh, it's okay,' I stammered. 'I-I'm new here, I arrived yesterday, up at the cottage, I needed some supplies and–' I realised I was babbling, and shut up.

'Let me help.' He turned and spoke in rapid Italian to the

lady behind the counter. She laughed at something he said, and took my basket from me.

'Do you speak Italian?' he asked.

'Oh yes. My mum always spoke to me in Italian when I was little. I was actually looking forward to seeing how much I can remember.'

'Oops,' he said, laughing. 'I'll let you take it from here then.' He stepped back.

I handed over my euros – admittedly, I had some trouble understanding the numbers but with the lady's help and a bit of fumbling, I managed to pay eventually and left the shop with a couple of heavy bags of groceries. I stood in the piazza, debating whether to go straight home or to the bar for another coffee.

'My name's Mark, by the way,' Sexy Stubble Guy said, suddenly appearing next to me.

'Oh, okay. Hi, Mark,' I said, feeling like an idiot. 'I'm Jennifer.'

'Pleased to meet you, Jennifer.' He held out his hand. As I shook it, I noticed a woman standing nearby who looked up, startled.

'Jennifer?' she called out. 'Your mother phoned and said you were coming, but she didn't say when. I'm your Aunt Liliana. Ah, I am so happy you've arrived at long last!' She gasped. 'The cottage, it's a disaster, we wanted to get it ready for you; you must have thought we were terrible, terrible people.'

Her Italian was very fast but somehow I managed to keep up. Finally, my chance to speak the lingo.

'No, no,' I said, eager to reassure her. 'I only arrived last night, the cottage was fine. I'm going to clean it up today. That's why I'm here, I had to buy some things.'

'I will help you,' she declared firmly, leaving me with no option but to accept her offer. After only a few minutes, I was already feeling overwhelmed by this friendly woman.

'We'll go and get the others. We'll all come to help, and you can meet the rest of your family.'

I sighed. So much for some quiet time for reflection. 'That would be lovely.' I turned to Mark. 'I'm sorry,' I said, with a shrug. 'I've got to go. We'll chat another time, maybe?'

A shadow crossed his face, and then he smiled at me. 'Sure, no problem. You said you're staying at the cottage, right? That one outside the village? I've heard lots about it.' He winked. 'Anyway, here's my number too, in case we miss each other. The next time you're in the village, call me and we can meet up.'

I took his business card and dropped it in my handbag. 'Okay. I'll be in touch.'

Aunt Liliana dragged me across the square and led me along a narrow road that quickly became a steep slope, chattering the whole time. She marched up the street; I tried to keep up with her, but soon had to rest. I put my bags down and leaned against the wall of a house, gasping, trying to get my breath back and stop the trembling in my legs. She turned and looked at me, a huge grin on her face.

'Oh, you tourists, it's always the same! You'll get used to the climb, although your legs will ache for a few days.' She burst out laughing. 'Come on, it's not far now.'

I grunted and forced myself into motion once more, my calves complaining the whole time. Her house was in one of the back streets, right at the top of the slope. I puffed my way up the road as she opened the front door and waited impatiently.

'Come in, come in, *prego*, they're all here, I'll introduce you.'

I was greeted by a chorus of Italian salutations and enveloped in hugs and kisses, my ears filled with loud exclamations and a chaotic jumble of people all talking at once. Bewildered, I tried to join in but ended up just standing there, grinning insanely at everyone, completely lost for words.

Aunt Liliana soon took control of the situation. 'That's

enough, everyone. Look at poor Jennifer, she can hardly think for all the confusion you're making. Come, let's go and sit down.' They stood back as I trailed after her into the kitchen, blushing furiously.

'Now I'll introduce you properly, Jennifer, one at a time.' She glared at the others.

'Please, call me Jen,' I said.

'*I* will call you Jennifer. They can do as they want,' she declared.

I put a hand over my mouth to cover a smile, amused by everyone's contrite faces. I'd heard of the Italian matriarch, but it was quite something to see one in action. Even though I was overwhelmed by their welcome, I could tell I was going to enjoy my stay in Italy.

6

The rest of the family turned out to be Uncle Dante, Aunt Liliana's long-suffering husband who didn't seem to speak much but merely nodded in agreement with his wife, and their grown-up children Lorenzo, Piero, and his wife Giulia, whose eight-year-old daughter Beatrice was at school, and Agnese. I noticed that Giulia was pregnant, her bump showing under her cotton dress, and I felt a small wave of jealousy wash over me. I pushed it away and tried to concentrate on the introductions.

'This isn't our whole family, we have more relatives down in the valley but we rarely see them since my mother died.' Aunt Liliana sniffed in disdain, as though it were a disgrace to have such a small group gathered together in one place. I was secretly grateful there were only six of them, I could hardly imagine what it would have been like if everyone had turned up.

'And there's Tommaso,' Lorenzo added. 'He lives over the other side of the village, but we don't see much of him either.'

'Tommaso prefers his own company to ours,' Aunt Liliana said. 'I'm sure you'll meet him eventually.'

'You'll stay for lunch.' Uncle Dante's booming voice startled me, it was the first time he'd spoken.

'Oh no, I couldn't, it's too much,' I said, but I was drowned out by Aunt Liliana.

'Of course you must, we were going to eat together anyway and one more person won't hurt. You can tell us about England, about your mother. We haven't seen Rita for such a long time; we speak on the phone but it's not the same. It's a shame your great-grandmother Luisa is no longer with us, she would have loved to have seen you.' And on and on it went, like being buried under a ton of earth.

Aunt Liliana busied herself with the pots and pans on the stove, and Agnese took an extra set of cutlery and plates through to the dining table. I resigned myself to not getting any work done in the cottage, and started to relax and enjoy the day.

The food was exquisite, spaghetti bolognese with a home-made sauce, followed by tender roast pork drizzled with the cooking juices, and sautéed courgettes that, I was informed, had been freshly picked that morning. There was never a lull in the conversation, everyone chatted easily together while they ate. I watched as they broke every rule I'd ever been taught in England: talking with their mouths full, using their knives to scrape up sauce and then licking them, breaking a chunk of bread off the loaf and wiping it around their plates, leaning on their elbows, laughing and joking. Aunt Liliana prided herself as a wonderful cook, and told me every detail of the preparation process, while I copied my cousins and broke off a piece of home-made bread to mop up the delicious pasta sauce left on the plate.

I mostly listened as they talked about their lives, jobs, and living in the mountains, secretly envious of their laid-back life-style and lack of concern about material things. It was like taking a trip to the past, to an easier way of life. I wondered if that was the magic Mum had spoken about.

'So, how are you finding the cottage?' Giulia asked. 'We

wanted to give it a clean before you arrived, but we got confused with the dates. We didn't think you were arriving for another two weeks.'

'I only got here late yesterday evening,' I said, hastily swallowing a mouthful of courgettes. 'I haven't had a chance to do anything yet. I had a quick look this morning, and everything seems okay. There's no gas or electricity, though.'

'Oh, we'll sort that out. Piero will phone straight after lunch and get it switched on, won't you?'

'Of course, it should take a couple of days at the most. You have water, yes? I think Dante turned it on last week.'

'Oh yes, that's working fine. There's a wood-burning stove, but I have no idea how to use it.' I looked hopefully at them. If part of my new lifestyle meant cooking on that stove, then I'd have to learn how to operate it.

'I will show you how,' Aunt Liliana said. 'It's easy when you get the hang of it.'

'Great, at least I can have a coffee in the morning then.'

'Ah, a true Italian.' Lorenzo nudged his brother. 'You see, Piero, I told you she would be more Italian than English. Look how she ate her pasta, and now she says she loves coffee!'

They all started talking at once again, this time about the pros and cons of being either English or Italian. I let their insults about English food and coffee go unchallenged, sensing that it would be pointless to get into an argument about it. Especially when most of what they said was true. Agnese glanced over at me and gave an apologetic shrug. I smiled back at her, trying to let her know I wasn't offended. I liked Agnese; she seemed very shy and hardly spoke, but I'd have bet anything she wouldn't let anyone take advantage of her gentle personality.

'So, tell me about my grandmother,' I said, when I managed to get a word in. We had finished eating and sat companionably at the table waiting for the coffee percolator to boil, as if we'd been doing it all our lives.

'Do you mean Luisa, your great-grandmother?' Giulia asked.

'Oh, Mum's told me about her. I mean, of course I'd like to hear more, but I'm curious about my grandmother too.'

'Bruna?' Agnese asked. The room suddenly fell silent.

'Yes. Mum said she left here when she was twenty-one, that she went to live in England. I don't remember Gran much, she died when I was little. Mum's never really talked a lot about her.'

Aunt Liliana ran her hand through her grey hair. 'Well, let's see...'

'Hush, woman, we don't need to talk about that,' Uncle Dante said abruptly.

'But–'

He slammed his fist down on the table. 'I said no,' he roared. 'Go get the coffee, and no more talk of these things.'

I stared at him, shocked. Everyone else pretended to ignore him, although the cheerful chatter of a few moments earlier was gone.

Aunt Liliana nudged me. 'Take no notice,' she murmured. 'Did you enjoy your lunch?' she asked, raising her voice, as she went into the kitchen.

'Yes, it was delicious,' I exclaimed. I had no idea what was going on, but I didn't dare ask any more questions about the family. The tension broke, and normal conversation resumed.

Aunt Liliana returned with a tray of steaming coffee cups and passed them around the table. Uncle Dante brought out a bottle of grappa, and added a generous dash to his coffee cup. He glanced at me and raised his eyebrows, offering the bottle.

So much for being out of the reach of temptation here in Italy. I managed to find an inner strength, even though my whole body was crying out for the bottle. 'N-no thanks, I prefer my coffee as it is.'

He grunted in reply and handed the bottle to Piero and Lorenzo. I turned my head and started talking to Giulia, trying not to breathe in the alcoholic fumes as they wafted over the table. With lunch finally over, the women got up and cleared the table while the men sat on the sofa and talked politics.

When we'd finished tidying up, Aunt Liliana gathered together a huge bag of cleaning materials. 'Tomorrow, the girls and I will come up to the cottage and help you sort it out,' she declared.

'Oh no,' I protested. 'That's not necessary.'

'Nonsense. Agnese, Giulia and I will give you a hand.'

I looked at the others helplessly. 'But Giulia's pregnant.'

'I'll only do light work,' she promised.

I gave in gracefully, it was the only way.

7

The family turned up bright and early the next morning, full of energy and loaded with bags of bleach, polish, rags and detergents. I'd already made a start in the kitchen and scrubbed down the table and work surfaces so I had somewhere clean to eat.

My first priority was learning to use the wood-burning stove, as my caffeine deficiency was causing me considerable problems. Aunt Liliana bravely took on the task of teaching me.

'Come on, Jennifer, I've already shown you three times how to light it, it's not that difficult.' She stood back with folded arms, watching as I attempted to copy her actions. But try as I might, I couldn't do it. I managed to get the scrunched-up balls of newspaper lit, but every time I shut the door the flames slowly died out. Agnese and Giulia tried to keep a straight face, while Aunt Liliana became more and more agitated. They took turns showing me how to open the grate to control the air flow, but it was beyond me.

'I'll just use the cooker when the gas is back on, it'll be easier in the long run,' I muttered, wanting to give the stove a kick. I decided I'd google it later on and see if I could work it out on my own.

'I've brought a thermos of coffee, I'll make one up every morning until you've got gas and electricity again,' Agnese said, producing a huge flask from her handbag.

'Oh, Agnese, you're a saviour,' I exclaimed. 'Coffee before we start then?'

The day passed in a blur as we dusted, tidied up, washed windows, furniture and everything that could be washed, and threw away anything that couldn't, stopping only for a quick sandwich at lunchtime. We started in the kitchen and living room, working our way through the cottage. Aunt Liliana was a fantastic organiser and kept us in line, giving us each a task and not letting us rest until we'd finished it, only to assign us the next one. But it worked, and by the end of the day the downstairs was looking a lot better.

'Tomorrow we'll do the corridor and the pantry, then we will start upstairs,' she declared.

'Oh yes, the pantry. I've seen inside, what was it used for?' I asked, curious to find out. 'And why isn't there a window?'

'That's the herb room, where Luisa stored all her, what would you call them? Herbal remedies,' Agnese replied.

'What?' I was even more confused.

'She was a healer, the last one of the family,' Aunt Liliana said.

'A healer?'

'Oh, it's nothing, it was only an old woman's hobby,' she replied.

. . .

It took us a week to clean the cottage. Every morning the three women arrived and we worked until late afternoon. I had gas, electricity and a basic internet connection after only a couple of days, helped by the fact that Giulia's sister worked for the local council and knew the right people to contact. She was a lifesaver, as I couldn't get the hang of the wood-burning stove. Giulia, on light cleaning duties as she was pregnant, took over cooking for us at lunchtime, and every day we sat down to an enormous plate of pasta with delicious home-made sauces. I hoped all the cleaning would counterbalance the calories I was consuming every day.

One afternoon I stood outside the back door with Agnese, breathing in the fresh mountain air and enjoying a few moments of quiet. Our chores done for the day, we were waiting for Giulia and Aunt Liliana to finish.

'How come the cottage has two entrances?' I asked Agnese. 'Isn't it a little unusual, having such a grand drive leading up to the back of the house?'

'That's because it was originally part of a large manor,' Agnese replied. 'This whole area was ruled over by the Innocenti family, who were very powerful until about a hundred years ago. The cottage was part of the estate and the drive led to the main house, but that was torn down, I don't know when. Only the cottage remained. It's been a part of our family since the dawn of time, as far as I know.'

'Haven't you ever looked into your family's history? It sounds interesting,' I remarked.

Agnese did that typical Italian shrug I was starting to recognise. 'It's never really crossed my mind. Why don't you do it? It might give you something to do while you're here.'

'That's not a bad idea, I might give it a go,' I said, stretching. 'If I can ever find the energy after all this cleaning.'

At long last, everything was gleaming. The tiles on the floor were visible, the parquet upstairs waxed and polished, the broken window replaced, and everything smelled fresh and new. We stood back and admired our handiwork.

'I don't know how to thank you,' I said, and I meant it. I'd loved having the women in the cottage, chattering while we worked, the time passing so quickly that it was no effort at all. And I knew that I was going to miss having them close by. To tell the truth, I was quite scared of being by myself again. I didn't want to have to think about the past, the mistakes I'd made, of having to face the future alone. Being with these women had been a buffer to my memories.

'We've enjoyed it, and it's been lovely getting to know you,' Aunt Liliana said. 'Finally I get to see Rita's daughter, after all these years.'

'Don't worry, we'll be dropping in so often you'll be sick of the sight of us,' Giulia said. 'Don't think we're going to abandon you up here at the cottage. But we will leave you alone this weekend, so you can enjoy some of the peace and quiet you came here for. And Bea wants to meet her cousin,' she added. 'She's talked about nothing else the whole week.'

'Please, do drop in whenever you want,' I said. 'And I'd love to meet Bea too!'

8

All week long, I hadn't even thought about touching a drop of alcohol; not because of any magic in the cottage, but because I was so damned tired from cleaning. I was in bed by eight o'clock every night and asleep one minute later.

One weekend. A whole weekend on my own.

'You can do this,' I told myself sternly. No more excuses, no more putting things off. Two days to think. I still had to find the magic Mum had talked about, if it really existed. Now that the cottage was in order, maybe I could finally relax and get in touch with my surroundings.

I got up on Saturday morning and decided to do some weeding. After a couple of hours, I concluded that whoever said it was good therapy should be shot. I found nothing therapeutic about kneeling on sharp gravel, digging up weeds with a blunt knife. Standing up afterwards was torture – my knees popped, my muscles protested at having to stretch and my shoulders felt so hunched that I was sure I looked like Quasimodo. But the few square metres of drive I'd cleared looked fantastic.

I stretched my whole body, trying to loosen the cramped nerves, and turned around in a circle, inspecting my hard work.

I groaned at the sight of the weeds growing amongst the bushes in the garden, the ivy spreading over one side of the cottage and threatening to block an upstairs window, the ancient trees bowing over from the weight of their untrimmed branches. I threw down my knife and stormed back indoors, defeated for the day.

'A gardener, that's what I need,' I said. I found that being alone made me talk out loud much more often. 'I'll ask Aunt Liliana on Monday, she'll know someone.'

After all that fresh air and gardening, I could have done with a cold glass of wine. I clenched my hands into a fist, my desire for something alcoholic consuming me. I started opening the kitchen cupboards like I'd gone crazy, knocking things over in my frenzy to find a bottle of something, anything, then slamming them shut in fury when my shaking hands found nothing. Of course, there wouldn't be anything in the cottage, we'd taken everything out when we cleaned. But nobody had touched the garage yet. Perhaps... I ran out to the ramshackle garage, with its sagging roof and broken windows. Nobody in their right mind would go inside, it looked like it would fall down with the slightest breeze.

'Oh, sod it,' I exclaimed and threw the doors open. A thick layer of dust covered everything and long cobwebs draped down from the ceiling. I carefully stepped inside the garage and saw a big old dresser with secateurs, a trowel, old seed packets, and a myriad of other gardening implements scattered across the top. I crouched down and pulled open the cupboard doors at the bottom.

There were rows of tall wine-shaped bottles stacked neatly inside, a small handwritten label affixed to each one.

'*Frutti di bosco*,' I read out loud. 'Fruits of the forest. *Uva nera*. Black grape. *Prugna*. Plum. *Lampone*. Raspberry. *Mela*. Apple.' I counted thirty bottles and reread the labels. 'Fruits of the forest, black grape, plum, raspberry and apple.' It sounded like a mantra. 'Oh, Grandma Luisa, thank goodness you liked to make your own wine.' I could have wept. Thirty bottles. With a bit of care, I'd have enough to last me a couple of months, maybe longer. After all, I wasn't going to drink a whole one every day.

I grabbed a cloth, dusted off each bottle and took them back into the cottage. I found the perfect hiding place in the cupboard in the hallway, which I could lock with a key. My alcohol. Hidden safely away from prying eyes. A habit I somehow couldn't break, not just yet. I didn't want to let Mum down, but I knew I couldn't stay off the booze forever. Not until I found that damned magic she'd kept on about.

I took out a bottle filled with a deep-red liquid and read the faded label. 'Hmm, fruits of the forest. Sounds delicious.' I imagined going back to the kitchen, taking a corkscrew out of the drawer and hearing the cork come out with that oh-so-familiar popping sound. I could almost smell the sweet aroma of the wine, my mouth watering as I imagined that first sip, the warm, fruity liquid sliding down my throat...

'No!' I quickly placed the bottle back into the cupboard and slammed the door shut, locking it. I had to be strong, try to resist.

Since weeding as a distraction hadn't worked, I grabbed a book and a sun lounger and headed to the garden. I set the lounger up in a cool, shady spot under a large tree that looked to be at least a hundred years old. There was a slight breeze that took away the heat of the afternoon sun, and the sound of bees droning among the branches of the tree helped me to relax. A few pages in, my eyelids fluttered and I drifted off to sleep.

'La dolce vita, eh?' I heard a voice call out.

I woke up with a start and saw Mark standing over me. 'Wh-what?' I mumbled, confused. 'How did you get in?'

'I'm sorry, I didn't want to scare you.' I squinted as I looked up at him, the afternoon sun directly behind his head. 'The gate wasn't locked. I hadn't heard from you all week, so I thought I'd pop in and see how you are. The village is buzzing with news of your arrival, your family are so excited you're here.'

I struggled to follow what he was saying as my head was still a bit fuzzy from my short nap. 'We've been cleaning, the cottage was in quite a state,' I managed to say. 'I was going to call you next week, I needed a couple of days to recover–' I wanted to say, 'from my family' but suddenly felt guilty after everything they'd done for me. 'From the hard work,' I finished lamely, as I sat up and swung my legs over the edge of the lounger.

Mark laughed. 'You don't need to tell me about Italians and needing to recover from them,' he said. 'I've been here since I married my Italian wife, that'd be fifteen years now. We're divorced,' he added, noticing my frown. 'The marriage lasted ten years, which I consider a miracle, seeing as they were always interfering. Her mother was always dropping in, telling us how to live our lives, what we should be doing, eating, even thinking! I couldn't take any more in the end, and I told my wife it was either her mum or me. And here I am, divorced.'

I couldn't help smiling. 'You could have gone back to England.'

'Ah, I love it too much here. The countryside, the wonderful weather, even some of the people. You can't get this in England.'

'You might find someone else.' He was definitely good-looking enough.

'I might,' he agreed vaguely.

I suddenly realised that I was sitting down on a comfortable sun lounger while he was still standing. 'What a terrible host I am. Let's go inside and I'll make a coffee.'

He chuckled. 'I'd prefer something stronger, seeing as it's after five o'clock.'

I stood and led the way back to the cottage. 'Unfortunately, I haven't got anything in, only water, juice or coffee,' I said, my palms sweating. There was no way I was going to share my wine with anyone else.

'I'll remember to bring a bottle next time.'

I opened the back door and gestured him inside. 'That's okay, I don't drink anyway.'

Rule number one: keep all temptation out of the house. And rule number two: ignore the fact that there's a cupboard full of wine just down the corridor!

We sat and drank coffee, making small talk. I found him pleasant enough, but my mind kept drifting to the wine. It was a relief when he finally declared he had to go.

'Call me soon, I'm free most mornings. We can go for a coffee if you like.'

'Okay,' I replied.

'Are you all right? You seem a bit distracted.'

'Oh, I was doing some gardening earlier, the sun's given me a headache.' Why wouldn't he leave? I could feel the wine calling, singing to me, its lure dragging me towards it, irresistible.

'Bye, then.'

'Yeah, sure, bye,' I said breezily. I'd closed the front door before he was halfway down the garden path. *He'll think I'm so rude*, I thought, giggling, *but I don't care.*

I couldn't hold back anymore. I ran to the cupboard, unlocked it, and took out the bottle of fruits of the forest wine. I placed it on the kitchen table and took a corkscrew out of the cutlery drawer, anticipating the ritual uncorking with growing excitement. The pop of the cork, the delightful smell as I inhaled its rich fruit scent with musky undertones; then an image of Mum standing before me with folded arms leaped into my head, a disappointed expression on her face.

'I'm sorry, Mum,' I whispered. 'I can't, not right now. Please understand.' The image disappeared and all I could see was the open bottle on the table, the empty glass next to it. That glug glug sound as I poured the wine, the glass filling with the deep-red liquid, not a drop spilled as I gave the bottle a final twist and put it back down with a flourish.

'One glass,' I murmured, 'only one.' I squeezed the cork back into the bottle and replaced it in the cupboard in the hall, locking the door. I removed the key and put it in a kitchen drawer, out of temptation's way. The glass was still on the table, waiting for me. I wanted to drain it in one gulp; my body was crying out for its sweet nectar, but there was a small, masochistic part of me that wanted to make me suffer for this prize.

I carefully carried the glass outside to the sun lounger, picked up my book, and sat down. 'You're going to enjoy this drink,' I told myself sternly, 'just like anyone else would. A nice, relaxing glass of wine after a hard day's work in the garden.' I put the glass close to my nose and breathed in. My head was filled with the scent of wood and spices, with a strong overtone of raspberries, strawberries and blackberries, a wonderful aroma that made my mouth water. I took a sip, closed my eyes, and waited. The flavour was an intense fruity mix that hit the back of my throat, followed by an instant warmth spreading through my stomach. It felt so good, so right, so natural.

By the time I finished the glass, the sun had disappeared behind the nearby hills and the air was growing chilly. The last birds swooped crazily in the sky, their final moments of freedom before it was time to roost. A dragonfly flitted in front of my face, startling me.

'Oh, shoo,' I said, watching as it flew away. I was feeling relaxed, happy, more at peace with the world than I'd felt in a long time. The dragonfly came back, perched on the arm of the sun lounger, then flitted away again as I moved my hand. I smiled. When it came back a third time, I stayed completely still. It hovered in front of my nose, flew a few metres to my right, returned, then flew away again in the same direction. Curious, I watched it. It repeated the same movement several times.

'It's almost as if it wants me to follow it,' I whispered. Then I laughed out loud. 'Good grief, get a grip. You've only had one glass!'

But something was happening. My senses felt sharper than usual; I could hear insects moving in the grass at my feet, the leaves above me sucking nutriment from the tree, birds' feathers rustling in the wind as they flew high in the sky. Strange, sweet perfumes floated through the air that I'd never sensed before, unrecognisable but somehow familiar. I could feel the vibrations coming from the dragonfly's wings as it beat them at an impossible speed to hover before me.

As if in a dream, I got up from the lounger and followed the dragonfly. It led me down towards the end of the garden where I hadn't yet had the chance to explore, through a small gate in an overgrown hedge to a wild, unkempt area. Here there were fruit bushes strangled by weeds, and brambles grew over everything, catching on my clothes as I made my way through the tangled undergrowth. It was strangely alluring, this patch of unexpected wilderness.

The dragonfly stopped a few metres ahead of me, hovered for a few seconds, then flew straight up in the sky and disappeared out of sight. I went over to where it had been a moment before and saw that there was a huge mass of ivy growing up from the ground. The sky was getting darker, but I could see a shape underneath the ivy. I pulled a few strands, and suddenly a large clump came away in my hands. I looked closely at what I had uncovered and screamed.

9

I stood in the kitchen, trembling, my hands shaking as I poured a glass of tap water. The calm, relaxed feeling was long gone, and my head pounded with unanswered questions. I kept replaying in my mind the moment the ivy had fallen away, uncovering what lay beneath.

A tombstone.

Who the hell was buried there? I started to think I'd dreamed it, there couldn't possibly be a grave at the bottom of the garden. I bitterly regretted drinking the wine.

One day. That was all it had taken, one day of solitude and I'd immediately turned to alcohol. *Mum's wrong. I'm too weak, I'll never get through this.* I'd tried so hard. I'd even locked the bottles away, but it was stronger than me, the pull was too much to resist. I remembered how I'd felt after drinking the glass of wine, those strange sensations, the dragonfly, and I wondered what on earth my great-grandmother had put in the wine to make me react that way.

I suddenly felt exhausted, as if I had lead weights in my pocket. I finished the water and left the glass in the sink for the next morning. Even though it was only 8pm, I didn't want anything to eat. I wanted to crawl into my bed and sleep until the next morning. *Tomorrow I'll deal with things. Tomorrow.*

Rather than the oblivion I sought, however, my dreams were filled with confused images of dragonflies darting through a garden full of graves, landing on the headstones with their wings humming so loudly that I had to cover my ears. I ran haphazardly, trying to catch them before they woke up the slumbering inhabitants in their coffins. I tripped over the edge of a grave and fell heavily to the ground, the freshly dug cold earth caressing my cheek, a maggot writhing inches from my nose. A bony finger broke through the ground, turning to point at me, and I wanted to scream, but instead inhaled mouthfuls of dirt. I was choking, suffocating, unable to move, my eyes fixed on the grey bones of the rest of the hand inching their way towards my neck. I willed myself to wake up. My mind kept screaming *This is only a nightmare, it isn't really happening*, but I continued to gasp for air, desperate for the oxygen my lungs needed. Finally I knew no more, and drowned in blessed darkness.

The sun woke me early the next morning and put an end to the nightmares. I felt as if I'd run a marathon, and my nightshirt was damp and clammy where I'd sweated during the night. After a shower and two very strong cups of coffee, I felt slightly more human. I stared out of the kitchen window at the garden. From here, I couldn't see the hedge I'd gone through the evening before and everything seemed the same as usual. But it wasn't, and I didn't know if it could ever be the same for me again. The idea of someone being buried out there sent shivers down my spine. I had a sudden thought. *Was it even legal to bury someone in your garden? Will I have to call the police?*

I rinsed out my coffee cup and the percolator, trying to delay the moment I'd have to go back into the garden. After the nightmares I'd had, that was the last thing I wanted to do, but I knew I had to go and check it out. I tidied downstairs, putting away a couple of magazines, rearranging the ornaments on the mantel-piece over the fireplace, but eventually I had nothing left to do.

I was hesitant as I slowly walked down the path towards the gate in the hedge. It was a warm day, the air filled with the sounds of chirping birds and insects scuttling about on their daily business. The magic I'd sensed the evening before was gone, though, and I felt only dread as I reached the gate.

I could clearly see where I'd passed while following the dragonfly, crushed grass and weeds showing the way. I opened the gate and went through. There were bushes and plants every-where, some very old, their twisted branches dark and thick under masses of weeds, while others were much smaller and lighter in colour. This part of the garden was protected by an old, moss-covered stone wall on three sides and the hedge and gate where I'd entered on the fourth. Several trees stood against the wall, covered in pretty white blossom. I wandered over to look at them, sure that they were apple trees. A slight breeze blew through the garden, and clouds of blossom floated in the air around me, like confetti being thrown over a bride's head, settling in my hair and on my shoulders. I reached out and caught some in my hand, the delicate flowers tickling my palm.

I didn't know how long apples took to mature, but I guessed that by the autumn I'd have enough to make plenty of cakes and pies, maybe even some jams. I thought I'd give cider a miss, for obvious reasons, and besides, I had my great-grandmother's apple wine. I whirled round, and saw a row of grape vines in a corner, and over there some blackberry bushes... I realised I was standing in my great-grandmother's garden, where she had grown the fruit for her wines.

'She'd be turning in her grave at the sight of her garden looking like this. I'll have to sort it out.' I quite liked the idea of taming this wild area and tending the plants, and started to feel excited. Finally I had something worthwhile to fill my time. Then my gaze fell to the pile of ivy in the middle of the garden, thrown haphazardly over the grave in my panic to leave the previous evening. The excitement drained away, leaving a dull numbness in its wake.

I dragged myself over to it and stared at the headstone, set like a giant full stop in front of me. I brushed the dirt and moss off and crouched down to read the inscription.

Sei nata per essere amata da me, ma non ero all'altezza. Mi dispiace.
Malva, settembre 25 1960 – settembre 28 1960

Three days old. The baby had been three days old when it died. I ran my hand over the writing, trying to understand. 'You were born to be loved by me, but I wasn't good enough. I'm sorry.' A tear rolled down my cheek. 'You poor baby,' I murmured.

Glancing down, I saw that the grave was covered in weeds. I cleared them away with my hands, ripping them out of the ground, faster and faster, until the marble base was completely free. I sat down on the ground and cried, for the unknown child here before me, and for my own children, so cruelly taken before I had the chance to hold them in my arms. My chest hurt from the pain I had inside and my whole body ached with the love I could have given them and would never have the chance to experience again.

10

It was too much for me. The gardening could wait, I would come back tomorrow and start putting everything in order. Not today. Not with all this pain. No, today I would finish off the bottle of wine I'd started, and forget everything for a while.

'Jennifer!'

I jumped as someone called my name.

'Jen, are you here?'

'Coming,' I yelled back. I tried to dry my tears, then realised that my face would be red anyway and gave up. Walking back to the cottage, I saw Agnese standing by the back door, waiting for me.

'There you are,' she said, relieved. 'I just came round to see if I can bring Bea tomorrow afternoon. I thought you'd gone out, and I'd have to go back home.' She paused and stared at me. 'Are you okay? Your face is a bit red, like you've been cry... Oh.'

I gestured, embarrassed. 'It's nothing, I'm all right, really. Do you fancy a coffee?'

'It looks like you need something stronger,' she said.

I thought of Luisa's wine in the cupboard in the corridor. 'Maybe later. Let's start with a coffee.'

We went into the kitchen and I prepared the percolator, adding an extra heaped spoonful of coffee. I needed something to pick me up.

'Why were you crying?' Agnese asked.

'You Italians are pretty direct, aren't you?' I remarked, but I wasn't annoyed. I was starting to get used to their ways.

'And you English are very good at changing the subject.'

'I guess we are.'

'So?'

I hesitated, unsure whether to tell her. 'I-I found a gate at the bottom of the garden.'

'You found Luisa's sanctuary. We call it the Grove.'

'The Grove,' I repeated. 'What a lovely name.'

'Yes, and very apt, don't you think? She loved going down there, tending the plants and trees, picking the parts she needed for her remedies. I'm sure you'll find a few balms and lotions in the pantry, some of them may still be good to use. She showed me how to make some, it was interesting watching her at work.'

'Yes, I'm sure it was. But I found something else down there, it was quite a shock.'

'Oh?'

'It was a grave,' I blurted, unsure how to say it gently.

'Ah, the grave.' She didn't seem shocked by my revelation.

'You knew about it?'

'Of course. It's the baby's grave, we all know about it.'

'What? Why is it there, in the garden? Why isn't the baby in the cemetery?'

'She died before they could baptise her, and Bruna didn't want her buried in the cemetery. She wanted her here, close to the family, where Luisa could look after her.'

'Bruna? It was Bruna's daughter?'

'Yes. It was very hush-hush. She had the baby before she met George but wouldn't tell anyone who the father was. The poor thing died a few days later, and she was distraught. Then she married George and escaped to England, to get away from everything.'

'Now I understand why Uncle Dante didn't want to talk about her. How do you know all this?'

'Aunt Teresa told me. I often went down to the valley to visit her, she loved telling me all the family gossip. No one else in the family would tell me anything. Although Luisa said some strange things towards the end, but a lot of it didn't make sense.'

'How did the baby die?'

'Teresa said they found her dead in her bed. Bruna was hysterical.'

I felt like crying as well. I could only imagine Bruna's pain, together with the stigma of giving birth to an illegitimate child, and then finding it dead. 'Poor Bruna,' I murmured, and then I did start crying again, much to my embarrassment.

Agnese looked alarmed. 'It happened years ago. Why are you so upset?'

I blew my nose, avoiding looking at her. 'I-I can't have children, I keep miscarrying, my husband left me because I started drinking, nobody will ever talk to me about it, not even my mum, and when I saw the headstone today it set me off crying and now I can't stop,' I said miserably.

Agnese came over and hugged me. 'Oh, Jen, I'm so sorry. You can talk to me, maybe it will help.'

'I wouldn't know where to start, I've kept it inside me for so long.'

'Start at the beginning,' she suggested.

I didn't realise I had so much pain inside me, so many tears, so much heartache. It helped that Agnese was a good listener; she let me talk without interrupting and encouraged me to go on when I faltered. We sat in the kitchen for ages, talking, crying, hugging, until finally I had nothing else to say. I felt strangely empty, as if I'd got rid of a heavy burden I'd been carrying for so long without realising it. We were silent for a while, each lost in our own thoughts.

'You know, you could talk to Uncle Tommaso about the baby,' Agnese suddenly suggested.

'Uncle Tommaso?'

'He's Bruna's brother, he was still living at home at the time, and I know that he and Bruna were close. He can probably tell you more, although he's a bit funny about who he talks to. If he doesn't like you, he'll chase you away.'

'As long as he doesn't have a gun,' I quipped. The look on Agnese's face wasn't too reassuring. 'Maybe I'll go and pay him a visit.' If I was desperate enough.

'I have to go now,' Agnese said. 'Will you be okay?'

'Yes, I'll be fine.' I felt a bit embarrassed after all the crying I'd done. 'I'm not always like this, you know. But thank you for listening, it's been a big help.'

She hugged me goodbye, and I watched as she walked out of the front gate, giving her a little wave as she closed it behind her. I reluctantly went back indoors, the cottage suddenly empty. I was hardly aware that I was heading towards the wine cupboard until I found myself standing before it, the key magically in my hand. I took out the bottle I'd started the day before, got a glass from the kitchen, and, even though it was the middle of the day, went upstairs to bed.

I'd never considered myself a weak person; after everything I'd been through I'd always been proud of my ability to face things head-on and deal with them on my own. At that moment, though, gulping down the wine, I felt that I was losing control of my destiny.

I lay back on the bed and watched the clouds scurry across the incredibly blue sky, pushed and moulded by invisible hands to become those fantastic shapes everyone likes to look at, imagining they can see faces and animals. But all I could see was my life floating away out of reach, the umbilical cord that tethered me to the earth trailing behind it, frayed, swinging uselessly in the air. I finished the wine and put the glass on my bedside table, then closed my eyes and let the drink transport me to that dark, dreamless place I called salvation.

11

I woke, terrified, from another nightmare. The wine glass on the bedside table fell to the floor with a crash as I flung my arms about. I fumbled for the light switch, sighing with relief as the room lit up. Glancing at my phone, I saw it was three in the morning. I knew I would never get back to sleep, so I went downstairs and turned on my laptop. The internet was slow but usable, and I decided to do some research on Bruna and her baby.

Two hours later I admitted defeat and closed the laptop. The Italians were obviously not as efficient as the English; trying to find a newspaper article from the 1960s in a small village in Tuscany was about as easy as finding the proverbial needle in a haystack. It suddenly occurred to me that maybe the baby's death hadn't been reported. Would that be possible? Surely a doctor would have had to sign the death certificate; maybe Luisa had managed to find a way to keep it out of the papers.

Whatever had happened, I knew I'd have to find the courage to speak with Uncle Tommaso. The thought of facing him and his gun wasn't something I was looking forward to at all. I cursed out loud. I knew this wasn't about Tommaso and his possibly psychopathic personality. This was about me, about those soul-destroying circumstances that had slowly worn me down over the years and moulded me into the bitter, messed-up person I was now. The bitter, messed-up alcoholic, I berated myself sharply. How the hell had I got into this state? I lay down on the sofa, closed my eyes, and let the memories of those awful days when I stopped drinking flood in.

Mum made an appointment with her GP and together we explained my drinking problem. Dr Alden didn't really take me seriously, though. She merely lectured me about the damage I was doing to my liver and the rest of my body. She pulled a few random leaflets from the holders on the wall of the small exami-nation room and handed them to me. Glancing at them in disdain, I found they were about self-help groups. I couldn't see the point of those.

She also prescribed some medicines that would help during the 'weaning-off' period. There was no in-depth interview about why I was doing this to myself, or what had triggered it. *Why should she care anyway*? I thought bitterly. *No one else does, not even Mum or Paul, and they're supposed to love me. What hope have I got with an overworked doctor who has fifty patients to get through in one morning*?

Mum talked me into going to one of the self-help groups. She drove me there and said she'd return in a couple of hours. It was either stay out in the cold or go into a warm building and have some coffee. I chose the latter. It was awful. The attendees were middle-aged people feeling sorry for themselves and talking about how easy it was to relapse. I refused to go back. So Mum drove me to another one, which had a mixture of age groups. There were a couple of thirty-five-year-olds and some youngsters, but again they were mostly older people.

I liked this one more, so I kept going, finding some solace in the fact that there were others in my situation. I listened as they talked about their problems, inwardly cringing as they burst into tears, and became even more determined not to lower my guard and reduce myself to their state. There was no way I was going to share my innermost secrets with a bunch of strangers, or open up to their curious stares and invasive questions.

The nights were the hardest to endure; waking up drenched in sweat, shaking uncontrollably, thirsting for something alcoholic, anything. I would turn on the TV in my bedroom and use the mindless late-night programmes as a distraction from my cravings. Mum would sometimes come in and join me when she heard the TV was on. I tried not to wake her because she was looking more and more exhausted from the stress and worry. I knew she checked the wardrobe, the chest of drawers and the furniture for hidden bottles, but she needn't have bothered. With no job, I didn't have any money to buy booze. She offered to give me some pocket money but I refused. I had to avoid temptation.

My withdrawal symptoms made me paranoid and nervous of my own shadow. I obsessively cleaned my room, as the slightest speck of dust sent me into a panic attack. In the mornings, I polished all the surfaces until they gleamed. After that, I hoovered, and carefully scanned my room for more dust, and then I polished again. I always did this in the same order, remembering to replace each item exactly where it had been. Otherwise I'd think that someone had been in my room, watching me as I slept, ready to take me away at the slightest hint of weakness.

I had to co-ordinate my wardrobe as well. My clothes were neatly lined up in grades of colour, like a paint chart. Summer wear was to the right and winter wear was to the left. Mid-season wear was in the middle, obviously. Tops and skirts from shortest to longest, then shorts, and finally trousers. Any item that didn't fit in with the colour or length system went in the bin.

Mum peeked in at me from time to time but only tsked, shaking her head. She had no choice but to put up with my obsessions, as long as they were confined to my bedroom. When I started to scrub the kitchen surfaces with a cloth soaked in bleach one day, she exploded.

'Enough now, Jen! Everything's clean, I did it this morning. Look at your hands, they're red raw. Stop it, please stop.' She burst into tears and collapsed on a chair, sobbing furiously.

I hung my head in shame. 'I'm sorry, Mum. It's just that I heard the doorbell ring, and I thought they'd come for me, they were here in the house, and I wanted to run away, hide, before they could get me.' The words gushed out in a stream, my speech getting more and more confused.

Mum got up and hugged me. 'There's no one here, Jen. It was only the postman, I had to sign for a special delivery. No one came in, and no one's coming to take you away. I won't let them.'

I nodded, but I knew she didn't understand. My fears were real. I had a constant feeling of dread in my chest from the moment I woke up to the moment I went to sleep. My heart pounded and I sweated constantly. But I couldn't tell anyone, just like I couldn't tell anyone about the things that had started this all off in the first place.

I pushed everything back down to that secret hideaway deep inside of me, the deep pit where even I wouldn't venture if I could help it. Alcohol had helped; as I didn't have that anymore, I turned to my obsessive paranoias. Anything to avoid facing the pain.

12

Over the next few weeks, I slowly felt more human. My face lost its puffiness, I had less headaches, and I was sleeping better. I didn't fly off the handle anymore at the slightest thing and my paranoia was easier to control. I managed to confine my OCD to my room, and left Mum to deal with the rest of the house, apart from adjusting the odd wonky picture on the wall. I didn't even jump when the doorbell rang. Instead, I held my breath and stood still, paralysed, until I understood who the visitor was. I was proud of the progress I was making, and every day was a tiny step forwards toward my goal of staying sober.

Then the divorce papers arrived, and it sent me over the edge, back into a heightened state of agitation. The fear rose up in me again at the thought of Paul abandoning me, and it tugged at my secret place, urging me to dive back down into the pit. I spent the day in my room, pacing, scratching at my arms until they bled, a sudden craving for wine hitting me with all its force. By the time I had to leave for a meeting, I was a wreck, both mentally and physically. I almost cancelled going, but I knew that Mum had high expectations for me, as I'd been doing so well. This meeting was a milestone, six months without alcohol, and I had been looking forward to celebrating with the group. Mum had been talking about it all week, so excited that I'd finally reached this point. I couldn't tell her about the letter, scrunched up in my trouser pocket like the piece of rubbish it was.

Attending a meeting was the only time I went out of the house alone, and it was only a short ten-minute bus ride, with the bus stop a few metres away from the community centre. When I left the house, my head was swirling with thoughts I hadn't had for a long time, my hands clenching and unclenching as I waited for the bus. The journey passed in a blur, and I suddenly found myself standing on the street, watching the tail lights of the bus disappear into the murky night.

The community centre was only metres away, warm and welcoming. But I turned left instead of right and went into the nearby corner shop. The owner said hello, then went back to his conversation with a customer. The bottle of gin was in my pocket before I knew what was happening. I wandered round the aisles for a bit, then said goodbye as I walked out of the shop. Stunned that I was now a thief as well as an alcoholic, I walked to the nearest bench, sat down and took a swig. And then another. And another. Until the bottle was empty.

'Shit.'

A passing man looked at me strangely.

'What do you want?' I yelled.

He turned his head and hurried on. I stumbled to my feet and saw the community centre door. Ah, that was where I was supposed to be.

Everyone turned as I crashed through the door and staggered over to an empty chair. 'Sho shorry I'm late,' I slurred. I took hold of the chair and sat down, my heart nearly stopping as I hit the floor instead.

'Who moved the chair?' I glared angrily around me. Fifteen stony-faced people glared back.

Rob, the co-ordinator, rushed over to help me up. 'Have you been drinking, Jennifer?' he asked gently.

'Sho what if I have? It's not against the law, is it?'

'No, but it is against our group's policies.' He gestured to a nearby chair. 'Sit down. I'll get you a coffee, it'll help you sober up.'

'Maybe I don't wanna sober up.' I stamped my foot.

'Jennifer, we're here to help you,' he said. 'Talk to us. Tell us what's wrong.'

The others smiled in encouragement. I stared at them, my mind buzzing.

'Whatsh wrong,' I started, then belched. I tried again. 'Whatsh wrong, is that I wanna drink and you assholes won't let me!'

'Don't throw away all your hard work,' Rob insisted. 'Don't let the drink win.'

'I don't give a shit. You can take your stupid group and shove it up your arse.' I delighted at their shocked gasps. 'I'm going home and I don't think I'll be back.'

My dignified exit was somewhat ruined by my tripping over a chair, lunging forwards, then banging my shoulder on the door, but I didn't care. I felt exhilarated, I was finally doing what *I* wanted to do. The feeling lasted until I got home. The look on Mum's face deflated me.

'Don't say anything, Mum. I'm sorry. I'm going to bed now.'

It took two days of lying in my darkened bedroom for the headache to pass. Mum brought me food and drink but she didn't sit with me this time. I had two long, lonely days to think about, well, about everything. Unable to distract myself with my other obsessions, I couldn't avoid the pit, hard as I tried, and this time it dragged me in headfirst.

The drinking had started seven years earlier, after my first miscarriage. Paul had continued as normal, as if nothing had happened. He told me we could try again when I was ready, while I wanted to mourn my unborn child, the end of my dreams. I missed imagining my baby growing inside me, that anxious anticipation of its first kick, wanting to know if it was a boy or a girl. All those plans, all those dreams. And then, nothing. Only emptiness, a black hole that sucked my future into it.

At first I didn't drink that much, just enough to dull the pain and get through the day. Then I miscarried again, and then a third time. After that I didn't want to try anymore, I didn't want to suffer anymore. I discovered the only thing that took away the pain was the drink. If only Paul had been willing to talk about our lost children, but he used his work to distract him. No one wanted to talk about my babies with me, even Mum changed the subject when I tried. So I drank. More and more. Then I found a job and that helped for a while. Until my colleagues invited me to go with them to the pub for lunch. And the rest, as they say, is history. I no longer needed to find someone to talk to; when I drank, the demons went away and I could pretend things were all right. Even though it wasn't, even though I was destroying everything in the attempt to enjoy my 'perfect' life.

I spent those two days wallowing in misery. The few mouthfuls of food I managed to get down churned in my stomach, threatening to force their way out again, so I stuck to sipping water every now and then. My dry, cracked lips felt taut and strange, my skin was clammy to touch and I seemed to ooze gin from every pore. The smell was unbearable.

Eventually, I was able to get up and have a shower. Feeling better, I went downstairs for something to eat. Mum pottered round the kitchen making some sandwiches while I held a steaming mug of coffee between my hands. The shaking had stopped but I went from feeling freezing cold to boiling hot within seconds. I suddenly found my appetite and I chewed enthusiastically on great big mouthfuls of bread, while Mum nibbled her sandwich like a mouse without saying a word.

'Okay, I get it. It's the silent treatment for now, is it?' With some food and coffee in my stomach, I was starting to feel more normal, and my fiery temper returned with a vengeance.

Mum slumped in her chair. 'I don't know what to say to you, Jen. I'm tired of worrying about you, wondering what state you'll come home in, if you'll find a bottle of alcohol and not have the willpower to resist. You've already lost your husband, your job, and now your support group. What do you have left?' A tear rolled down her cheek. 'You're my only daughter, my only child. Ever since your father died, I've done my best for you, I've tried so hard. And now I look at you and ask what I've done wrong.'

I saw the desolation on her face and felt sorry for the hurt I'd caused. 'You've done nothing wrong, Mum, you've done everything right. It's me. I can't face life anymore. Ever since, you know, the babies...' I stopped, unable to go on. The mouth of the pit yawned before me, daring me to jump in.

She scratched at her neck, looking at me as if she wanted to say something. I looked at the red marks her nails had left, wondering if this was going to be the moment of truth. Then she coughed and glanced away, and the moment passed. The pit closed, and I breathed a sigh of relief.

I stretched out on the sofa and yawned, exhausted after my early start. We'd never spoken about the babies again. I never told Mum about the pit, and how close I'd been to falling into it, never to come out again. We'd simply skipped over the important bits and concentrated on the silly, superficial things, putting a temporary bandage over my problems so that I could travel to Italy and 'find myself'. Stumbling upon the grave had led to me picking at the bandage, slowly unravelling it, until the unhealed wound was once more out in the open, ready to fester if I didn't take care of it. I thought that if I found out what had happened to Bruna's baby, perhaps I could find the strength to face my own demons. I promised I would start looking into it, as soon as I had the energy. I knew that I couldn't put it off forever.

13

Giulia and Agnese brought Bea to the cottage the next day after school. She entered the front door like a whirlwind, running excitedly through the rooms, chattering non-stop. As far as I could make out, she was telling me about her day at school, her friends, and how she loved to come and visit Luisa when she was alive.

'Bea, enough now,' Giulia said finally, exasperated with her daughter. 'Go out in the garden and pick some flowers for Jen, so she can put them in the kitchen.'

Silence fell when she ran out of the back door.

Giulia turned to me with an apologetic expression. 'She's great, but she can be a bit much at times. She's been so looking forward to meeting you.'

'Oh, don't worry,' I replied. 'It's like a breath of fresh air after the weekend I've had.'

'Jen said it was quiet here by herself,' Agnese quickly explained to Giulia.

'Yes, after having all of you here last week, I felt bit lost, I have to admit,' I said, relieved she hadn't mentioned the grave.

Giulia laughed. 'I'll leave Bea with you for a couple of days, if you like. That'll cure your need for company.'

I made a coffee for the three of us, which we took into the garden. Watching Bea running about, picking flowers and chasing butterflies, made me wonder what it had been like for my mum when she'd come to visit Great-grandmother Luisa. The garden must have been incredible back then, if Luisa had been dedicated to living naturally. And the Grove, why hadn't Mum told me about that? I was sure she would have mentioned the child's grave if she'd known about it.

'No, Bea, not in there,' Agnese called. Bea stopped outside the gate to the Grove and turned to us, pouting.

'Why not? Nonna Luisa used to let me go.'

'Only if she was with you, remember? She told you some of the plants are dangerous, you can't go in alone.'

'So, come with me.'

Agnese glanced at me. 'I don't know which plants you can touch. Just stay in the main garden for now, okay?'

Bea grumbled and stamped her feet, but soon got distracted by a lizard scuttling past her and chased it through the long grass.

'Thanks, Agnese,' I said.

Giulia looked at us and frowned. 'Have I missed something?'

'Jen found the grave the other day, and it shook her up a bit,' Agnese replied.

'Of course. We all take it for granted, it's a part of the garden,' Giulia said. 'We forgot to tell you about it. I guess it could be quite a shock if you don't know it's there.'

'Just a bit.' I was glad I hadn't told Agnese about the dragonfly leading me to the grave, they'd have thought I was mad.

'What have you got planned for this week?' Giulia asked. 'I know Liliana is going to insist you go around for dinner every day, so you won't have a chance to feel lonely again.' She winked.

'Oh, I don't know,' I said, running my hand through my hair. 'I'd like to find someone to give me a hand to sort out the garden, and I thought I'd go visit Uncle Tommaso to get some advice about the Grove. I'd like to bring it back to its former glory.'

'Good luck with that.' Giulia sniggered.

'What, sorting out the garden or Uncle Tommaso?' I asked.

'Hmm, both. I'll ask Piero if he knows someone who can help out. You'd better prepare yourself before going to Tommaso's, he's quite a character.'

'So everyone keeps saying. But I think I'm going to need his help, there are so many plants and bushes that I've never seen before, and I've no idea how to look after them.'

'Tommaso hasn't been back since Luisa died, he says there are too many ghosts here for him. But give it a go; who knows, maybe he'll change his mind.' Agnese patted my arm. 'At least you've got plenty to keep you busy. Otherwise it can get a bit boring, there's not a lot to do up here in the mountains.'

'I like it, the peace and quiet,' I said. 'It's so different from where I lived in England. I like being able to do things at my own pace, when I want, without the hustle and bustle of the town, the constant traffic, people everywhere, deadlines. This is exactly what I need right now.'

'Look, look, Jen, here's a bunch of flowers for you.' Bea came running up with her arms full of brightly coloured weeds, some dropping to the ground as she careered towards us.

'They're beautiful, Bea. Come, let's go and find a vase, then you can decide where to put them.'

I helped her carry everything back to the cottage, glad that the conversation with Giulia and Agnese was over.

I got a glass vase out of one of the cupboards and put it on the table. Bea carefully arranged the flowers, moving them about until she was satisfied with her composition.

'There,' she declared.

I added some water from a jug. 'Where do you want them, Bea?'

She picked up the vase and put it on the windowsill by the sink. 'Here's perfect, they've got plenty of light and you can see them when you wash up.' She turned and smiled, and I gave her a big hug.

'Thank you, now it really looks like home in here,' I said.

A little while later they left, promising to visit again. Bea took hold of my hand, suddenly shy, and gave me a quick kiss on the cheek.

'I'm so glad you're here,' she whispered, and scampered down the path, waving goodbye without turning back.

Agnese and Giulia both kissed me goodbye, then raced off down the road after her, shouting at her to stop and wait for them. Laughing, I went back into the kitchen.

Sitting at the table, I looked at the flowers on the windowsill, delicate pale blues clashing with vivid greens and yellows, and the occasional red poppy in amongst them. The little girl had created a stunning arrangement, she definitely had an artistic eye for colours. A bee flew in through the open window and landed on one of the flowers, making it bend slightly under its weight. Its quiet hum and vibrating wings reminded me of the dragonfly, which made me think of Mark's visit and how I'd been in a rush to get rid of him. I blushed, filled with guilt. *Maybe I should phone him and arrange a coffee to say sorry*, I thought. *Just one date, get to know him*. I got my handbag and rooted through it for his business card, shoving everything aside until I found it right at the bottom. I grabbed my mobile and dialled his number before I changed my mind.

14

We met at ten the next morning in the town square of Gallicano, in front of the only newsstand in the place. Mark was dressed casually in beige chinos and a polo top, a faint shadow of stubble covering his chin.

'No work today?' I asked.

'Nope. I'm a freelance translator, I work when I want. I decided to take the morning off so we don't have to rush.'

'Where are you taking me?' I wondered if we'd have to walk past the elderly gentlemen already sitting outside the bar, but Mark took hold of my arm and steered me in the other direction.

'We're going to see the Chiesa di San Jacopo,' he informed me.

'A church? I thought we were going for coffee.' I'd only had one at home, and had been looking forward to another two, at least.

'It's right at the top of the town and the views are incredible. It'll be worth it. And there's a bar next door,' he added, winking at me.

I relented. 'Okay, let's go and see this church.'

It was a steep climb up the narrow streets, and my calves

were protesting once again by the time we reached the top. Mark pointed out various places of interest, laughing at my red face and gasped comments.

'Don't worry, you'll get used to it,' he said.

'I'll have to,' I retorted, 'or I'll die from a heart attack.'

He was right; the view from the church was truly incredible. I could see the town spread out below, the narrow streets winding among the clustered houses, people taking a morning stroll, stopping to greet each other with a kiss on the cheek, gesticulating while chattering excitedly. I tore my eyes away from the fascinating sight of Italian social behaviour and gazed at the half-tamed mountain opposite. Dense forests crowded around small patches of cultivated land, interspersed with the occasional house, as if the locals were determined to fight nature and claim any piece of ground they could. I marvelled at how anyone could dream of taming this wild region, and why they'd even want to try.

Mark's voice suddenly brought me out of my reverie. 'Was I right about the view?' He grinned. I imagined the answer was obvious from the expression on my face.

'Yes, it's beautiful. I never thought it would look like this.' I turned towards him. 'What about some coffee now?'

'Just one more thing, then I promise we'll get that coffee.' He led me along the side of the church to a large iron gate. Inside was a cemetery, the headstones barely visible among the long grass and weeds. I shuddered, but it didn't have the same effect on me as the grave in the garden at the cottage. Here there was a feeling of serenity, of long-dead people slumbering under the ground, content with leaving behind their bleak earthly lives in exchange for an untroubled eternal rest.

'This isn't used anymore, but there are graves in there dating from the 1300s,' Mark said. 'It's usually locked, but every now and then the priest will let a few people in to have a look around. There's a crypt right at the back that belonged to your aunt's family, the Innocenti. I read about them when I first arrived here; they were a rich, influential family in medieval times, and controlled the whole area back then.'

I pointed at a statue of an angel, hidden behind a tall, leafy weed. 'That's unusual.'

'Now there's a mystery waiting to be solved. It marks an unnamed grave, no one has ever discovered who's buried there. But there are a couple of the Innocenti missing from the crypt, so it's presumed that it's one of them. No one knows for sure, though.' His voice trailed off, but his eyes glinted mischievously. 'So, shall we go for a coffee? Or do you prefer a glass of wine?'

I followed him back towards the church, debating with myself whether to tell him about my drinking problem. I turned around a couple of times, my eyes searching until the angel was out of view, strangely drawn to it.

'Mark.'

'Hmm?'

'Wait, I need to tell you something.' I took a deep breath, uncertain as to how he would take it. 'I can't drink alcohol, none at all,' I told him, watching his face.

'Ah. Because?'

'Because I'm an alcoholic.' There, I'd said it, for the first time ever.

'I see. Thanks for telling me, Jennifer. Or can I call you Jenny?'

'I prefer Jen, if you have to,' I replied.

There was an awkward silence, then he straightened his shoulders and offered me his arm. 'Coffee it is, Jen,' he declared. I heaved a sigh of relief, thankful it had been so easy to tell him.

We sat outside a characteristic bar, watching the world go by as we drank our coffees and quietly chatted. I liked Mark, but there was something about him I couldn't quite put my finger on, something that made me feel uneasy. The odd comment here and there, an irritable expression flitting over his face at something I said, or interrupting me if I spoke for too long. I decided he'd be all right as a friend but nothing more.

'We could go sightseeing tomorrow, if you like,' he said, after a long pause turned into an embarrassing silence. 'There's plenty to see here. We can go to Lucca for a cultural outing, or we can go further up in the mountains. There's a sanctuary, or a river where we can have a picnic, or–'

'What about the caves?' I interrupted him, remembering Umberto's advice. 'I've heard they're quite spectacular.'

'La Grotta del Vento?' he asked, surprised.

'Yes, the taxi driver told me about them. I'd like to go and see them.'

Mark frowned. 'Sure you don't want to see the sanctuary? The monks will take you on a guided tour, it's very spiritual.'

'I'm not all that keen on monks and sanctuaries,' I said, laughing. 'I'd much rather go to the caves.' I saw a look of anger pass over his face, but it was gone before I could ask him what was wrong.

He snorted. 'All right, the caves it is. It'll be an early start, though, better to get there before the crowds. Now drink up, we'll take the scenic route home so you can see the rest of Gallicano.'

I was so tired by the time we got back down to the square that I refused his offer of lunch. 'No thanks, I think I'll make my way back to the cottage and have a rest.'

'If you're sure. I've got to get back anyway, get some work done so I can take the day off tomorrow.'

Confused by his hot and cold behaviour, I clutched my handbag closer to my body and stepped back. 'Okay. What time tomorrow?'

He glanced around, as if checking whether someone was

listening to us. Satisfied that we were alone, he leaned forward. 'About half past eight. That way we can do the first tour at ten.'

'Fine, see you tomorrow then.'

'Great. Enjoy the rest of your day,' he said, already turning to go.

Frowning, I started on my long walk back to the cottage.

I spent the rest of my day with my laptop down in the Grove, googling the various plants to try to identify them. It was a long, laborious task, but it took my mind off Mark and his mood swings, and kept me from thinking about my stash of wine bottles. I was determined to stay off the drink this time, especially if I kept having nightmares.

By the end of the afternoon, I had a long list of plants, which I would then have to research individually to find out how to care for them. I sighed. It looked like I'd need Uncle Tommaso after all, it would take me months to learn everything I needed to know.

I stood and contemplated the Grove, trying to imagine Grandma Luisa diligently tending the plants, choosing the various parts for her herbal remedies, carrying her wicker basket full of sweet-smelling cuttings back to the cottage to start turning them into ointments and salves that would cure the locals. How did she know which ones to use? Aunt Liliana had said Grandma was a healer, as if it was the most natural thing in the world for her to be.

I swayed, my legs wobbling as the long day caught up with me. I left the Grove, closing the gate behind me, and made my way up the garden to the cottage. It was only when I got to the back door that I realised I hadn't seen a single dragonfly all afternoon.

15

Mark arrived the next morning at eight thirty on the dot with a squeal of brakes, horn blasting, as I was finishing getting ready.

'Hi, Jen,' he called as I locked the front door behind me.

'What's all the noise about?' I grumbled. 'You'll have the neighbours complaining.'

He looked around, puzzled. 'What neighbours? You live in the middle of nowhere, the most I've done is scare a few sparrows. I guess they'll be "tweeting" you any moment now.'

I groaned. 'It's far too early for that sort of pun.' He held the door open for me as I got into the car. 'You are taking me for a coffee first, right?'

He got in the other side. 'There's a bar up at the caves. There'll be time for quite a few coffees.' I was glad to see he was in a better mood than the day before.

'As long as it's within the next hour,' I said, trying to add some levity into my voice.

'Oh yes. The caves are up in the mountains. It's a bit of a tortuous road, but it only takes about half an hour to get there.'

'Great. Let's go and see these caves then.'

. . .

He wasn't joking about the tortuous road. It wound around the side of the mountain, huge boulders suspended above us, only held back by what looked like chicken wire. I gulped each time we passed under one, terrified that the wire would break just at that moment and completely flatten the car, with us in it. *At least it would be quick and relatively painless*, I thought as I looked at the outer edge of the road. With no barriers, it would be easy enough to go over the edge as we went round one of the hairpin bends, especially at the speed Mark was going. And that, I imagined, would be relatively slow and extremely painful, as the car rolled over and over down the steep mountainside, banging and thumping its way to a gradual halt in the valley below. I closed my eyes and tried to stop imagining so much.

We finally arrived at a parking area with a touristy restaurant on one side and a drab-looking building on the other. We seemed to be the only ones there. I got out of the car, my body stiff with tension after the terrifying drive.

'Is this it?' I asked.

'Yeah. I agree it doesn't look like much, but if you turn round...' He paused dramatically, so I did as he said. And gasped. I hadn't really taken much notice of the scenery, scared as I was of becoming an indelible part of it. I saw that we were surrounded by mountains, woods, rocky tors, and that wonderful tranquillity you only find when immersed in nature.

'This is why I wanted to get here early, before the tourists arrive,' Mark said. 'What do you think?'

'It's beautiful, absolutely stunning. Well worth the early start.'

'Come on, let's go and get a coffee.'

. . .

The tourists started arriving a while later, huge coaches billowing dark clouds of exhaust fumes. We watched them spill out and make their way towards us.

'Peace is over,' I said. I'd enjoyed our quiet cup of coffee outside on the terrace, soaking up the atmosphere.

'Let's go and get our tickets. It's going to get packed in here.'

A little later, there was a long queue of people waiting for the guided tour through the caves. Everyone chatted excitedly, and I saw a few teenagers taking selfies underneath a low-hanging rock. I nudged Mark. 'If that falls, I wonder if people will try to help them or just take photos of it.'

'They'll probably help after they've uploaded the video to Facebook,' he replied, laughing.

I took out my phone. 'Shall we? Seeing as everyone else is doing it.'

'Maybe later.' He turned brusquely away from me. I put my phone back in my bag, hurt. He must have seen the expression on my face because he said, 'We're about to go in. Look, that's the guide. We'll take a photo after, when everyone's gone.'

'All right,' I said, but I wondered why he kept changing his moods so quickly.

'Okay, everybody, our tour is starting,' the guide called. 'Follow me, and don't get lost.' We all followed obediently.

He turned towards a heavy door at the back of the cave. 'Brace yourselves. When I open this door, there's usually quite a breeze that comes out, as the tunnel is much colder than outside and the air rushes through.' A strong wind blew around us when he heaved the steel door open, as if the mountain was sighing at the tourists walking through it, disturbing its slumber of thousands of years.

'I feel like we're intruding,' I whispered to Mark, sensing the mountain's displeasure at being awoken every day by hordes of noisy people.

'What?'

I sighed. He obviously didn't feel it. 'Nothing.'

We went along a tunnel and found ourselves in an enormous cave.

'This is Bear Hall,' the tour guide explained. 'We've found evidence of cave bears that lived here thousands of years ago. Over there you can see some of the actual bones.'

We turned towards the glass case he indicated, some people oohing and aahing.

'Can we take photos?' someone asked from the back.

'Yes, of course, I only ask you don't use your flash too much,' the guide replied. The teenagers immediately stood beneath a mock skeleton of a bear, grinning inanely as their phones clicked.

We followed the guide in single file through the narrow tunnels, marvelling at the incredible natural sculptures we passed, formed by drops of water over the millennia. Every now and then the tunnels opened into large caverns, filled with brilliant white stalactites and stalagmites, breathtaking twisted shapes standing silently to attention as we passed.

'Now be careful,' boomed the guide. 'The tunnel descends here for quite a few metres; it's not slippery but watch where you put your feet. This is the Giant's Abyss, where there is an underground river.'

I could feel the dampness on my face from the humidity in the air and I pulled my cardigan tighter to me, the cold seeping into my bones. Mark noticed me shivering.

'You okay?' he asked, putting his arm over my shoulders.

'It's a bit cold, that's all.'

'There are several small ponds down here, left behind by the river,' the guide explained. 'The water looks milky, but it's only an effect of the lights. Now, the next cave we're going to enter is called the Hall of Voices. The dripping water echoes around the walls and sounds like far-off voices of people talking. This was a base camp for explorers, and those who remained here waiting for the others found it very unnerving. When we're all inside, I'm going to turn off the lights so you can understand how it was for them.'

We huddled together inside the cave, some looking visibly scared at the notion of being in total darkness when the lights were switched off. I had to admit I felt a bit nervous. It wasn't easy to ignore the fact that there were thousands of tons of rock above our heads, and that it wouldn't take much for it to collapse on us. I took comfort from the thought that these caves had been here for millennia, and would probably still be here at the end of the world.

The guide turned the lights off. No one made a sound, and after a few seconds I could hear it. A soft staccato sound, as if a few people were having a conversation some distance away. It reminded me of when I was little, hearing the television programmes downstairs while I was trying to get to sleep, that muffled sound as if they were broadcasting through cotton wool. I thought if I strained my ears, I might be able to make out words or sentences.

After a few minutes, the guide turned the lights back on and there was an audible sigh of relief.

'Follow me, we're almost at the end now,' he called.

Mark pulled my arm and made me wait until everyone had left the tunnel behind the guide.

'What's up?' I asked.

'I saw something back there, down a side tunnel. I want to go and have a look,' he said, smiling at me.

'Shouldn't we follow the group? We'll get left behind.'

'It's just down there, not too far. We'll be back before you know it. I bet they'll still be outside the cave.'

'Okay.' I wasn't too convinced. I glanced at him and saw a

triumphant look flicker over his face, gone so quickly that I thought I'd imagined it.

'Let's go,' he said.

Holding my hand, he led me back through the cave entrance and a short way along the tunnel, until we arrived at an unlit passage that branched off to the right, down a flight of steps.

'Let's take a look,' he said.

'Why would anyone want to go down there?' It looked like a scene from a horror movie, the steps swallowed up by the darkness below. All that was missing was the man-eating monster lurking around the corner.

'I don't know, maybe we can find a stalactite that's fallen and smashed into pieces. That would be a great souvenir to take home. Or are you too chicken?'

I grunted. 'Me, chicken? Of course not.' I tried not to think about what could be down there, cursing all the horror books I'd ever read. 'But we won't get told off for stealing part of Italy's national heritage or anything like that, will we?'

'Of course not, silly.' He laughed. 'After you.'

I made my way down the steps, keeping one hand on the wall. The light from the main tunnel filtered to the bottom, but it was difficult to see more than a few inches ahead. I heard Mark's footsteps behind me and carried on, turning into the lightless tunnel when I reached the bottom. I slowly made my way forward, trailing my hands along the wall to avoid banging into the rock, my eyes straining in the semi-darkness. It was an exhilarating feeling, leaving the group to explore on our own, and I felt a flicker of excitement at the thought of breaking the rules like this.

Without warning, the lights in the main tunnel behind me went out.

16

'Hello?' I called. My voice echoed around me, bouncing off the cave walls. 'Mark, are you there?' I couldn't hear anything, except for a consistent dripping of water murmuring incomprehensible words further ahead. I turned, my arms outstretched, but there was nothing there. I continued to turn, shuffling my feet a few inches in every direction, until I was completely disorientated. I stopped, aware that I had no idea of which way would take me back to the group.

'Mark!' I shouted louder, my voice startling me. I could hear a note of hysteria creeping in, and it scared me. My imagination went crazy, filling my head with improbable outcomes, as I understood that I was alone. I could usually handle anything, but the thought of being lost in the caves, doomed to wander the catacomb of tunnels, made me shiver with fear. I tried to stay calm and think. I'd only turned off the path for a few minutes at most, surely Mark would have noticed I wasn't there. But I saw a fleeting image of his sneering face in my mind and I wondered if he would raise the alarm. He'd been right behind me on the steps, reassuring me that we'd catch up with the group in no time, but I realised that I hadn't heard him since entering the lower tunnel.

'Okay, breathe,' I whispered, not wanting to start the echoes off again. This part was completely dark but if I walked forward a little I should come across the main tunnel and the steps taking me back to the group. If I was going in the right direction.

Panic took hold of me and I started to walk more quickly, stumbling over rocks and stones, rubbing my hands along the wall to keep my bearings. My breath came in deep gasps, fear taking over everything else. I tried to move faster, straining my eyes for a glimpse of light and a way out. I suddenly tripped and fell, bashing my forehead against the wall of the tunnel. I collapsed onto my knees and cried out, wincing as pain shot through my head and down to my neck. My probing fingers found something wet and sticky above my eye and I felt the beginning of a lump.

'Shit,' I wailed. 'Shit, shit, shit!' My voice reverberated around the tunnel, mocking me. I lifted my head but it felt heavy, almost too heavy to move. Then I saw it. Up ahead, there was a light. I blinked, trying to focus on it, unsure whether to trust my vision after the knock I'd had. It was definitely a light. I gathered myself together and stood, my legs shaking. I walked forward, keeping my eyes on it, trying to stop myself from dashing madly along the tunnel.

The steps came into view, dimly shining in the light from the main passage that led to the Hall of Voices. I walked more quickly, relieved. Now I knew where I was.

'Jen?' Mark ran down the steps. 'I've been looking everywhere for you. Didn't you hear me calling?'

I shook my head, feeling numb. 'I was in the tunnel,' I mumbled, half-collapsing in his arms. 'I thought you were behind me, but you'd gone.'

'I told you it was better we turned back, otherwise we'd

remain too far behind,' he said, holding me. 'When I reached the group, I realised you weren't there. I came back to search for you.' He looked more closely at me. 'What the hell have you done to your head?'

'I fell,' I said tiredly. 'Let's go, I want to get out of here.'

'Yes, let's find the group. They'll be at the exit by now.'

'Wait, didn't you tell them I was missing?'

'No, I didn't want them to organise a search party or anything. I knew where you were, it was only a matter of coming to get you.' His face was a sickly pale colour under the artificial light, giving him a macabre appearance.

'I can't believe you. I could have got lost, gone down the wrong tunnel, I could have been anywhere, and you didn't even bother telling the guide.' I stormed off, leaving him standing there.

'Don't be like that, Jen,' he said, running after me. 'I had everything under control.'

'I was scared out of my wits,' I said, without stopping to wait for him. 'I panicked. I fell over and hurt myself. Anything could have happened.' I turned and glared at him, but his innocent expression made me even angrier. I shook my head with helpless rage. 'Oh, let's just get out of here.' Sobbing, I went towards the exit, the blue sky a welcome sight through the large cave opening.

The group was milling about outside, the guide counting heads. 'There you are,' he said, visibly relieved. 'I kept doing a recount, I thought I was two people short. Where on earth did you get to?'

'Ask him,' I replied, and stomped over to the bar.

Mark followed me inside. 'Go and sit over there, I'll order.'

I did as he said, still fuming. The place was filling up as more tourists arrived, noisy chatter booming across the room, the aroma of coffee hanging heavy in the air. I took some deep breaths, trying to use my calming techniques with little success.

'Here you go.' Mark sat next to me and placed two glasses of white wine on the table.

'What's that?'

'Wine, to help you relax. I imagine you need it after your shock.' He pushed a glass towards me.

'But I told you I can't drink alcohol,' I snapped. 'I'm an alcoholic, remember?' I pushed it away, leaving a smear of condensation on the table's surface.

'Go on, just this once. It's purely for medicinal purposes, right? You need something stronger than coffee after what's happened.'

'No, I can't,' I insisted. 'You'll have to drink both of them.'

'Oh, I'm driving. I can't drink both.' He looked disappointed. 'Maybe you can have a sip, rather than waste it. A small taste isn't going to ruin your efforts, is it? I really am sorry for what happened in the caves.' He picked up his glass and swallowed a large mouthful.

I shrugged, my resolve wavering. An image of the dark tunnel came into my mind, I could almost feel the rough rock beneath my hands once more. I reached out and wrapped my fingers around the stem of the other wine glass.

'Just a sip,' I whispered.

A glass of wine later, I'd calmed down a bit. A couple more glasses after that, I was feeling mellow. Not enough to accept Mark's apology, but enough to get into the car and let him drive me home. I hadn't wanted to drink any wine; I'd gone to the bar for a coffee, but I'd let him talk me into having a few glasses. It was for medicinal purposes, I told myself, anyone would be entitled to a couple of drinks after an experience like that. My head spun as the car negotiated the steep, winding road back down the mountain, and I dozed off.

'Hey, sleepyhead, wake up. We've arrived.' Mark shook my shoulder, stirring me from my slumber.

'Washn't shleeping,' I mumbled. Christ, was I really that drunk?

'Let me give you a hand,' he said, grinning. He ran round to the passenger side and opened the door. I scrabbled about with my seat belt and finally managed to release it. I tried to get out of the car in an elegant manner, but my foot twisted beneath me and I almost fell to my knees.

'Oops. Here, I've got you. Don't want you hitting your head again.'

'I can do it myshelf.' I glared at him. My trembling legs said otherwise, and I found myself grabbing at his arm.

'It's okay, I'm here,' he laughed. 'Let's get you indoors.'

When I woke up, the bedroom was cast in strange shadows from the last rays of the setting sun shining through the shutters. I fumbled for my phone and swiped it. Eight o'clock. I groaned. My head was thumping, my throat dry, and I desperately needed the toilet. I turned the bedside light on and almost screamed. Mark was in bed with me! I tried to control myself, not wanting to wake him up. I quietly slid out of bed, realising only then that I was naked, and crept into the bathroom.

'Oh my God, oh my God,' I groaned, looking at my shadowy reflection in the mirror. My bloodshot eyes confirmed what I already knew: that I had drunk too much. I suddenly rushed to the toilet and threw up, gasping for breath as I vomited. I washed my mouth and face when I'd finished, grabbed my dressing gown from the hook on the back of the door and wrapped it tightly around me. There was a knock on the door.

'Jennifer? Jen, are you okay?'

A sudden rage came over me. It was his fault I was in this state. I'd told him I couldn't drink. He knew what a few glasses of wine would do, and he'd taken advantage of me.

I threw open the door. 'Get out,' I shouted.

'Wh-what?'

'Get dressed and get out of my house,' I screamed at him.

'Jen, honey, I think–'

'Don't you dare "Jen, honey" me.' I was furious.

'But I–'

I was determined not to let him finish a sentence. 'I said, get out.'

He glared at me, then turned and went back into the bedroom.

A few minutes later he came out, dressed. I was still as angry as ever, if not more.

'I think you're being very unfair,' he said. 'You were all right with this earlier, I would never–'

'But I'm not all right with it now,' I retorted. 'And I was drunk, as you well know.' I stood there before him in my dressing gown, my chest heaving, with so much anger inside me that I thought I'd explode.

He raised his hands in defeat. 'Okay, okay, I'm going,' he said. I watched him go downstairs and open the back door.

Pausing, he turned to me. 'You'll regret this,' he said quietly and went out, slamming the door behind him.

I sank to the floor and cried, partly from relief that he was gone, mainly from a deeply ingrained hatred towards myself. I waited until I heard his car roar off down the road, then I gingerly got to my feet. Legs shaking, I poked my head round the bathroom door. Everything was quiet, proof that he'd gone. I couldn't face going back into my bedroom, too embarrassed to see the evidence of my drunken exploits, so I went to the guest room instead. The bed was already made up with crisp, clean sheets provided by Aunt Liliana. I gratefully lay down.

My head was still spinning but the nausea had passed. I concentrated on my breathing, slowing my heart rate down by focusing on a point on the ceiling, until my eyelids became too heavy to stay open and I fell fast asleep.

17

I woke to the sound of dripping water and for a split second imagined I was back in the caves, wandering about in the dark. I came to with a start, then slowly calmed down as I realised I was lying in bed, covered in soft blankets. I went over to the window and opened the shutters, looking out at a grey sky with low-hanging clouds, rain making everything sodden and miserable.

I closed the window, tears prickling at my eyes as images of the previous day came to me. I blinked them away, furious at myself for having lost control like that. While mentally berating myself I heard it again, a constant drip, drip, drip.

'What the hell's going on now?' I stormed out onto the landing and saw a puddle of water in the middle of the floor. 'That's all I need,' I groaned. I'd wanted to wait before starting repairs on the outside of the cottage, but I guessed I'd have to get it sorted as soon as possible. I grabbed a bucket from the bathroom and placed it under the leak as a temporary measure.

· · ·

A long, hot shower later I felt slightly better; a cup of coffee helped me reach a more acceptable level of sociability. Unable to stay in the cottage alone any longer, despite the rain, I went to visit Aunt Liliana.

I rang the doorbell, looking like a bedraggled rat, rivulets of water running down my body and pooling at my feet.

'Oh my God, look at the state of you! Didn't you bring an umbrella? And what on earth have you done to your head?' she cried as soon as she opened the door. I touched the bump on my forehead, wincing at how tender it felt. I hadn't dared look at myself in the mirror, so had no idea how bad it was.

'Come in, let's get that seen to,' she said, hustling me inside the door.

I hesitated. 'The others?'

'No, nobody's here, I'm all alone. Giulia and Agnese went to the shopping mall down in the valley, the men are at work. Come on, you're soaking.'

I followed her through to the kitchen and sat down while she hurried about, gathering her medical supplies together. She handed me a towel to dry myself off, and I realised belatedly that I was dripping all over the floor.

'Oh, leave it, it's only water,' Aunt Liliana said when she saw me glance down. 'Stop looking so guilty. Now, this is going to hurt a bit,' she added, dabbing some liquid on a gauze strip, 'but it will reduce the swelling. Good job Luisa left me some of this.' I closed my eyes as she gently swabbed the cut, and flinched when she touched my forehead. The liquid was cool on my skin and brought instant relief to the throbbing pain.

'There. It's clean, but you're going to have a nasty bruise for a while.' She pursed her lips. 'How on earth did it happen?'

Panicking, I said the first thing that came into my mind. 'I went out in the garden last night for a stroll, and bumped into a branch.' I gave her an embarrassed smile. 'I really whacked my head, saw stars for a moment there.'

'Tsk. You've got to be more careful up at the cottage alone. What if you'd knocked yourself out?' She handed me the bottle of liquid. 'Here, use it three times a day until the swelling's gone down.'

'Thanks.' I noticed it was still raining, although the sky was starting to brighten. 'I'm going to have to find someone to fix the roof, it was leaking this morning.'

'Yes, Giulia mentioned you needed a handyman. I think Piero is looking into finding someone, but it's a busy period, you might have to wait a while. I'll send Dante over to patch the roof up in the meantime.'

I was glad the others weren't there. It was pleasant listening to her gentle chatter and her voice was a balm for my aching head. My mind started to drift as she talked, going back to the previous day's events. I couldn't believe that Mark had left me in the tunnel – had he done it on purpose? The more I thought about it, the more suspicious I became. He'd bought me a glass of wine afterwards, to calm me down he said, but then he'd ordered more. What kind of a bastard would get an alcoholic drunk? I felt sick again.

'Jennifer? Are you all right?' Aunt Liliana's worried voice brought me back to the present with a jolt. 'You looked like you were drifting off. You can never be too careful with a bump on the head, maybe I should take you to the doctor.'

'No, no, I'm fine, honestly. I'm sorry, what were you saying?' I smiled sweetly and hoped she would forget about the doctor.

She peered closely at me, as if trying to see through my skull to any possible brain damage, then relented. 'Well, you tell me if you feel dizzy or sick, yes? Another coffee?'

'That would be lovely,' I exclaimed, my voice a little too loud at my relief that she wasn't going to call an ambulance. I looked out of the window while she busied herself at the stove, and saw it had stopped raining.

'I might go and visit Uncle Tommaso this morning.' The idea had just come to me, but now was as good a time as ever. 'Didn't you say he lives by himself?'

'Yes, in a small house at the edge of the village, but no one ever goes to see him. I went there a few months ago to make sure he was still alive. Someone's got to keep an eye on the grumpy old sod. He sent me away, shouting and yelling that he didn't need mollycoddling, he'd let me know if and when he needed anything. That's nothing unusual, though, he hates company. The only person he ever got on with was Luisa, and since she died he does his best to show how much he dislikes everyone else. Why do you want to go and see him?'

'Agnese said he helped Luisa look after the plants in the Grove, and I wanted to ask his advice on how to care for them. It's pretty overgrown, and I'd like to get it back to how it was when Luisa was alive.'

'That's a lovely idea,' Liliana said, hugging me. 'Luisa would be so happy, and it would keep you busy for a while.' She glanced at me and blushed.

'Have you been talking to Mum?' I asked.

'She phoned me a few days ago and told me about your... problems. I'm sorry, I didn't know about you and your husband.'

'Yes, well, I came over here to sort myself out,' I replied. 'And I'd appreciate it if you didn't tell everyone else.'

'Of course not. You take all the time you need. I promised your mum I'd keep an eye on you, that's all.'

'Okay,' I said, relieved.

'Yes, well, you go and see Tommaso. Tell him I sent you and start talking right away about the Grove, it might help. But if he starts shouting, get out of there as quickly as possible!'

18

I approached Tommaso's house with some trepidation after Liliana and Agnese's warnings. But I had to find out, I had to know what had happened to the baby. The house appeared run-down, its weathered shutters badly in need of a few coats of varnish, the windows so grimy they didn't even reflect the morning sun. The patch of ground at the front was full of weeds and several rusting objects, so old I couldn't make out what they were. A huge metal gate and fence barred my way and I looked for a doorbell.

An ugly brown and white mongrel charged towards me, yapping loudly, and made me jump. I stepped backwards as it put its nose between the metal bars of the gate and snarled viciously, upper lip curled back, showing off its razor-sharp teeth.

'It's okay, I'm not going to hurt you,' I said, realising how stupid that sounded. It was more likely the dog would rip my ankles to shreds. It kept on barking, and my head started to throb. Surely, if Tommaso was at home, he would have come out by now to see what all the noise was about? I saw the doorbell at long last and, standing as far away as possible, reached out to ring it.

'What the hell do you want?' came a voice from the back of the house. 'I've told you people over and over again, I don't want to buy anything, my house isn't for sale, and I definitely don't need saving from God!' A silver-haired man came stomping towards me. I couldn't help thinking he looked exactly like his dog, and half expected him to start barking at me too.

'Uncle Tommaso–' I began, but he interrupted me.

'Uncle? I'm not your uncle, I've never seen you before. What do you want? Why can't people leave me alone? You think I don't know what they say about me in the village?' He grabbed hold of the gate with grubby hands and glared at me, drops of sweat on his forehead. 'All I want is to be left alone, understand?'

I didn't know what to say. His anger radiated from him in invisible waves, crashing over me as if trying to flatten me. My shoulders sagged in defeat.

'I-I'm sorry. I wanted to meet you. Aunt Liliana suggested I come and speak to you about the Grove.' I turned to go.

'Wait!' he shouted. 'The Grove?'

'Yes. I-I'm staying at Great-grandmother Luisa's cottage. The Grove is so overgrown, and I wanted to sort it out, but I'm not really a gardener, so Aunt Liliana said to speak with you, because you used to help Luisa, and she said you'd know what to do.' The words came tumbling out together; I hardly paused for breath in my hurry to explain everything before he sent me away.

'The cottage?' he mumbled, staring at me. 'You're staying there? Who are you?' He bent down and stroked the dog, who had stopped barking but was still snarling at me. 'Hush now,' he said, and the dog lay down at his feet, watching me, but silent at long last.

'I'm Rita's daughter,' I said, relieved that both he and the dog had calmed down. 'I live in England but, well, it's a long story. I've come over here to stay at the cottage while I sort myself out.'

'Rita?' he said, looking closely at me.

'My mother. Bruna's daughter.'

'Bruna?' he snapped.

'Y-yes,' I said, startled at his tone of voice.

He ran his hand through his white hair, making it stand up on end. When he spoke, his voice was calmer, but he had a wild expression in his eyes.

'I guess you'd better come in then,' he said, and opened the gate. I expected the dog to rush out at me, but it remained at its master's feet and glared at me, reminding me exactly who was in charge.

The inside of his house was as dirty, if not dirtier, as the outside. I followed him into the living room, which was sparsely furnished. The dog jumped up onto the only armchair, clouds of dust rising up into the air, shimmering in the subdued sunlight. Tommaso went over to a small table where there were two wooden chairs and gestured to me to sit down.

'What's your name?'

'Jennifer. Everyone calls me Jen.'

He snorted. 'Not very Italian, is it?'

'No, not really.' I was determined not to let him goad me. 'I was born in England, Mum didn't want to give me an Italian name that would make me stand out too much. She suffered enough with her own when she was at school, and had to shorten Margherita to Rita to avoid any problems. I didn't understand at the time, but now I know why she did it. I quickly found out that kids can be very unkind. They used to sing the Cornetto song at me during breaktimes, just because they knew my mother was half Italian.'

'Ashamed of her heritage, was she, your mum?' Tommaso frowned at me.

'Not at all. But things were different when she was growing up.' I tried to change the subject. 'I found the Grove, at the bottom of the garden. It's a very beautiful place.'

He actually smiled at that. 'Mamma loved the Grove. She told me some of the fruit trees and bushes had been there for hundreds of years.'

Mamma? Of course, Luisa was his mother! I had to keep him talking. 'Hundreds of years? Is that possible for plants?'

'If Mamma said it, then it's possible,' he retorted. 'She knew everything about the cottage. It has been in the family for generations, did you know that?'

I nodded, hoping to encourage him to continue. 'Will you tell me what you know?'

'About the Grove or the family's origins?'

'Both.' I held my breath.

He looked at me. 'Why should I?'

'Because it's my heritage, I'd like to find out more about my family.' I leaned forward and gently touched his hand.

'All I know is what Mamma told me. It's an extraordinary story but she was adamant it was true.'

I waited, not daring to interrupt him.

He picked up a pair of glasses from the table and rubbed them on the corner of his shirt, squinting to see if they were clean. 'She said the house has been in our family since the 1300s, when Europe was devastated by the plague. An English girl arrived here and married a noble from the Innocenti family. They lived in the cottage, rather than the main house, and it passed from daughter to daughter, up to today.'

I looked at Tommaso, his leathery face staring at me earnestly, and saw once again that wild light in his eyes, barely contained intense nervousness coursing through his body, and wondered whether I should believe him.

'Mamma said the girl was a healer,' he continued, lost in his thoughts. 'She created the Grove, she planted the fruit trees and made medicines that helped people get better. Not from the plague, but from normal illnesses, afterwards. She lived till the ripe old age of ninety, and her daughter took over from her, and so on, right up to Mamma. Then it ended there.'

'Bruna didn't want to carry on the tradition?'

'Bruna? Huh.' He spat on the floor. The dog jumped up and barked loudly. 'Shut up, you,' he yelled. 'No, Bruna didn't want to have anything to do with all that. She left for England, as you damn well know.' He stood and paced around the room.

'I found the grave,' I said, trying to see if that would calm him down. 'Agnese said you could tell me what happened, why they buried the baby there.'

'Grave? What grave?' A confused look appeared on his face, then his eyes suddenly snapped wide open. 'Who are you?' he bellowed. 'What do you want? Always people here snooping, asking questions; leave me alone, I tell you.' He gestured wildly with his arms. 'Get out. Get out of my bloody house before I set my dog on you!'

I sat, stunned at this sudden onslaught. 'B-but, Uncle Tommaso, you know who I am. I'm Jennifer, Rita's daughter. You were telling me about–'

'Jennifer? Rita? I have no idea who you are.' He strode over and grabbed me by the arm, pulling me up from the chair. 'Get out!' he roared, dragging me to the front door. The dog barked angrily around my feet, its teeth snapping at my ankles. I found myself on the doorstep, as Tommaso slammed the door behind me.

Shaking, I left the house, almost running as I got to the gate.

Aunt Liliana tried to comfort me. 'There, there, Tommaso's like that with everyone,' she said, placing an enormous slice of *casta-*

gnaccio in front of me. 'Eat this while I get you a cup of tea. Isn't that what you English like when you're in shock?'

I smiled, even though I was still trembling. The Italians had such funny notions about the English. 'Yes, that would be lovely.' I bit into the cake. 'Wow, this is wonderful. Did you make it?'

'Of course. You don't think I bought it, do you? No, it's made with my own hands. There are chestnuts, raisins, walnuts and pine nuts in it.'

I grimaced. 'Not too many calories then.' I closed my eyes as I savoured every mouthful, devouring the cake in minutes.

'Here's your tea.' She handed me the delicate china cup and saucer.

'Thanks.' I looked at the slice of lemon floating in the cup and repressed a sigh. Teaching Italians to put milk in tea was an uphill struggle. 'But he was fine until I mentioned the grave, then he suddenly turned weird.'

'He was devastated when Bruna left. He adored her and she spoiled him rotten when he was little, him being the younger one. He was one of the first to hold the baby when it was born, and he helped dig the grave when the poor thing died. He finds it hard to talk about it.'

'I guess I'll never know then.'

'You could try one last time. Come by tomorrow morning and I'll give you some *castagnaccio* to take to Tommaso as a peace offering. He was always partial to my cake. And don't mention the grave for the time being.'

'If you're sure.' I really didn't fancy a second round with Tommaso and his dog, but my curiosity was getting the better of me.

'And maybe pass by the butcher's first, and get a big bone for that mongrel of his,' she suggested with a wink.

19

The next morning I left Aunt Liliana's house with a still-warm cake in one hand and a plastic bag containing a meaty, smelly bone in the other. I walked across the piazza, saying hello to people as I passed, and greeted the elderly gentlemen already sitting outside the bar, soaking up the morning sun.

As I walked down the narrow dirt track that led to Tommaso's house, I saw a bundle of brown and white fur come hurtling towards me.

'Shit,' I yelled, and looked for somewhere to hide. But there were only bushes nearby, not even a tree to jump behind. I stoically stood my ground and waited for my fate.

'Bella. *Bastarda*! Come back here.' I'd never have thought I'd be so relieved to see Uncle Tommaso. My relief soon turned to fear as he hurled a stream of insults at me, his arm raised high above his head, ready to pound me into the ground.

The dog stopped at the sound of its master's voice and turned, cowering. '*Bastarda*,' Tommaso hollered at the terrified animal. 'I opened the gate and she ran off.'

She? Ah, so maybe the insults weren't aimed at me then.

'Are you all right?' he asked. 'Bella didn't bite you, did she? She's not nasty, she's a softy really, but she feels she has to protect me.'

'I-I'm fine, Uncle Tommaso,' I replied, without thinking.

He narrowed his eyes, staring at me. 'Uncle?'

'Y-yes.' I wondered if there was going to be a repeat of yesterday. 'I'm Jennifer, remember?'

'Ah, the English girl,' he exclaimed, laughing loudly. 'Rita's daughter, right?'

'You remember me?' I said, hardly daring to believe it.

'Yes, you came to visit me, when was it, the other day, yes?'

I smiled at him, hoping the relief I felt wasn't too obvious. 'Yesterday. I thought I'd come and see you again. And I've brought you some *castagnaccio* from Aunt Liliana. It's still warm, look.'

He leaned towards me and sniffed appreciatively. 'Ah, Liliana, she knows how much I love her cakes.'

'And this is for your dog, maybe she'd like something to chew on.' I handed him the plastic bag. *Rather than bite my ankles*, I thought.

'Come back to the house then. I'll make a coffee and we can eat some cake.' He whistled to the dog and I followed my uncle along the dirt track, already dry and dusty even though it had rained the previous day. Trying to keep up with his vigorous pace, I guessed he wasn't as old as he looked, despite his white hair and leathery, wrinkled face.

This time I didn't try to talk about Bruna, the baby or the grave and, to my surprise, spent a pleasant couple of hours in Tommaso's company. He knew everything there was to know about the fruit bushes in the Grove and gave me plenty of advice on how to care for them. We avoided talking about the family, but he had plenty of gossip regarding the villagers. He'd known most of them since he was a child, and relished telling me about scandals that had happened before he was born.

'Mamma told me about a woman from the village, Caterina. It was after the war. Her husband came back after being away for two years and found her in bed with his cousin! Mind you, they all knew something was going on, because she always wore lipstick and stockings – things that weren't easy to come by in those days, you see – and they kept wondering how she got them. And she thought she was something so special, all hoity-toity, looking down her nose at everyone. Turned out she'd slept with a load of American soldiers during the war, and they were still sending her presents. Her husband threw her out of the house; last they heard she was on a boat to America, off to one of those soldiers. Even her own family disowned her.'

I almost choked on my coffee. 'I always imagined you Italians as being faithful, putting family first. You know, being Catholics and everything, especially in those days.'

'Hah!' he snorted. 'Men and women are the same the world over, my dear, regardless of religion and family.' He looked sad for a moment, then perked up again. 'I must tell you about the butcher, Grassi. This is only a story, mind, you'll have to decide if you believe it. After the war, there was a shortage of, well, of everything, really. There was never enough to eat, especially in the small villages. The cities fared a bit better. This Grassi, he's slaughtered all the cows he had, but it's not enough, people were still demanding meat. So he starts selling game – pheasants, quail, hare, rabbit – you name it, whatever he could catch, he sold it. Said hunting was good, wildlife was abundant. Then people started to mention their cat was missing, only the odd one here and there at the beginning, but then it became more and more frequent. And old Grassi always had a well-stocked counter. But they finally had enough to eat, so no one said anything. Then the economy picked up and he stopped selling game and went back to selling beef and pork. But the story has it that they knew what they'd been eating.' He chuckled at the tale he'd probably told a hundred times already.

'If it is true, I don't know whether to laugh at his craftiness or to feel sad because they were so hungry,' I said, shocked that he was so relaxed about the whole thing.

He shrugged in that oh-so-Italian way. 'It doesn't really matter, does it? They survived the war, and he helped get them through it. We Italians are very good at ignoring the how and why, and just concentrating on the here and now.'

By lunchtime we'd eaten half the cake and Bella had chewed most of the meat off her bone. Tommaso put a saucepan of water on the stove.

'I'm going to make some pasta for lunch, if you'd like to stay.'

'Oh no, really, I don't think I could eat anything, I've eaten so much cake. I think I'll go back to the cottage and do some gardening, burn off some of those calories.'

He glanced over at me. 'If you want, I could come over this afternoon, give you hand.' Shocked, I didn't answer immediately. 'It was only an idea,' he said grumpily. 'I quite understand if you don't want me around. I haven't got anything else to do.'

'Of course I'd love you to come over,' I said. 'I was surprised by your offer, that's all. Aunt Liliana said you preferred your own company.' I stopped, annoyed with myself. Just when things were going better, I had to say too much.

To my relief, Tommaso laughed. 'And she's right, when it comes to those interfering busybodies. But you're different. I like you, and I'd like to help you restore Mamma's garden.' He rubbed his hands together. 'I'll be over about three, if that's all right.'

. . .

I was already working in the Grove when Tommaso turned up with Bella at his heels. I couldn't help thinking that Bella was a most inappropriate name. I'd never seen such an ugly dog in all my life.

'Hi, I'm glad you came,' I called out as he opened the gate.

'I said I would, didn't I?'

I tensed up at the grumpy tone of his voice. It wasn't a good start.

He stared at the garden, curious. 'I haven't been in here since Mamma, you know... since she died. It's a bit overgrown, isn't it?'

'A bit.' I watched Bella sniffing around the plants, following a trail only she could pick up, thankful I'd replaced the ivy on the grave before my uncle had arrived.

'You know, Mamma told me it used to be called the Dragonfly Grove.'

'What a pretty name. Why did it get shortened to the Grove?'

'I don't know. Probably 'cause most of the dragonflies disappeared. Mamma said she always called it the Grove, and so did her mother. I guess the original name got lost over the years.'

'Pity, I like it.' I wondered how many dragonflies there had been before.

'Well, less chat, let's get on with things. Where do you want me to start?' Eager to get on, his eyes lit up as he looked at the plants and trees, and his face relaxed as he reached out and gently stroked the new buds of fruit. A lizard scuttled by and he smiled as he watched it disappear under a stone.

'I'm clearing the weeds so they don't choke the plants, like you told me to do.'

He turned to me and frowned. 'Don't touch that one in the corner over there.' He gestured to the far wall, where there was a tall, overgrown plant with large leaves and bell-shaped purple flowers.

'I haven't got that far yet.'

'Leave it alone, I'll deal with that one. It's poisonous, you see. Mamma never let me go near it when I was little. The leaves, berries, flowers; if you touch 'em, you need to wash your hands right away. It's lethal.'

'I'll let you deal with that one then.' I was grateful I hadn't reached that point of the garden, and realised how much I had to learn. I briefly wondered what such a poisonous plant was doing in here, but dismissed the thought. I handed him a pair of gloves. 'You could start pruning the plants I've cleared if you want. I don't really know how to do that and I'm scared of damaging them.' I handed him the rusty pruners I'd found in the garage.

'First we need to sort these out.' He turned them over in his hand, tutting and shaking his head at the state of them. 'They're probably blunt, and I need to get rid of the rust. I'll be back in a moment.'

I watched him disappear into the garage, and smiled as he started whistling a cheerful tune. I wondered how long it had been since he'd whistled like that.

We worked together all that afternoon, me clearing weeds and Tommaso pruning and trimming the bushes. Bella ran around, digging holes and spraying dirt everywhere, snapping at wasps and flies. She finally ran out of energy and lay down in the shade, tongue dangling out of her mouth as she watched us hard at work. I noticed that even the dog avoided going near the centre where the grave lay, still mostly hidden by weeds and ivy.

20

We worked together in the Grove for the next few weeks, starting from the outer edge and working our way inwards. Tommaso arrived at eight on the dot every morning and let himself in. It seemed that the bone had definitely helped with Bella accepting me, and my ankles were safe. Every morning she launched herself at me, slobbering my hand with wet doggy kisses, then crunched a handful of dog biscuits while Tommaso and I drank our first espresso coffee of the day. Then it was out into the garden for the rest of the morning.

I enjoyed my new, relaxing routine: I worked with Uncle Tommaso during the day, then walked down to Aunt Liliana's for dinner and a chat with the family. I liked getting to know them, and felt a special bond growing between myself and Agnese. I hoped we would become friends, God knew I needed some! I phoned Mum every Wednesday and Saturday to keep her up to date with everything. I was surprised by how much I missed her, even though I was enjoying my freedom. Mark had tried ringing me a few times but I never answered his calls. He could go to hell as far as I was concerned.

Tommaso was surprisingly talkative during our lunch

breaks, even though he'd sometimes go off on a tangent or forget what we were talking about. I still saw that wild look in his eyes, but he seemed a lot calmer than the first day. I kept a careful eye on him, though, observing his mood as we drew closer to the grave. I'd covered it with ivy the best I could, trying to hide it from him, but I had to admit, I was worried that he'd go crazy again, and this time there was nowhere for me to run.

I realised that I hadn't thought about alcohol or Luisa's wine ever since we'd started our gardening project. Even when watching TV after dinner, my only concern was about planning the next day's work. I imagined that this could be the magic of the cottage Mum had talked about.

That final morning, everything started as normal. We drank our coffee and ate some croissants Tommaso had brought with him. They were still warm and we relished every mouthful. It promised to be a hot day and we decided to get as much work done in the morning as possible, so we could rest in the afternoon. The Grove was almost finished; there was only the area in the middle to finish off, with the grave silently waiting for us. Tommaso seemed oblivious but I couldn't help feeling tense.

I pulled the weeds out by their roots, savouring the satisfying ripping sound as they released their hold in the earth. I threw the clods into the wheelbarrow behind me and picked up the small gardening fork. I turned the soil over, breathing in the unmistakable smell of rotting vegetation and freshly turned earth, and used the trowel to place a dollop of manure at the base of the bush.

'That's right, now turn the earth again to mix it all together,' Tommaso said approvingly, standing behind me with his hands on his hips. 'You're a good gardener, girl, I'll give you that, but there's still so much more you need to know and I'm too old and tired to teach it to you.' He sighed. 'Mamma used to have a book, a recipe book for those creams and potions she made. It was passed down from daughter to daughter through the generations, each one adding to it. After Bruna left, there was no daughter to give it to. Mamma had to pass it on, though, otherwise the secrets would have been lost. The Grove is old, much older than you'd think. All these bushes, planted so long ago.' His voice faded as he lost himself in reminiscing.

I was touched by the faraway look on his face. 'Shall we call it a day?' I was tired and sweaty, and couldn't wait to get under the shower. It had been a long morning.

'All right,' he replied, coming back with a jolt. He looked around. 'We've done a good job today, haven't we?'

'Fantastic,' I said, looking at the freshly trimmed plants, everything neat and tidy. I stretched my arms, and the trowel slipped from my grasp. It made a dull, metallic sound as it hit the ground.

'What was that?' Tommaso asked, and bent over to pick it up.

'Don't.' It was too late. He'd noticed the grave.

He stood, staring at the ivy-covered headstone. His face paled, and he suddenly looked much older. Bella trotted over to see what was going on, whining, then lay down at his feet, her ears perked, her nose sniffing the air. He reached down and absentmindedly stroked her head.

'I remember the day the baby was born.' He spoke so quietly that I had to move closer to hear his voice. 'Poor Bruna, she was in labour for forty-eight hours, we thought it'd never come out. But then, there she was, this pink, screaming bundle with a powerful set of lungs.' He turned towards me, a tear rolling down his weathered cheek. 'I'd forgotten,' he whispered. 'I'd forgotten about the grave, how could I forget?'

'It's all right.' I tried to soothe him, shocked by the devastated look on his face.

'I need to tell someone,' he murmured. 'Please, dear God, I need to say–'

I touched his arm. 'Let's go indoors, Uncle Tommaso. I'll make us a cup of tea and you can tell me everything.'

He followed me back up to the cottage, Bella behind us. I gestured for him to sit at the kitchen table, then pottered about making the tea, giving him time to compose himself.

I sat down with him, two cups of steaming tea in front of us, a bowl of water on the floor for Bella. I remained silent, letting him gather his thoughts and speak when he was ready. I didn't have long to wait.

'B-Bruna was so beautiful,' he began. I nodded. Mum had some black and white photos of her when she was in her teens, and she'd been extraordinarily beautiful.

'I was the youngest of the three of us. No one else in the family had much time for me but she did. She looked after me when Mamma was working in the Grove, or making her medicines, or tending the sick in the village. Mamma and Teresa were happy to leave Bruna to it, they had their own lives, their own things to do. My father told her to stop mothering me, that I'd have to grow up, learn to do things by myself, but she refused. He was jealous of me, taking up her time.' He paused, breathing heavily. I smiled reassuringly at him, not knowing what to say.

'Then Bruna got pregnant. Mamma was so upset, shouting and screaming at her, telling her what a stupid girl she was. My father was more understanding, he calmed Mamma down and told her these things sometimes happen, that we had to help her.'

'How old were you?' I asked.

'Oh, about eight. Old enough.' He furrowed his brow, the creases in his forehead becoming even deeper. 'My father was a strict Catholic, he went to church every Sunday and prayed before going to bed. He'd never have approved of sex before marriage, and especially not having a baby. I couldn't believe he was being so calm about it. So I watched him. And Bruna. She refused to say who the father was. I wanted to find out, so I could go and beat him up, make him suffer for what he'd done to her.'

My heart broke at the thought of this eight-year-old boy determined to seek revenge for the wrong done to his sister. Fascinated by his story, I could never have imagined his next words.

21

Tommaso continued to speak, lost in his memories. 'I followed her when she went to the village, watched everyone she spoke to, but she seemed perfectly normal with everyone. Then, one evening, I was sitting in a corner playing with my tin soldiers. Mamma was washing the dishes, my father was in his armchair, listening to the radio, and Teresa had already gone outside. Bruna was helping Mamma, drying the dishes. Mamma told her to go and lie down as she looked tired. She had to pass by my father's armchair to get to the stairs, by now her stomach was getting bigger and it was difficult for her to squeeze through. I liked to watch her waddle about, it amazed me how something could be growing inside her like that. I saw my father reach up and take hold of her hand to stop her, and then he whispered something. I couldn't hear what he said, but I clearly saw the expression on her face. It was of pure hatred, and it shocked me. I'd never seen such a look ever before, not from anyone, especially not from Bruna.' Tommaso rubbed his hand over his hair, making the white wisps stand up in all directions.

'She hissed at him, "Don't you ever touch me again, you dirty bastard." That I did hear, although I didn't understand at first.

She snatched her hand away and stormed out of the room. Mamma didn't even turn round, she just tossed me the drying-up cloth and told me to take over. I looked at my father; his face was white with anger, his lips locked tightly together, and his eyes were fixed on a point on the wall.' Tommaso took a sip of tea, then put the cup down with a shaking hand and wiped his mouth carefully with a napkin. 'And then I knew.'

'He was the father of Bruna's baby,' I whispered, shocked, but at the same time horrified that I wanted to hear more.

Tommaso grunted. 'I tried to ask her about it, but she told me to keep quiet and not breathe a word to anyone. I said she could talk to me if she wanted to. But she never did.'

'Oh God, Uncle Tommaso, I'm so sorry.' I understood why he'd gone a bit crazy, anyone would have under the circumstances.

'But that's not the worst of it,' he said. His eyes were wide, staring at me, and I felt he was almost pleading with me to let him unburden himself after all this time.

'Go on,' I said faintly, bracing myself. But nothing could prepare me for what he said next.

'Bruna killed the baby.'

'What? No, that's impossible.' I stared at him, incredulous. 'Aunt Liliana said Bruna was so happy when the baby was born, that she never got over her death.' I looked at Uncle Tommaso, imploring him to say he was lying.

But he shook his head. 'Yes, she loved her, but over the years I've come to realise that she never wanted the child,' he said sadly. 'How could she, when it was her own father who got her pregnant? Every time she looked at her, it must have reminded her of what had happened. One afternoon she went upstairs for a nap, then we heard her screaming a couple of hours later. She came running out of the house with the baby in her arms, but it was too late. Malva was dead. Natural causes, Mamma told Papà, Teresa, everyone in the village. But I was there when it happened. I heard Bruna say she was so tired, she only wanted to sleep.' He buried his face in his hands, an enormous sob escaping his throat. I reached over and touched his arm, uncertain of what to do. He sat up straight and looked at me with a haunted expression. 'Mamma told her she must have suffocated the baby in her sleep, without meaning to.'

I put my hand over my mouth, unable to take in what he was saying. I couldn't believe that Bruna had killed her own baby, it was a concept I couldn't comprehend. But I had to ask one last thing, I couldn't let it finish like this. 'You've known your father was the father of Bruna's baby, and you've never told anyone?'

'Bruna made me promise. I couldn't go against her wishes. Then she left for England, just like that, and left me here alone, knowing what I knew. I wanted to kill my father, I swore that as soon as I was old enough, I'd make him pay for what he'd done. But I never got the chance. He died of a heart attack the year after she left. So the bastard got away with it.'

'And Luisa? Do you think she knew?'

'Mamma? No, I don't think so. She did tell me once that she was glad he'd died, so she didn't have to keep imagining him with his other women. It seems he bedded half the women in the village, one time or another. But no, I don't think she knew. She'd have killed him herself if she had. She loved us kids, she would have defended us to the death, if necessary.' He stood and went over to the sink, and looked out of the window. 'I never married, I couldn't. How could I trust anyone after everything that happened? I moved out as soon as I could, there were too many bad memories, but I always came back to help Mamma in the Grove. It gave me peace, being there, close to her, to our heritage. My family always meant so much to me, until *he* destroyed it that day.'

I went over to him and patted his arm. 'Thank you, Uncle Tommaso.'

'What for?' he replied gruffly.

'For trusting me enough to tell me. That means a lot.'

'Don't you go telling the others. It's our business, mine and Bruna's, it's nothing to do with them.'

'It's all right, I won't say anything.' I was taken aback by his sudden outburst. Bella jumped to her feet, whining again, alert to her master's moods.

'Good.' He snapped his fingers and Bella ran to his side. 'I'll be going now. It's late, I'm sure you need a rest after our hard work. I'll be back tomorrow morning.' And he was gone, leaving me alone in the cottage to mull over everything he'd told me.

22

The next morning at nine, there was no sign of Tommaso and Bella. I'd already drunk two coffees and was pacing nervously around the kitchen. He had said he would come, but after his reaction at seeing the grave, I was worried about him.

I glanced at the clock for the hundredth time. Nine thirty. 'Oh, sod it,' I grumbled. I grabbed my keys and set off for Tommaso's house. The sun in Italy was already hot at this time of the morning; not like England, I thought grimly, where you needed a jacket until midday even in the middle of summer. The stress made me feel hotter and sweatier, and I felt that my face was bright red by the time I reached the village square.

'Jen,' I heard someone call.

I gritted my teeth and turned round. 'Mark.'

'I wanted to see if you're all right. I've called you a few times but you never answer. We didn't part on the best of terms.'

'I don't want to talk about it, and I don't want to talk to you.'

'Okay, have it like that, if you want,' he retorted. 'Out jogging, are we?'

I felt a trickle of sweat running down my nose, all the way to the tip, and realised I must look a mess. I shuffled my feet, embarrassed, and tried to brush my hair out of my face, but it obstinately refused to obey.

'Yes, I thought I'd go for a power walk, get away from things for a while.' I glanced at him and saw yet again that smirk of his that made me want to punch him.

'Fed up with your family already?'

'Not at all. I'm going there later for dinner,' I said primly. I felt the need to goad him, so added, 'They're lovely people, so welcoming. Agnese and I are becoming good friends.'

He narrowed his eyes. 'Be careful who you trust, she's not all she seems.'

'That's the pot calling the kettle black,' I snapped, then immediately regretted letting him get to me.

'Well, I won't keep you,' he said coldly. 'Give me a call if you want to go out again one evening, I enjoyed our last date.'

'Go to hell.' Turning, I left him standing behind me, vowing I'd wipe the smirk off his face some time soon.

Tommaso's gate was locked as usual, and no one came out when I rang the bell. I called loudly, expecting Bella to come running over, but there was a deadly silence. My sense of dread grew, and I ran along the fence, looking for another way in.

There was a tree just outside the property with low-hanging branches. I clambered up it, scratching my legs and arms on the rough bark. I crawled along a branch overhanging the fence, and gripped on tightly as it bowed beneath my weight, expecting to hear a dry, snapping noise at any moment. Luckily the branch held, and I gingerly lowered myself to the ground, inside Tommaso's garden at last.

I ran over to the house and tried the door, but it was locked. I peered in through a nearby window, rubbing my hand over the dirty glass to get a clearer view. I jumped back as Bella threw herself at me, barking and whining, her nose leaving smear marks on the glass.

'Hold on, Bella,' I yelled. I looked around desperately, wondering how the hell I was going to get in. I couldn't break the window, not with Bella there. She'd cut her paws to shreds on the glass. I ran round the outside of the house, checking each window, but they were all closed. I tried the back door, hardly daring to hope. To my surprise, it opened. Bella rushed out and jumped up, her front paws on my legs. I lifted her into my arms, and she licked my face, frantically wagging her tail.

'Okay, Bella, it's all right,' I said, stroking her head. 'Where's Uncle Tommaso?' She wriggled to be set free and I gently dropped her to the ground. She took off into the house and I ran after her.

I found him in the living room. Uncle Tommaso was sitting upright in his armchair as if he was sleeping. But there was no gentle snoring noise, no small puffs of air as he breathed in and out, and his skin had a grey pallor. There was an unpleasant odour in the room, and the air was still, as if all life had been sucked out of it. Bella looked up at me and whined, wagging her tail uncertainly. My steps were hesitant as I walked over to Uncle Tommaso and my hand shook as I reached out and touched his.

I was right: he was dead. Standing there in shock, I half expected him to open his eyes and shout 'Boo!'

I'd never seen a dead body before, and it wasn't how I'd imagined it would be. I stood there for a while, looking at him, memorising every wrinkle, every craggy line on his face, the way his scalp showed through his wispy white hair in places, wishing I'd had the chance to know him longer and hear more of his incredible stories. Then my brain suddenly started working again. I took out my phone and called the family.

'The doctor thinks it was a heart attack,' Aunt Liliana said, sniffing and dabbing at her eyes with a handkerchief. 'He was

HELEN PRYKE

only sixty-five, even though he looked a lot older. He carried the weight of the world on his shoulders, always has done since Bruna left, but that's hardly the right age to die. I'm going to miss the old devil, even if we didn't get on very well.'

I hugged her. 'Me too. I got to know him over the last few weeks, and he told me lots of stories about the village and when he was younger. It was good fun working with him too.' A thought suddenly struck me. 'You don't think it was the work, do you?' I asked, horrified. 'Maybe it was too much for him.'

'I don't think so, dear. And even if it was, he spent his last weeks doing what he loved the most, working in the Grove. He couldn't have asked for more. I think you made him happy, and God knows he needed it.'

I'd had to shut Bella in the bedroom when the doctor and the police arrived, since she tried to attack anyone who went near Tommaso. I could hear her barking and scratching at the door as I talked with Aunt Liliana.

'What's going to happen to Bella?'

'Bella? Oh, the dog. I don't know,' she said. 'It seems as wild and antisocial as Tommaso was. I suppose it'll have to be put down.'

'No, absolutely not. She's all right once you get to know her, she only wants to protect Tommaso.'

'You take it then. No one else will want it. We never understood what Tommaso saw in the creature, it's ugly as sin. You can keep it at the cottage, you've got the space.'

'What about when I go back home?' I asked.

'We'll decide when the moment comes. Oh, there's the doctor, I wanted to have a word. I'll tell Agnese to give you a ring later, make sure you're all right.' Aunt Liliana hurried over to the doctor, our conversation forgotten.

After everyone left, I let Bella out of the bedroom and patted her head. 'It's just you and me now.' She looked up at me with mournful brown eyes, her tail between her legs. 'Come on, let's get you home.' We went downstairs and I searched the kitchen for her food, bowl and lead, noticing that the cupboards were practically empty, apart from a few packets of pasta and some jars of sauce. A wave of sadness crashed over me at the thought of the lonely existence Tommaso had had. I gathered Bella's things together as quickly as possible; I wanted to get out of the house.

As I pulled the door to behind me I heard a hushed, whispering sound and felt a light breeze on the back of my neck.

'Rest in peace, Uncle Tommaso,' I murmured, and closed the door with a click.

Bella seemed a bit lost at first. She followed me everywhere, as if she were afraid that I'd disappear too. I didn't work in the garden that day, or the next. I felt it would be wrong to carry on creating life when Uncle Tommaso was dead. The grave remained untouched, thick ivy still covering it. It would stay that way until I found the strength to finish the work.

The coroner returned the verdict of a heart attack and, given Uncle Tommaso's age, everyone accepted it. Except me. I couldn't help having some doubts. I'd watched him working in the Grove, hardly out of breath as he ripped weeds out by their roots or chopped branches off the fruit trees. He'd carted wheelbarrows of detritus out into the main garden, ready for a bonfire, going to and fro without needing to sit down and rest. I'd been more out of shape than him, unused to the physical exertion. But I kept my thoughts to myself, I didn't want to create problems for my family. He was at peace now, that was all that mattered.

. . .

The funeral was three days later. When it was over, I decided the Grove couldn't wait any longer. I grabbed some gardening tools from the garage, whistled to Bella, and we made our way down to the Grove. I was determined to tackle the grave that morning, tear away the remaining ivy, and clean the marble. It seemed the least I could do.

After I'd removed the weeds, I got a bucket of water and a wire brush and set to scrubbing the grave. Wiping the sweat from my eyes, I stood back and looked at my handiwork. The marble headstone gleamed in the sun, a beautiful creamy-white colour once the moss and lichen had been removed. I ran my fingers over the engraved writing.

'Rest in peace,' I whispered. The Grove was in order; the bushes cut back and tidied up, the tree trunks clear of weeds and ivy, their branches already covered in fruit. I found that I was looking forward to seeing how much produce I'd get.

'But what are you going to do with it when it's ripe?' I asked out loud. Bella glanced at me, then went back to sniffing around my feet. 'Hey, Bella, know any recipes for peach wine?' She barked at me. 'I didn't think so. Bet Uncle Tommaso did, though.' I paused. 'What was it he said, Bella? That Luisa had a recipe book... didn't he say that?' I looked at her but she ignored me.

'I'm sure he did,' I mused. 'What else?' I thought back to that day in the Grove, just before Tommaso saw the grave. 'He said the book was passed down from daughter to daughter, but Luisa didn't have any daughters left to pass it on to. Tommaso was the only remaining child, as her other daughter Teresa died some years ago.' It was difficult trying to piece together the Italian side of the family, there were so many of them. My head felt like it was going to explode, so I gave up for the moment.

'Come, Bella, I think we've earned ourselves a nice treat this afternoon.' She trotted next to me as we went back to the kitchen. I'd been thinking about the bottles in the hall cupboard for a few days, trying to resist, flashbacks of what had happened the last time I'd given into temptation helping me stay strong. Today, however, I reasoned that after everything we'd been through, we both deserved something special.

Ten minutes later we were out on the patio, Bella gnawing on an enormous bone and me with a glass of Luisa's wine in my hand.

'This is the life, eh, Bella?' I said, already giggling just from breathing in the fumes. Bella was too busy crunching the bone to take any notice of me. I took a long sip, and leaned back in my chair.

I thought about Uncle Tommaso and tried to replay the conversation we'd had that day. The wine seemed to help clear my head, and I could remember everything.

'There were no daughters left, but Luisa had to give the book to someone,' I murmured. It suddenly dawned on me. 'She had to give it to someone, but there were no daughters, so that someone had to be... Uncle Tommaso.' I was amazed I'd managed to solve the puzzle. Usually wine had the opposite effect and turned my mind into a hazy fog. Now the only problem was how to get in to Uncle Tommaso's house and search for the book.

23

'Of course you can have the keys to Tommaso's house, dear, it's kind of you to offer to help,' Aunt Liliana said, fussing about in the drawers of the large oak dresser. 'I've been meaning to get up there myself, but with one thing and another... I'll try to go next week, sort through what to keep and what to give away. I know they're here somewhere. I always kept a spare set, you never knew when the old fool would need some help. Not that he'd ever phone, no. A couple of years ago, I dropped in to see him on the off chance. I found the silly bugger out in the garden at the bottom of a ladder, unable to get up, with that smelly dog of his running around like crazy. Turned out he'd been there for two days. He'd fallen and put his back out. Took three men to pick him up and get him back in the house. I told him, "You have to carry your phone with you at all times, so you can call us if something like this happens again. You're not getting any younger." And do you know what he said?'

I shook my head, imagining stubborn Uncle Tommaso withstanding the onslaught of Aunt Liliana's wrath.

'He patted his shirt pocket and said, "Got my phone right here, woman, but I didn't want you fussing, just like you're doing right now." I tell you, I was flabbergasted. That foolish old man might have died out there, and he could have called us at any moment!'

I burst out laughing at Aunt Liliana's furious face. She relaxed, chuckling with me. 'He was stubborn and annoying, but I miss him,' she said softly.

'I know. I didn't get to spend enough time with him, but I liked him. He was a real character.'

Aunt Liliana sniffed loudly, wiping at her nose. 'Here,' she said, handing me a set of keys. 'Take your time, I'm sure there's lots of stuff to go through. He was a bit of a hoarder, didn't like to throw anything away. Feel free to keep anything you find if you want, it's your heritage. But I'd like some photos, if you come across them. I think Luisa must have given some to him, I never found them up at the cottage. They were taken after the war, all the family together; Luisa, Ernesto, Bruna, my mum, and Antonio, before... well, we don't speak about that now. I remember Mamma showing them to me one day at Luisa's, but we never saw them again after that.'

'Of course I'll keep an eye out for them,' I said, grateful I would be allowed to keep whatever I found. 'I'm sure Bella will be happy to see her home again.'

'I'm glad you took her in, the pair of you seem to be getting on well. Tommaso loved that mongrel, he'd have hated anything happening to it. Here, take these cakes for a snack, I'm sure you'll get hungry while you're up at the house.' She handed me a paper bag, a delicious vanilla aroma making my mouth water.

'Thanks.' I gave her a hug.

'What was that for?'

'For being you.'

'Oh, get on with you,' she said, slapping my shoulder, but I could see she was pleased.

.　.　.

It was odd being back at Uncle Tommaso's house again. The rooms echoed with my footsteps and it felt as if it was only an empty shell, its soul missing. Bella appeared agitated and kept close by my legs, bumping her nose against me whenever I stopped.

I went into the living room and stared at the armchair where I'd found Tommaso. A shiver ran through me and I turned away.

'Okay, Bella, where do we start?' Bella wagged her tail at me and trotted off into the kitchen.

'Good a place as any,' I said, and followed her. She stood by the place her food bowl used to be, looking quizzically at me.

'Typical dog, always thinking of your stomach. Shoo, Bella, you've already had breakfast.' Looking hurt, she went out into the garden to chase some birds. 'Let's get started,' I said, and began by opening cupboard doors.

It didn't take me long to go through the rooms in the house. Tommaso didn't appear to be a hoarder; the kitchen cupboards were practically empty, with only the bare essentials necessary for cooking and eating. It was the same story in the small living room and in his bedroom upstairs. I felt like a trespasser, searching through his things, but I focused on the fact that I had to find those photos for Aunt Liliana. Upstairs, his bedroom and bathroom were as bare as the other rooms.

I slowly turned the doorknob to a third door and found a room that appeared at first glance to be an extension of the garden. I understood why my aunt had said he was a hoarder. Plants, small bushes, transparent plastic boxes with some very unusual insect specimens inside, skulls, skeletons, snake skins; anything of interest that Tommaso had picked up over the years had found its way into the room. I shuddered, hoping there was nothing alive in there. I cautiously entered and glanced into the various containers, marvelling at the preserved creatures inside.

There was a desk underneath the window, covered in sheets

of paper. I picked them up and saw that they were filled with drawings of dragonflies, from every angle and in every position, from resting on stems of plants to soaring in full flight. It was incredible how he'd managed to capture the delicate fragility of their wings, the brilliant colours, the depths of their bulbous eyes. Almost as if he'd drawn the insects while observing them from close up.

'Impossible,' I murmured, but I remembered that evening the dragonfly had led me to the grave, as if it had been waiting for me. I sat down in the room's only chair, the one where Tommaso had probably sat for countless hours, staring out of the window or concentrating on his drawings. I shuffled the sheets of paper together and stacked them into a neat pile. I thought of framing some, putting them up in the cottage. They would make it seem more like home. *There I go again, thinking of the cottage as home.* Somehow, the place had worked its way into my heart, and I had a feeling it would be difficult to leave.

I opened the drawers underneath the desk one by one. They were full of pens, pencils, erasers, elastic bands, bits of paper, all the usual things you'd expect to find in an artist's desk. But in the last drawer I found something different. A large wooden box, with a dragonfly carved on the lid and bronze handles at the sides. I carefully lifted it out and placed it on the desk.

Bella trotted into the room, her paws clicking across the tiled floor. She wagged her tail at me, then lay down with her head on my feet, sighing happily.

'It's good to be home, isn't it, Bella?' I said, scratching her head. Her tail thumped a couple of times. 'Right, let's see what's in the box, shall we?'

I ran my hand over the engraving, feeling the cool, smooth wood under my fingertips, following the tiny crevices that outlined the dragonfly's body. It was truly stunning, its intricate design etched into the wood in minute detail. I wondered if

Uncle Tommaso had carved this himself. Looking inside, I saw a bundle of old photographs. I lifted them out and flicked through them, smiling at the black and white pictures of a family I'd never met. Luisa and Ernesto stood at the back of the group, their hands on their children's shoulders in front of them. Ernesto was a giant of a man, towering over the whole group, a dark frown on his face. Luisa was turned slightly away from him, looking wistfully at something in the distance. I looked closely at the children, who all stood in a row. The tall blonde girl must have been Bruna, I recognised her from the photos Mum had shown me; next to her was Teresa, Aunt Liliana's mother, then a boy; the mysterious Antonio, I presumed, as he was almost as tall as Teresa, too big to be Tommaso. I wondered what had happened to him. There were several faded photos of these people, frozen in time, my family I'd never met. I wished I'd had the chance to get to know them.

I laid the photos down on the desk and looked back inside the box. There was an envelope with my name on it, and as I picked it up I noticed a thick leather-bound book at the bottom. I took that out as well and placed my treasures on the desk next to the photos.

The envelope felt crisp and new, and the scrawling, immature writing made me think that Uncle Tommaso had written it. I took a deep breath, opened the envelope and pulled out a single sheet of paper.

Jennifer,

I didn't expect to enjoy our time together over the last few weeks as much as I did. I'd been meaning to go back to the Grove for some time, but kept putting it off. It took you, girl, to give me a reason to return.

I have one more thing to tell you. Your great-grandmother was the last of the healers – a tradition that has been passed down through the generations of our family for many centuries. When Bruna refused to take on the role, it broke Mamma's heart and she believed it would die with her. I believed that too, until I met you and I saw how much you love the cottage and the Grove, almost as much as she did. Read the book, Jennifer. Maybe one day your name will be in it, with your recipes. Only you can decide.

I've left you the book with their knowledge and cures, added to over the centuries by all the healers. And my mother's recipe, the one that gave me the way out. My mother had her faults, but what she did, she did because she loved us and for that, I forgive her. This will make no sense to you but, believe me, some secrets are best left untold.

Don't be angry with me, I am tired of living and I want to be at peace. It will be painless and quick, quite the opposite of the cancer they found a few months ago.

Uncle Tommaso.

I read the letter in Uncle Tommaso's voice, picturing his hands shaking as he wrote each word. Tears pricked at my eyes. That last paragraph had me thinking. So it wasn't a heart attack as the doctor had said, Tommaso *had* killed himself. I wondered how; which recipe had he found that would give him such a painless death and release him from the cancer's grip?

Bella whined. 'Are you bored with staying still for so long?' I said as I scratched behind her ears. 'I'm pretty sure this is what we were looking for. Let's go home and start reading the book, shall we?'

She jumped up and barked, eager to go. I didn't blame her. It felt creepy being in Tommaso's study with the dead insects and animals staring at us with lifeless eyes. I put everything back in the box, and added Tommaso's dragonfly drawings as well.

. . .

Aunt Liliana was over the moon with the photos. Her eyes filled with tears as she looked through them. 'Oh, you have no idea how happy you've made me,' she said, hugging me tightly. 'I thought they were lost, and I so wanted to see them once more.'

'Can I make some copies? I'd like to show them to Mum when I go back home.'

'Of course. There's a shop in the village, I'll get them done tomorrow. But there's no need to take them back to England, your mum's coming here in a few days.'

I stared at my aunt, dumbfounded. 'What? When?'

Aunt Liliana seemed a little flustered. 'I'm sorry, dear, I didn't realise you didn't know. I spoke to her yesterday and she said she'd like to come over to see the cottage and her family. I think she said her flight would be arriving Friday.' She leafed through some pieces of paper by the telephone. 'Yes, you see, I wrote it down. The flight number and arrival time.'

'I only spoke to her the other day, she didn't say anything to me.'

'I think it was a spur of the moment thing,' Aunt Liliana said, trying to reassure me. 'She'll probably phone you later to let you know.'

'Hmph.' Why was I always the last one to know everything around here? Then I remembered something Aunt Liliana had said when she'd given me the keys earlier.

'What did you mean, you don't talk about that now?'

'Wh-what?'

'When you were telling me about the photos, you said there were photos of the family before, then you said you don't talk about it,' I insisted. I was fed up with not knowing anything about my family and feeling excluded all the time.

'Oh, ah, well. It was a long time ago, there were a series of tragic events in the family. We don't really talk about them because, you know...'

'I know about the baby,' I said. 'I found the grave, and when Tommaso came to help in the Grove he saw it and fell to pieces. He told me about Bruna killing the baby.'

'You can understand why we don't talk about it then. Sometimes things are too painful and we keep them inside, where they can't harm anyone.' She folded her arms and avoided looking me in the eyes.

I realised she wouldn't tell me what she knew of the story, perhaps she didn't trust me enough. Tears prickling at my eyes, I picked up the wooden box and whistled for Bella. 'I'd better get back to the cottage.'

'I'll get those copies done for you,' she called after me. I raised my hand in acknowledgement but didn't turn around.

After dinner, I poured myself a large glass of Luisa's wine and sat down on the sofa with the recipe book. Bella was lying on the rug, belly full, snoring softly as she slept. I glanced over at her, comforted by her presence. I was glad to have her with me, she was good company on nights like these.

I sipped at my wine as I opened the book and started looking through the pages. I marvelled at the beautifully written recipes, amazed to think that many of them were hundreds of years old and written with a quill and ink. Some of the pages had drawings on them, and I recognised a few of the plants from the Grove. The recipes seemed quite innocuous, and mainly consisted of steeping leaves and flowers for several hours before drinking. However, the range of ailments they purported to cure was incredible: mouth ulcers, psoriasis, gastroenteritis, emotional imbalances, broken hearts; the list went on. One entry made me smile. I knew it had been written by my great-grandmother as she'd included the date.

Signora Conti swears by the cream for her haemorrhoids, says nothing else will ease the swelling and pain. She can even sit down again now. Success! It seems we have perfected the recipe at long last. 4th June, 1951.

'So it's not all fame and glory then, being a healer,' I murmured. 'But judging from the notes, their ointments and cordials seemed to work.'

The lights in the room suddenly flickered several times. Bella woke with a jump and barked angrily. Startled, I almost spilled my wine over the book, but managed to recover it before any damage was done. I leaped up off the sofa, meaning to put the glass on the coffee table, and the book fell to the floor.

'Shit,' I muttered. I'd learnt that the electrical grid here in the mountains was unreliable at the best of times; there must be a thunderstorm about somewhere nearby. I put down my glass and bent to retrieve the book. Several pages had come loose and lay strewn about. Praying it was reparable, I picked everything up. I made myself comfortable once more, then flicked through the book trying to find where the pages had come from. A folded piece of paper fell onto my lap.

Bella came over to investigate, sniffing at the book. I gently pushed her away. 'Don't want you slobbering over everything, Bel. Let's see what this is.'

I carefully unfolded the paper and saw from the elaborate signature at the bottom that it was written by my great-grandmother Luisa. As I read the first sentence, my blood ran cold. I took a very large swig of wine, desperately in need of it, then another. Surprised, I noticed that the glass was empty. Everything faded away, the living room, Bella, the cottage, until it was just me, alone in the light from the lamp beside me. I felt as if I was suspended in time, bodiless, a lone spirit lost in the cosmos. There was a flickering all around me, like an old black and white film about to start, and an image appeared projected on the wall in front of me, only I was the one on screen, in the middle of a set that was curiously familiar. My eyes widened as the film started, watching the woman who was meant to be me; or was I meant to be her? My head started to spin as she hurried along the street, hugging the collar of her coat tighter to keep the chill of the evening air out...

LUISA

1940 – 2014

24

1940-1943

Luisa hurried along the street, hugging the collar of her coat tighter to keep out the chill of the evening air. She always finished late on a Friday; Signora Bianchi would punctually arrive one minute before closing time and keep them there for ages while she looked through all the fabrics, ribbons and buttons, only to leave without buying anything. Luisa hated working in the haberdashery and couldn't wait for the other girl, Sara, to have her baby and return to the shop. Then she could go back to being a housewife and spending her days in the Grove, hopefully before spring was over.

She passed the bar, thanking her lucky stars that at least she didn't have to work there. It was always full of rowdy workmen, spending their week's wages, intent on getting drunk. Including her husband. Ernesto dropped in every Friday night, regular as clockwork, which gave her time to get home and prepare dinner.

She heard a noise and stopped to listen. There it was again, a scuffling sound coming from the alley along the side of the bar. She hoped it wasn't rats, they'd had problems the year before with the disgusting vermin.

She stepped into the alley, straining to see in the dark. More noises; whatever it was, it was bigger than a rat. The side door opened and the raucous sounds of men laughing suddenly filled the night. A bag of rubbish flew into the alley, thrown by an unseen hand, and then the door banged shut once more. In that brief moment when the light had flooded the alleyway, she'd seen them. A man and a woman against the wall, her white pudgy legs wrapped around his waist while his naked arse pumped backwards and forwards, grinding into her, both of them grunting and groaning. He looked round at Luisa just as his body contorted and he came, a crazed, triumphant look on his face.

Luisa turned and ran, as fast as she could, all the way to the cottage. She slammed the front door closed, threw her bag on the sofa, and rushed up to the bedroom. Huge sobs shook her whole body as she sat there, stunned, the image of her husband and the woman replaying over and over again in her mind.

When Ernesto came home sometime later, she was lying on the bed, still wearing her coat. He sat down next to her, the bed sagging under his weight. She could smell the alcohol on his breath and it made her feel sick. He reached out to touch her.

'Don't.'

'Come on, Luisa, don't be like that,' he said, slurring his words. 'It's not what you think.'

'I know what I saw.' Her voice sounded hollow. 'And you know I saw you.'

'She's only the local tart, everyone's had a go at one time or another.'

'And tonight it was your turn?'

'It didn't mean anything, Luisa. I love you.' He leaned over, trying to kiss her.

'I said no!' she shouted, pushing him away. 'You think I want you touching me, after seeing you with that, that–'

She screamed as he covered her with his body, grabbing her

arms. 'You're my wife, and you'll let me kiss you, or so help me God!' he yelled. He kissed her roughly, cutting her lip with his teeth. She struggled to get away, suffocating under his weight, his fingers digging into her arms.

'Stay still, damn you.' He hit her, hard, with the back of his hand, and she stopped moving, stunned. He pulled at her dress, tugging it up above her waist, then pulled down her knickers.

'Wh-what are you doing?' she whimpered. He didn't reply, but unbuttoned his trousers. 'No, no, no,' she screamed, terrified.

'Shut up or I'll hit you again,' he said, pulling down his trousers.

Tears streamed down her face as he gripped her hips and forced himself into her, his hands leaving bruises on her legs and arms, his mouth biting her nipples through her clothes, leaving her sore and bleeding. He lay on top of her when he'd finished, panting heavily. She shoved him off and sat up.

'Don't you ever do anything like that again,' she shouted.

He looked up at her, bemused. White-hot anger surged through her, shocking her with its intensity. She got up and walked towards the door, then changed her mind and went back to stand over him.

'If you touch me again after you've been with one of your whores, I'll kill you,' she said quietly, and slapped him on the cheek with all the force she could muster. A bright red mark instantly appeared on his skin. She stormed downstairs, went into the kitchen, and leaned against the sink as she stared at her reflection in the curtainless window.

Luisa pushed the pram down the street, glancing in at the baby's sweet sleeping face every now and then. Ernesto hadn't touched her since that night, but that was all it had taken to conceive their daughter. Bruna was so innocent and unsuspecting, and

Luisa wondered how she could feel so much love for this tiny being created in such violence.

'Morning, Luisa,' she heard as she passed two women talking outside their front doors.

'Morning, Flora,' Luisa replied, ignoring the sniggering behind her back. It was common knowledge that Ernesto was working his way through the women in the village, but everyone usually had the decency to keep quiet about it. Now that Luisa had Bruna to care for, she no longer had to work in the haberdashery and put up with the other women staring at her in pity or triumph. She enjoyed pottering about her garden up at the cottage and only went into the village once a week to pick up anything they needed and to visit her mum.

Noticing that Bruna had fallen asleep, Luisa sat down on a bench and took out the book her mother had given her the day of her wedding to Ernesto. Barely two years earlier, it had been the happiest day of her life. Before war had broken out, before their lives had been turned upside down, before they'd had to face the possibility of poverty and hardship like they hadn't known for a long time.

She knew that she should consider herself lucky. Due to the discovery that he had severe scoliosis during his medical examination, Ernesto hadn't been sent to the front. Instead, he worked in an ammunitions factory in Lucca, coming home every evening to her. His ego had been bruised at first, he'd wanted to go marching through the town in his smart new uniform with his friends. She'd had to convince him that he was needed at home, to protect her and the people left behind in the village. He'd seemed happier, and they'd had the chance to enjoy precious time together. Unlike many of her friends whose husbands had gone off to war, never to return.

Nineteen years old, with my whole future ahead of me, she thought bitterly. But she had been content back then, she was sure of it. Until that night at the bar. She shook her head, putting the image out of her mind. She held the book to her face, breathing in the musty odour of the ancient pages within it, and memories of her wedding day flooded her mind.

Emilia entered the room as cousin Fausta put the finishing touches to Luisa's dress and hair. Shooing Fausta out of the room, Emilia sat down next to Luisa and passed her a hand-wrapped parcel.

'So, my little girl's getting married today,' she said, her eyes misting.

Luisa nodded. 'Hard to believe, isn't it?'

'You're sure it's what you want?'

'Mamma! You're not going to try to put me off, are you?' Luisa said, laughing. 'It's a bit late for that.'

'No, of course not. Not after your father and I have spent so much money. It's just that being married, well, it's forever, Luisa, for better or for worse. You'll find out that he's got some habits that you'll grow to love, some that you'll put up with, and others that will drive you crazy. But you'll have to learn to put up with them, carry on regardless, no matter what. Once you're married, that's it, forever.'

Luisa giggled. 'I love Ernesto, Mamma, I have since the first time I saw him. I know he's the one for me, and I'll love everything about him, even if he does pick his nose.'

'We'll see if you still feel the same in thirty years' time.' Emilia's eyes filled with tears as she gazed upon her daughter. 'Look at you in that dress, it reminds me of when I got married to your father.'

Luisa looked down at the lace dress she was wearing, slightly yellow after so many years of being in storage. Her mother's dress fitted her perfectly, so no wonder it was taking her back to her own wedding day. Luisa wondered what being married to Ernesto would be like. Her courtship had been fun, walking through the village holding hands, stealing kisses whenever they could, and sometimes more if the opportunity presented itself. She'd never seen her parents kiss or even hold hands, but they'd respected and supported each other through the good times and bad. And even though they rarely showed affection to their children, they knew they were loved and protected. She hoped that she and Ernesto could be like that.

'I still remember when I first held you, you were so tiny and helpless,' Emilia said, shaking her head. 'Now look at you.'

Luisa smiled. 'Not so tiny now, am I? And definitely not so helpless.'

'This is my gift to you,' her mother said, gesturing to the parcel.

Luisa opened it, holding her breath. She'd waited nineteen years for this moment. 'Is it...?'

'The book? Yes, the same one that has been passed down from generation to generation, from eldest daughter to eldest daughter, on her wedding day.'

'Just like the cottage,' Luisa murmured. It was a family tradition; the cottage where Luisa had grown up would become her and Ernesto's home, and her mother would move in with her sister in the village.

'That's how it must be. I'm glad to leave, to be honest. Since your brothers and father went off to war, it hasn't been the same. But promise me you'll look after the Grove, Luisa.'

The Grove was as old as the cottage itself, with fruit trees and bushes that had been planted many centuries before. Luisa had always helped her mother tend the plants and use the fruit to make delicious jams and healing remedies that people would come from the valley to buy, and now it would be her turn to teach her children.

'I promise, Mamma,' she said.

'Good. You must read the book, it is full of recipes for using the plants from the Grove, but also for making cordials, wine, and many other things. People in the village swear by the medicines I make for them, and they will come to you as well.'

Luisa looked at the worn book in her hands, hardly daring to believe it was hers at long last.

Emilia took hold of her hand. 'You must also experiment and add your own recipes. Every healer in the family has written in this book.'

'Oh, Mamma, thank you.' She placed it carefully in the drawer of her bedside table, eager to start reading it later. 'Come on, otherwise Ernesto will think I've jilted him!'

25

Luisa sighed as she remembered the conversation with her mother. She had had hopes for the future, and dreams, all of them shattered by Ernesto. If only she'd known, she thought, but he'd kept that side of himself hidden until after the wedding. She'd wanted to enjoy her time as a newlywed woman, and had found a recipe in the book for preventing pregnancy. She'd carefully brewed the cordial and taken it religiously every day, and the first year had passed without any surprises.

Until Ernesto had found the bottle she hid at the back of the pantry and had demanded to know what it was. She'd told him, thinking he'd be as happy as she was that they'd been able to spend a whole year getting to know each other without the stress and tensions a baby would have brought. But Ernesto had finally unleashed his dark side, the part of him he'd carefully kept hidden during the long months of courtship and then marriage. He'd shouted at her, saying that she wanted to take away his virility, make him a laughing stock in front of the whole village when he didn't produce an heir, that she was a witch, like the rest of the women in her family. And when she'd tried to protest, he'd pushed her to the ground and threatened to hit her.

Shaking and whimpering in fear, she'd promised to never make the cordial again, and watched as he poured the mixture down the sink and then threw the bottle against the kitchen wall. That was the first time he'd hurt her physically during sex, pinning her to the floor with his body on top of hers, gripping her so tightly that he left marks. She'd felt humiliated afterwards, her scratched skin on fire from the rough floor, her dress torn where he'd pulled at it to get to her more quickly. He'd gone to the bar straight afterwards, and left her there, lying on the floor, sobbing in shock and pain. Somehow, she'd found the strength to get up and have a bath, to wash away the touch of him on her skin, the stinging soap cleansing her wounds and bringing her back to her senses. She'd been wary of him after that episode, but had never imagined that only three months later she would have found him in the act that would change her life forever.

Bruna awoke with a sudden wail, announcing that her hunger was more important than anything else. Luisa kicked a stone at her feet, watching it bounce down the street until it hit a wall and stopped. She put the book back in her bag, and stood up with a sigh. She shushed her daughter as she hurried along to her mother's house.

'Morning, Mamma,' she called out cheerfully as she entered. Doors were never locked in the village; everyone came and went as they pleased, dropping in for a coffee or bringing a plate of freshly made biscuits. No one was ever turned away or made to feel unwelcome, it was a part of village life.

'Morning, darling,' Emilia called back. 'Come through to the kitchen, I'm in here.'

Luisa picked up Bruna and left the pram in the corridor. 'I'm sure she knows when we're going to visit Nonna,' she joked, walking into the kitchen. 'She always wakes up and starts screaming as soon as we get close.'

Emilia took the baby in her arms. 'Of course she knows where she is, don't you, darling? You know that Nonna's going to spoil you rotten as soon as you're old enough.' She smiled at Luisa. 'How are you feeling today? You don't look as tired; did you get a good night's sleep?'

'Yes, for once.' Luisa rubbed her eyes. Bruna was only three months old, but she was definitely making her presence felt in the cottage, especially at night. Luisa had resorted to sleeping downstairs on the sofa with the cradle next to her, so that Ernesto could get some sleep. Even so, he usually came downstairs grumbling that the baby had kept waking him up. But she'd finally managed to get a few hours in a row that night, for the first time since Bruna was born. She almost felt human again.

'Did the cordial work?'

'Oh, Mamma, it was fantastic,' Luisa enthused. 'I put a few drops on her lips before feeding her, like you said, then put some on her forehead and pillow. She went out like a light and didn't wake up till four this morning.'

Emilia gave Bruna a big kiss. 'There's a good girl, I knew it would work. I can't understand why you didn't want to do it earlier, Luisa.'

'She's so little, I was scared of getting the dose wrong. And I hoped she'd sort herself out, like you said we did.'

Emilia looked slightly ashamed. 'I know I always said you were good babies, but it was all thanks to the cordial. I wouldn't have got through those first months without it.'

'Mamma!' Luisa laughed. 'I can't say I blame you, going without sleep is torture. At least madam here will hopefully get through the night now.'

Emilia peered at her. 'You look exhausted. Is everything else all right?'

'Yes, fine. I need to catch up on some sleep, that's all,' Luisa replied, her eyes not quite meeting Emilia's.

'And Ernesto? Everything's all right with him?'

'Yes, he's fine too, Mamma.' Luisa was starting to get irritated. 'He manages to sleep through anything, even though he always moans the baby kept him awake.'

'I know, men are usually lucky like that. I meant you and Ernesto, are you all right?'

'Of course,' Luisa replied, but her voice quavered a little.

Emilia looked at her, frowning. 'You've made your bed, now you have to lie in it, young lady,' she said. 'Like I told you on your wedding day, it's for better or for worse, there's no going back now.'

Luisa hung her head. 'I know, Mamma,' she mumbled. 'It's just that, when he drinks–' She was interrupted by the front door bursting open.

'We're back,' came a voice from the corridor. There was a commotion as coats and shoes were removed, then a rush of confusion and noise as Luisa's aunt and cousins poured into the kitchen, all talking at once. The moment passed; Luisa clenched her fists in frustration, and never spoke of it again.

When Luisa found out she was pregnant once more, she lay on her bed and cried for hours. Little did she realise that this was to become the pattern of her life for the next three years. After Bruna came Teresa, and then Antonio. Ernesto was over the moon that he finally had a son.

'Every man needs a son to carry on the family name,' he said, proudly holding Antonio in his arms while Luisa quietly suffered the attentions of the midwife.

She leaned her head back on the pillow, exhausted, as her husband took the baby to show everyone waiting outside. She could hear exclamations of joy as he was passed from person to person. Tears filled her eyes.

'I know, you're tired, aren't you?' the midwife said kindly. 'It's normal after giving birth, and you've delivered three in the last three years. And with everything that's going on with the war too. You should get a bloody medal! Go ahead and cry, it's fine by me.' She passed Luisa a handkerchief. 'I always keep one on me, most new mums need it sooner or later.'

Luisa dabbed at her eyes, grateful. But how could she explain that feeling of emptiness she had inside her in only a few minutes to the midwife?

The door opened and Ernesto waltzed in, the baby in one arm, a glass of whisky in his free hand, and an unlit cigar between his lips. He plucked the cigar out of his mouth, sloshing whisky on the floor, and burst into song.

Bruna came running in behind him, and threw herself at his legs. 'Papà, can I hold him, please? Papà, let me,' she squeaked, breathless from excitement.

Ernesto held the baby up high out of reach, and shook his head. 'You're too little, Bruna, you'll drop him,' he barked, pushing her away with his leg.

She fell back onto her bottom, a shocked look on her face. 'B-but I only want to see him,' she wailed.

Luisa beckoned her over. Bruna stood by the bed, large tears rolling down her cheeks.

'If you're really good, you can hold him later on, after you've had a bath. What do you think?' She didn't dare look at Ernesto. She could feel his fury from the other side of the room.

'All right, Mamma. I promise I'll sit still and I won't drop him.' She wiped away her tears with the back of her hand. 'I've never dropped Teresa, have I?'

'No, you haven't,' Luisa said. 'You're a big girl, I know you'll be careful.'

Bruna ran out of the room to the waiting relatives, laughing and skipping. The midwife glanced at Ernesto.

'Baby needs to eat now, if you'd like to hand him over to Mum,' she said quietly.

Ernesto hesitated, then passed the baby to Luisa. She put him to her breast, smiling as he hungrily latched on and started sucking. She lay her head back against the pillow, fighting the urge to fall asleep.

'I'll take away these things, then I'll be back to see how you're doing,' the midwife said, gathering up a bundle of soiled sheets and clothes.

As soon as she left the room, Ernesto spoke, forcing Luisa to open her eyes again. 'You shouldn't let her hold him, she's too young,' he snapped. 'Now that I've got a son at long last, I don't want anything happening to him.'

'What? Is that all that matters to you? Having a son? Don't your daughters matter anymore now?'

'My son comes first. I've waited too long for this moment,' Ernesto replied. 'By the way, I thought you could start making your special cordial again now. I don't think we need any more kids, do we? Three's more than enough. And now the factory's closed,' he paused and rubbed his arm where he'd had a ten-centimetre piece of shrapnel removed after the bombing, 'we can't keep on having kids. God only knows when I'll start working again.'

'I see.' Luisa didn't care; after giving birth three times, her body desperately needed a rest and she was more than happy not to have to go through a fourth pregnancy. 'You're right. We've already got three hungry mouths to feed, so let's stop there.'

26

Luisa worked in the Grove, while Bruna, Teresa and Antonio laughed and shouted as they played in the other part of the garden. She loved listening to them as she tended her plants, delicately pruning here, tying back shoots there, and digging out weeds with her trowel. Somehow the cottage had survived the war, its distance from the village sheltering them from the more brutal attacks and devastation that had hit the others further down the valley. She would be forever grateful that the Grove hadn't suffered any damage.

During the years, she had worked her way through the book, learning how to make each recipe, and her herbal medicines were popular with the villagers. The pantry was perfect for storing them, and was filled with bunches of drying herbs. There was always a pot bubbling on the stove, and the sweet aroma of herbs wafted around the house, permeating the walls and infusing everything with their perfume. Labelled bottles were lined up on the pantry shelves, ready for the villagers who travelled every day to the cottage with their maladies.

'Mamma, Signora Conti's arrived,' Bruna called. She loved to greet her mother's customers, and chatted gaily to them while Luisa prepared their cordials.

'All right, I'm coming,' Luisa called back. She carefully shut the gate behind her, making sure the latch was down. Teresa and Antonio were throwing a ball to each other, giggling. 'Be careful you two,' she said, ruffling Antonio's hair as she walked past him.

'Mamma,' he said crossly, shaking his head, then ran off to the other side of the garden.

Luisa went into the cottage, where Signora Conti was already sitting at the kitchen table, a glass of water in front of her. Bruna was spooning coffee into the percolator, concentrating hard on not spilling any.

'Morning, Luisa.'

'Have you come for your usual?' Luisa asked. Signora Conti suffered from piles and had already explained to Luisa in great detail the exact effects of this affliction. Luisa had listened intently, nodding every now and then, trying not to show her revulsion at the particularly intimate details. She'd adapted a recipe for some cream in the book, and now Signora Conti was a regular customer, telling anyone who would listen that if it weren't for Luisa's knowledge, she'd never have been able to sit down again.

'Ooh, yes please, Luisa,' she said, leaning back. The chair creaked under her considerable weight, the wooden back bending dangerously beyond its limit.

'And how is your, erm, problem?' Luisa asked.

'Oh, me piles are much better, thanks for asking.' She shifted in her chair and grinned. 'See, I can move about now without any more pain. They've shrunk to half the size. I don't even need me cushion no more!'

Luisa saw Bruna open her mouth to speak. 'That's fantastic news. And after only a few weeks' application, I'd say that was a miracle,' she said quickly, knowing only too well what her ten-year-old daughter's curiosity would lead to.

'So, tell me what you put in that stuff. Even the doctor couldn't believe it, had to see it with his own eyes.'

'Oh, you know, the usual ingredients,' Luisa replied. 'A bit of burdock and lungwort, with a sprinkling of sage and a little something else.' She didn't mention the final ingredient, the one that was in every single one of her home-made medicines. The secret of the centuries-old plant was passed down through each generation, only the eldest daughter knowing its properties and uses, its name lost over the years.

Signora Conti tapped her nose. 'I get it, there's a secret ingredient and you don't want to say what it is. Otherwise we'd all be making our own creams, right?'

'Of course,' Luisa replied. She glanced at her daughter. 'Bruna, isn't that coffee ready yet?'

From the noise of the percolator on the stove, it had been ready for a few minutes but Bruna had been too busy following their conversation. She turned around and quickly poured two steaming cups of coffee.

'There you are, Signora Conti, sorry about the delay,' she said.

The woman sipped her coffee and sighed deeply. 'Ah, I really needed this, you have no idea what a morning it's been. I met Carla in the shop and she kept me there for ages, telling me about the sickness down in the valley. Says lots of children are ill, and a few adults too.'

'What sickness is that?' Luisa asked, alarmed. She hadn't heard anything.

'Oh, what did she say it was?' Signora Conti gulped down the rest of her coffee, a pensive expression on her face. 'You know, that one with the high fever and cough, then they get a rash. Said they're falling like flies, the schools are half-empty.'

'Measles?' Luisa asked, dreading the answer.

'That's the one. Trust you to know what it was. But you can prepare one of your cordials if it arrives in the village, can't you? You're bound to have something to cure it.' She looked expectantly at Luisa.

'No, I'm afraid not,' Luisa replied sadly. 'I don't have anything that will cure those sorts of diseases. Just compresses to ease the pain of the rash and cordials to bring down the fever.'

'Really? 'Cause Carla said it was only a matter of time before it gets here too. Her grandchildren go to one of them posh schools down there, says her daughter's got ideas above her station and doesn't want them mixing with the likes of yours.' She gestured to Bruna, who blushed.

'I'd better start making some cordials then,' Luisa said, a heavy feeling in her heart. She remembered her mother telling her about an outbreak of scarlet fever many years earlier, and how helpless she'd felt as people had come to her for a miracle cure, only to see their child die a few days later. 'These illnesses are terrible, Luisa,' Emilia had said. 'We can't do anything, can't give them anything to make them better, only things to alleviate the pain and hope that prayers and time will save them. It was soul-destroying, not being able to do anything. I wouldn't wish that on my worst enemy.' Luisa broke out in a cold sweat and shuddered as Signora Conti continued with her doom-laden prophesies.

Luisa found out for herself exactly what her mother had been through during the scarlet fever outbreak. A week or so later, the villagers started beating a path to her door. Just a trickle at first, then it was as if the dam had broken. Desperate mothers knocking at the door every hour of the day and night, begging for salves for the painful rash and cordials to bring down their children's fever. Luisa snatched a few hours' sleep here and there, whenever she got the chance, but she felt permanently exhausted. Her mother came to stay at the cottage to help out, and between the two of them they managed to make enough supplies.

She made sure to keep her own children away from everyone, and wouldn't allow them to go down to the village, not even to school. Even though they protested vociferously, she stood her ground.

'Wait until the epidemic has passed, then you can see your friends again,' she told them, ignoring their sulking faces. Teresa stamped her feet and threw the nearest object at her mother, earning herself a slap from Bruna and a telling-off from Luisa. Antonio didn't seem to care. He didn't have many friends down in the village, and found schoolwork hard, so he was quite content to run about in the garden all day long.

Until the day he woke up with a runny nose and sore throat. By the afternoon he had a high fever, and Luisa and Emilia took turns sponging him with flannels soaked in cold water. Ernesto stormed indoors after work, his face black with anger.

'I told you to not to let the villagers come here!' he shouted at Luisa. 'They've brought the measles to the cottage, in my house, and now my son is ill.'

'I had to help them, Ernesto, they had no one else to turn to,' Luisa protested. 'I kept the children in their rooms whenever there were people here, I don't know how he got it.'

'You and your damned medicines, they're a curse. If anything happens to him, it will be your fault,' he said, slamming the door behind him as he headed off to the bar.

'Luisa...' Emilia began.

'Don't, Mamma. I'll deal with him later. Let's concentrate on Antonio now, shall we?'

Teresa and Bruna burst into the room. 'Mamma, can we go and see Antonio?' Bruna asked anxiously.

Luisa shook her head. 'You girls must stay away from him, with a bit of luck you might not have caught it.'

'He was infectious before he began showing symptoms,' Emilia said. 'Prepare yourself, Luisa, it's going to be a rough ride over the next few days.'

27

Emilia was right. The next morning, the three children had runny noses, sore throats and fevers. Antonio couldn't bear the sunlight in his eyes, so Luisa closed the shutters in his room and sat with him in the dark, dampening him with a cool sponge to try to bring down his temperature. Emilia made a chicken broth and came upstairs with three bowls on a tray. The girls gulped it down greedily but Antonio showed little interest.

'Mamma, he'll be all right, won't he?' Luisa asked, coming out of the bedroom.

'We're doing everything we can, Luisa, we can only pray it's enough,' Emilia replied.

They both jumped as they heard the front door slam. Ernesto stomped up the stairs, stopping outside Antonio's room.

'How is he?' he asked gruffly.

'No better,' Luisa answered. 'He doesn't want to eat, but Mamma says that should pass and he'll probably start to have more of an appetite tomorrow.'

'Humph.' Ernesto frowned at her, not convinced.

'The girls are coping well, thanks for asking,' Luisa added.

He didn't seem to notice the sarcasm in her voice. 'I knew they'd be all right, and anyway there are two of them.'

Luisa stared at him, shocked. 'They're all our children, male or female,' she said quietly.

'Don't start, woman, you know how I feel about this.' He went into Antonio's room, leaving the two women out on the landing.

'He's just worried, Luisa, he'll feel differently when this is over,' Emilia tried to reassure her.

The next day, all three children were feeling better and their fevers were almost gone. That evening they ate together in the kitchen, and even though Antonio was still quiet, Luisa dared to hope that the worst was over.

'Look at Antonio's face,' Teresa said suddenly, giggling.

'What?' Antonio looked at them, bewildered.

'Ha ha, look at those spots,' Bruna said.

Emilia smiled. 'That's normal, girls, with measles. Don't worry, you'll have them too by tomorrow.'

'Mamma, I don't feel so well,' Antonio said. His face went deadly white and he suddenly vomited on his plate.

'Eww, that's disgusting!' Teresa squealed, pushing her chair back hurriedly.

Luisa leaped to her feet and caught her son as he fainted. His skin felt burning hot and his hair was wet with sweat.

'Ernesto, take him upstairs to his bed.' She tried to keep her voice calm, but he must have caught the note of urgency as he didn't argue for once. He took his son in his arms and carried him out of the kitchen.

'And girls, you clean up this mess,' she said. They started to protest but one stern look from Luisa shut them up.

'Mamma, can you bring the medicine, please?'

Emilia got up, grim-faced. 'Girls, do as you're told and clear everything away. Your mamma needs all the help you can give her.'

'W-will Antonio be all right?' Bruna asked. Tears glistened in her eyes. Her brother was always so full of energy, seeing him like this was a shock.

'Of course he will,' Emilia said with forced brightness. 'He'll be fine by the morning.'

They stayed up all night, Emilia and Luisa going from one child to another, trying to bring down Antonio's temperature and comfort the girls, who were restless and agitated. Ernesto sat by his son's bedside, holding his hand and murmuring reassuring words over and over again. Antonio's black hair lay in stark contrast to the white pillowcase, his eyes moving restlessly as he mumbled, his sleep disturbed by horrific fever-induced dreams.

'We have to call the doctor,' Luisa said the next morning. The girls were covered in a thick rash but seemed to be on the mend. Antonio, on the other hand, burned hot with fever and wouldn't wake up.

'You call yourself a healer, but you can't cure your own son,' Ernesto said bitterly. He remained sitting at Antonio's side, his shoulders slumped in defeat.

'We've tried everything we could, Ernesto, you know that,' Emilia retorted. 'Luisa and I haven't slept for two days.'

'But your damn medicines don't work, do they?' he shouted suddenly. 'Pots boiling constantly on the stove, those bottles in the pantry, that stupid garden out there. All those hours wasted, and for what? Where's your magic now? Why can't you help Antonio?' Ernesto paused, breathing hard, then glared at Luisa. 'Unless you don't want to help him,' he said. 'Is that it? You hate me so much that you'd let your own son die?'

Luisa burst into tears. 'How can you be so ignorant?' she screamed at him.

Antonio stirred, sighing in his sleep.

'All right, the both of you,' Emilia interrupted. 'This isn't helping anyone, least of all Antonio. I'll go and fetch the doctor. You stay here, Ernesto, call Luisa if there's any change. And you, Luisa...' She glanced at her daughter's exhausted face. 'You go and get something to eat, and sit down quietly for a while.'

Luisa started to protest, then nodded. 'But you call me, if anything happens,' she said to her husband.

She left the room with Emilia, her heart heavy with foreboding. 'Can the doctor do anything, Mamma?' she asked quietly.

'At this point, we have to try,' Emilia replied, avoiding her daughter's eyes. 'Our medicines are no good now.'

Luisa, Bruna and Teresa sat at the kitchen table, too shocked to say anything, their eyes red from crying. Emilia busied herself in the background making a pot of tea.

'Where's Papà?' Teresa asked suddenly.

Luisa stirred, irritated by the interruption. 'He'll be here soon,' she snapped.

'Don't lie,' Bruna cried. 'He didn't care about anyone except Antonio, and now he's d-de-' She stopped, unable to continue.

Luisa went over to her daughters and wrapped her arms around them. 'I'm so sorry, girls,' she said, tears rolling down her cheeks. 'Your father's in shock at the moment, as we all are. He'll come back, you'll see. He loves you too, just as much as he loved Antonio.' She pretended not to see the look of disbelief on their faces, and hugged them close to her.

It was the morning of the funeral, and they were still stunned by the swift turn of events. The doctor had visited six days earlier and told them they were doing everything right, they only had to wait until Antonio got better. But he hadn't got better. He had got steadily worse, and he could barely breathe by the third evening. Emilia, Luisa and Ernesto had been by his bedside as his breathing became more and more shallow, until he had taken one final breath and died before their eyes.

Ernesto had let out an anguished howl, a sound that Luisa had never heard a human being make before and hoped never to hear again. He had picked up Antonio's lifeless body and crushed it to his chest, as if hoping to bring him back to life by the sheer force of willpower. Luisa and Emilia had left him there, lying on the bed next to his son, tears streaming down his face. Once downstairs, they had given vent to their own grief, holding each other while crying, wailing their desperation.

Stunned villagers had dropped by to express their condolences, bringing home-cooked food for the family to live on while they struggled to get through the days. The epidemic had passed, leaving several families in the valley grieving over the deaths of their children. Eight-year-old Antonio had been the only child to die in Gallicano.

A couple of hours later, they watched as the coffin was lowered into the ground, Emilia, Bruna and Teresa sniffing loudly as tears poured down their cheeks. Everyone in the village was there, lending solidarity to the two women who had worked so hard to save their children. Ernesto grasped Luisa's hand as workmen shovelled earth into the hole.

'I'm sorry, Luisa,' he said quietly.

She glanced up at him, startled. He stared off into the distance, as if lost in his own thoughts.

'I didn't mean what I said, you know, when Antonio was...'

'I know. It's all right, Ernesto, honestly. We were all stressed, it was a horrible time.' She squeezed his hand to let him know she had forgiven him.

He turned towards her. 'I'll try to be a better husband,' he murmured, putting an arm around her shoulder. 'And father,' he added, looking at the forlorn faces of his two daughters.

True to his word, he began taking more notice of the two girls, going on long walks with them in the countryside, helping them with their schoolwork, laughing at their conversations about hair and make-up. Luisa began to fall in love again with the man she had married. And when he asked her if they could try one last time for another baby, she didn't hesitate to say yes. He'd stopped going to the bar, the other women in the village no longer sniggered as she walked past them, and she became hopeful for their future.

Tommaso was born ten months later, conceived several weeks after they'd buried Antonio. Luisa looked at his wrinkled little face crowned with a shock of black hair and immediately fell in love with him. Bruna adored him, carrying him about in her arms and crooning lullabies, but Teresa didn't want to even look at him.

'He's not Antonio, Mamma,' she said after he was born. 'He'll never be Antonio, will he?'

Luisa shook her head sadly. 'No, darling, he won't replace Antonio, but he is your new brother. Come and say hello to him.'

Teresa ignored him from the start and continued to merely tolerate his presence. She could be a prickly character at the best of times, and resented this new intruder in their lives.

Ernesto seemed happy with his second son but kept his distance, as if afraid that his happiness would be destroyed once more. He remained close to his daughters, and Luisa was pleased to see that he no longer neglected them.

'The men in the village have asked me to drop in at the bar, to wet the baby's head,' he said to Luisa. She looked up from the magazine she was reading while the baby was sleeping quietly in his cradle.

'All right. Don't come home too late.'

'Really?' He looked surprised. 'I know you don't like me going there anym–'

'It's fine, really,' she interrupted him. 'You deserve it, you haven't been out for ages. Try to be back by eleven, so I can get Tommaso settled for the night.'

He leaned over and kissed her forehead. 'You're a wonderful woman.'

'And don't you forget it!' she said, laughing. 'Get on with you, and enjoy yourself.'

He left the room, whistling.

'Just not too much,' she whispered, her hands clenching the magazine.

He came back after midnight smelling of whisky, cigarettes and cheap perfume. Luisa said nothing as he climbed into bed beside her, but her heart broke one final time. She knew that she would never trust him again. Tomorrow she would tell him their marriage was over; she might not be able to divorce him, but from now on she would be his wife in name only.

28

Luisa smiled as she watched Tommaso chase a butterfly around the garden. He was an odd child, she thought; he seemed to avoid human contact as much as possible, but was fascinated by wildlife. She often found him sitting in the grass, absorbed in the behaviour of the ants by his feet, carrying insect wings or leaf fragments back to their nest. He hated rainy days when he was forced to stay indoors, it drove him crazy. If she wasn't careful, he'd sneak outside so that he could jump and splash in the puddles.

The only person he tolerated for any length of time was Bruna. Luisa was allowed to kiss him goodnight, or brush his hair, or straighten his clothes, but after a minute or so he would start wriggling to get away. With Bruna, instead, he would sit for hours on the sofa next to her while she read to him, or suffer her smothering him with kisses at bedtime. And Bruna adored him. She found Teresa to be too prickly and hot-tempered, so she devoted her spare time to Tommaso, who was a lot calmer.

Luisa turned her mind back to the plant she was tending. This particular bush needed special attention: it was centuries old and had been one of the first to be planted in the Grove. She bent her head and was soon lost in her own world, where nobody else existed.

Bruna threw her handbag down by the front door and sighed, happy to be home again. She headed into the kitchen, eager to see what her mother had prepared for her. She had just sat down at the table to eat when she heard the front door open.

'Is that you, Tommaso?' she called. 'Want some of this soup Mamma made? It's delicious.'

'That would be great,' her father said, striding into the kitchen. 'I'm starving.'

'P-papà.' Bruna's heart sank.

'Don't sound so pleased to see me.' He stopped and frowned at her.

'I thought it was Tommaso,' she said.

'Tommaso, Tommaso, it's always Tommaso with you,' Ernesto roared. 'It's like no one else exists here.'

'I-I'm sorry, Papà. I didn't think you'd be home till later.' She put her spoon down, her appetite gone.

'There was an accident, they sent us home early today,' he mumbled. 'Giovanni got his arm stuck in some machinery.'

'Oh. Is he all right?'

'Yeah, he's fine. Got a few bruises but he'll survive. Anyway, I came home to see how my favourite daughter is.'

'Th-that's nice.' Bruna desperately wished Teresa was there, but she'd gone to a friend's house.

'Where's your mother?' Ernesto asked.

'Out in the Grove, and Tommaso's out in the garden as well,' she said quietly. The few spoonfuls of soup she'd managed to eat lay heavy in her stomach.

'Good, good. They'll be out there for ages then, won't they?'

'I suppose,' Bruna said, feeling miserable inside.

'You finished?' he asked, gesturing towards her half-empty bowl.

'Yes, I'm not that hungry.'

'Neither am I. So, come and give Papà a hug then.'

She reluctantly got up and went over to him. He gathered her in a bear hug, his strong arms crushing her body to his. He stroked her hair, over and over again, until she thought she would scream. Then he said it, as she knew he would.

'Let's go for some of our special time. What do you think?'

She didn't answer, her eyes full of tears as he guided her over to the stairs. Slowly she walked up, each step feeling like she was walking through thick mud. Every time she felt like a condemned criminal walking towards the gallows. Her father had changed, ever since he and Mamma had had a furious row one evening. And now he had invented this special time, just for the two of them... and she wanted to die.

That evening at dinner, everyone seemed lost in their own thoughts. Luisa tried to ignore the others as she planned some new cordials, jotting down notes on a pad, her lips pursed as she thought about which ingredients would be best, but she kept an eye on her family. There was an undercurrent of tension in the room that unsettled her. Bruna quietly handed round the plates of pasta, adding an extra spoonful to Tommaso's, and Luisa saw him smile gratefully at Bruna, getting his hair ruffled in return. Ernesto shovelled forkfuls of food into his mouth, glaring at them.

'What's wrong with everyone tonight?' Teresa said, tactful as ever. 'It's like eating in a morgue.'

'Teresa!' Luisa said, shocked.

'It *is*,' she replied, pouting. 'Bruna looks like a wet weekend, you're busy with your witches' potions, and Tommaso never talks anyway. My family is so boring.'

'Go and find another one then,' Ernesto bellowed at her, fed up with her whining. 'If we're so awful, you know where the front door is.'

'I might just do that,' Teresa shouted back, tears springing to her eyes. 'You're so horrible to me, I don't know why. It's like you hate me.'

'Ask yourself why,' Ernesto said harshly.

'Ernesto!' Luisa put her pen down. 'Don't say things like that. Teresa, dear, your father didn't mean it, he's had a long day. Of course we don't hate you, we're all tired and grumpy. Let's finish up here and things will look better in the morning.'

Teresa didn't seem convinced. 'Every day it gets worse in this house. You know Cosimo, the baker's son? He's asked me to go out with him, everyone says he's madly in love with me. I'll probably marry him.'

Everyone looked at her, stunned.

'Ah, that got you, didn't it?' she sneered. 'What, didn't you think anyone could fall in love with me?'

'No, of course not, Teresa,' Luisa said. 'It's a bit sudden, that's all.'

'Not really. If any of you ever listened to me, you'd have noticed that I've been talking about Cosimo for a while now.' Their blank faces stared at her. 'See. That's exactly what I mean. Nobody cares.' She burst into tears and ran upstairs. They heard her bedroom door slam loudly.

'She never changes.' Ernesto shook his head.

Luisa bit back her reply. She hated what was happening to her family, but felt powerless to change it. Ever since Antonio's death, it was as if a bitter poison had seeped into their lives, eroding the closeness they'd once had, creating discord wherever possible. And, absurd though it was, she knew something, or someone, at the cottage was responsible.

29

Tommaso sucked his thumb as his mother yelled at Bruna, uncertain what was going on. He had watched from the back door the day before as his father stroked Bruna's hair, his arms holding her tightly to him, and noticed the tension in Bruna's body, as if she wanted to run away. Clenching his fists, he'd willed himself not to make any noise, knowing how his father might react if he discovered him there. Tommaso was an observer, he noticed things about people and animals that no one else did, and gauged their feelings from their subconscious actions. But when he saw his father lead Bruna up the stairs, he couldn't explain the uneasy feeling in his gut that told him something was wrong. He cringed as his mother's voice reverberated around the room.

'What do you mean, you're pregnant?' Luisa screamed. She felt as if she was going to faint, and had to hold on to the edge of the table to stop herself falling. Bruna stood before her, her head bowed low.

'I-I'm sorry, Mamma,' she whispered.

'Pregnant? How could you be so stupid?' Luisa narrowed her eyes. 'Who is he? The father, who is he?'

Bruna shook her head. 'I c-can't tell you.'

'Can't or won't? Or maybe you don't know who he is, maybe there's more than one candidate, is that right?' Luisa was bright red in the face, panting as she faced her daughter.

Tommaso sat in the corner of the living room, terrified by the scene before him. The toy cars he'd been playing with lay abandoned on the floor.

'No, it's not like that,' Bruna protested. 'Th-there was only one, but I can't tell you who. Please, Mamma, don't be so angry with me. I-it was a mistake.' She burst into tears. 'I knew you wouldn't be happy, but I didn't think you'd be like this.'

'Young lady, if you thought I was going to be lenient with you, you thought wrong! After all the talks we had, and you knew about the cordial. Did you even use it, you stupid girl?' Luisa yelled.

'Of course I did. It can't have worked. I did exactly as you told me, Mamma.'

Suddenly the front door slammed open.

'What on earth is going on here?' Ernesto demanded to know. 'I could hear the shouting out on the road. What's happened?'

'What's happened?' Luisa shrieked. 'I'll tell you what's happened. Young missy here has only gone and got herself pregnant, that's what's happened.'

'Mamma,' Bruna pleaded, tears streaming down her face. She sat down heavily on a chair and put her head in her hands, sobbing.

'What?' Ernesto said, walking over to her. He sat on the chair opposite her and rested his arms on the table. 'Is it true? What your mother said, is it true?' There was no anger in his voice, only concern.

'Y-yes,' Bruna snivelled, wiping at her nose with her cardigan sleeve. Tommaso saw she wouldn't look her father in the eye.

'Whose is it?' he asked quietly.

'I can't say.'

'She won't say, more like,' Luisa interjected angrily.

'Hush, woman.' Ernesto slammed his fist on the table. 'At this point, the damage is done. It doesn't matter who did it, Bruna is the important thing now.'

Luisa raised her eyebrows in surprise. 'It doesn't matter who did it? So who's going to pay for it when it's born, eh? If it's someone from the village, he has to be forced to face up to his actions and support his child. And preferably marry our daughter.'

'I don't want to marry him,' Bruna said.

'What you want isn't important, you must do the right thing by the baby and by yourself,' Luisa snapped.

'Enough,' Ernesto said. 'I'm still the man of the house here, and what I say goes. We'll help Bruna and take care of her and the child when it's born. If she doesn't want to marry the man, then she doesn't have to.'

'But–'

'No buts.' Ernesto looked sternly at his wife. '*We* will help Bruna.'

'You'll never find a husband after this,' Luisa spat, glaring at her daughter. 'Be it on your own heads then.' She stormed out of the kitchen, fury emanating from her every pore.

Ernesto glanced at Bruna. 'She'll calm down, you'll see.'

'I know,' Bruna replied.

'Bruna, is it...?'

She stood and walked out of the kitchen, leaving her father's question unanswered. Tommaso looked up as she passed by.

'I still love you, Bruna,' he whispered, but she didn't hear him. He could see his father, sitting at the kitchen table, his back straight, his shoulders taut. All sorts of thoughts ran through

Tommaso's mind, ugly thoughts that he pushed away as soon as they appeared.

Tommaso became Bruna's shadow during her pregnancy, never leaving her side whenever she went out. The villagers smiled at the sight of them: Bruna waddling down the street cradling her expanding stomach while Tommaso skipped along beside her, carrying her bags.

'Stop glaring at every man I speak to,' she whispered to him as they walked out of the butcher's.

'Was that him?' Tommaso replied fiercely.

'Who?'

Tommaso stared at her large stomach. '*Him*,' he said, gesturing towards the shop.

Bruna stopped in surprise, then wrapped her arms around him in a huge bear hug. 'Oh, Tommaso,' she said, holding him as he struggled to escape from her grip. 'Please don't do this. Who the father is isn't important, I just want you to carry on loving me and looking after me.'

He stopped wriggling and frowned. 'If I find him...'

'Come on, help me get these things home to Mamma, she said she needed them pronto.' Bruna smiled at her brother, but he noticed that her eyes didn't sparkle anymore, like they used to.

Tommaso spent the afternoon showing her the interesting things he'd found in the garden. The enormous black and yellow spider with its beautifully intricate web, the hole under the pine tree that was certainly a snake's nest, the thrush family that was raising a solitary cuckoo chick which had invaded their nest. When Bruna got tired, they lay down on a grassy patch and watched the clouds float by overhead.

'Do you ever see faces in the clouds?' Tommaso asked.

'Faces? No, I can't say that I do.'

'I do. All the time. See there.' He pointed at a grey cloud that was passing close by the sun.

'Yes.'

'Don't you think it looks a bit like Papà? With his hair going in all directions, like when he gets up first thing, and that pointy bit below could be his beard, when it's trimmed and tidy.'

'No, I don't see it. It doesn't look anything like him.' She closed her eyes and sighed deeply.

Tommaso turned and looked at her. 'You don't like to talk about Papà lately,' he remarked.

'Don't be silly.'

'Every time I mention him, you change the subject.'

'You're imagining things. I'm getting cold lying here, let's go inside and get something to eat.' She got clumsily to her feet, dusted off her skirt, and headed towards the kitchen.

Tommaso slowly followed her indoors, lost in his own thoughts.

30

Luisa stood at the kitchen sink, up to her elbows in soapy water as she washed the plates from the evening meal. She glanced over at Bruna next to her, noticing how pale she was. No matter how much the end of the pregnancy weighed on her, she still insisted on helping her mother in the cottage. Not like that snooty sister of hers, who considered herself above such trivial things. She snorted as she remembered how Teresa had come running down the stairs an hour earlier, enveloped in a cloud of expensive perfume, while declaring that she would be 'dining out' that evening. Luisa didn't understand how Teresa had ended up like that, she definitely hadn't put those grandiose ideas in her head.

'Go and sit down, Bruna, you're looking tired,' Luisa said gruffly to her daughter.

'If you don't mind, Mamma, I'd like to go and lie down for a while.' Bruna put the drying-up cloth on the draining board and leaned over to give Luisa a kiss. 'I'll see you in the morning.'

'Night.' Luisa gently squeezed her daughter's hand. Now that her initial rage over finding out that her daughter was pregnant had passed, she admitted to herself it would be wonderful to have a grandchild to coo over.

She watched as Bruna waddled across the room, her enormous stomach making it difficult to manoeuvre through the furniture. As she passed near Ernesto's armchair, he reached out and brushed his hand against hers. Luisa frowned when she saw Bruna retract her hand as if she'd been burned.

'Bruna, sweetheart.' She saw Ernesto's mouth form the words, then noticed an expression of pure hatred come over Bruna's face. Luisa recoiled from it, even though she was all the way across the other side of the room.

Luisa turned back to the sink, rage building up deep inside her, threatening to explode. Her hand closed tightly around the blade of the knife she was washing, until she looked down and saw the water had turned red. Swearing, she pulled the plug out and ran her hand under cold water, feeling as though her soul was flowing out of her body along with her blood. She picked up the drying-up cloth with her free hand and threw it at Tommaso, who sat in his usual corner on the floor, hitting him on the head.

'Don't just sit there, come and help me finish,' she snapped, then felt guilty as Tommaso jumped, a puzzled look on his face. Luisa turned her back on him, too upset to speak, as he silently started drying the plates.

Bruna's screams echoed throughout the cottage as her stomach contracted yet again. Beads of sweat burst out on her forehead and her face was contorted with agony. Luisa dripped water onto her lips from a wet sponge and ran her hand soothingly over her forehead, brushing back her sweat-soaked hair.

'Am I going to die, Mamma?' Bruna groaned, trying to find a comfortable position.

'Sssh, of course not,' Luisa replied. But she was worried. Her daughter had been in labour for almost two days, things were not progressing as they should. She leaned over and kissed Bruna's cheek. 'I'm going to the kitchen to get some things, I'll be back before you know it.'

She ran down the stairs and found Emilia already preparing a tray. The sharp knives glinted in the morning light, winking their joy at Luisa. She shook her head.

'No, Mamma, we can't,' she whispered.

'I've done this hundreds of times, Luisa, I could do it with my eyes closed,' Emilia replied, but her hand trembled as she put some clean cloths on the tray.

'You know the risks as well as I do. She's nineteen, she can do this by herself without our interference.' Luisa stepped around the table and took hold of her mother's arm.

'She's been in labour for almost two days,' Emilia snapped. Then her face softened. 'I'm sorry, I'm worried. She's not dilating enough, and that baby isn't going to come out by itself.'

'Can't we try the–?' Luisa began, but Emilia interrupted her.

'Hush. Ernesto said we weren't to use our remedies on her.' Emilia looked around nervously, as if expecting to see Ernesto glaring at her from his armchair.

Luisa shuddered, recalling her husband's face a few hours earlier, black with anger, refusing to listen to their explanations. 'But it will work. She's my daughter, your granddaughter; do you really think it's better to cut her open before at least trying the remedy? We could give it a couple of hours, and if things don't improve, we'll use...' She gestured at the tray, swallowing hard. The thought of her mother using the sharp kitchen knife on her daughter's belly made her feel sick. Luisa took the recipe book out of the cupboard where she usually stored it and flipped through the pages until she found the right one.

'Black cohosh, blue cohosh, ginger,' she read. 'Only the

roots, mind. And lobelia, steeped in hot water until concentrated, then add a few spoonfuls to a glass of water. Everything's in the Grove, you would only need to prepare the mixture. And add some...' She paused, but her mother understood and nodded. The special ingredient from the ancient plant in the Grove.

Tommaso came running towards them, his shirt half untucked and his shoelaces undone.

'Why aren't you at school, young man?' Luisa demanded to know.

'I-I can't find my books, Mamma,' he stammered, going bright red in the face.

Luisa took a deep breath, ready to shout at him to go to school, but her mother stepped in.

'Maybe he should stay home today, what do you think, Luisa? I don't think he'll be able to concentrate anyway.' She paused as a loud moan came from upstairs. 'Now, why don't you go back up to Bruna, and Tommaso and I will go out to the Grove and pick some herbs.'

Luisa looked at her mother in surprise. 'You mean...?'

'Yes. You're right, we've got to try everything before... that. Ernesto's already gone to work, he won't know. I'm sure Tommaso won't say anything, will you?'

'About what?' he asked innocently, then burst out laughing.

'See,' Emilia said. 'We'll prepare the infusion, you keep Bruna calm for now.' She gave Luisa a hug, then took hold of Tommaso's hand and the pair went out into the garden.

Luisa sighed, and made her way upstairs.

Luisa stood back and wiped her brow, glad that it was finally over. As the baby's wails filled the room, she felt like crying along with her new granddaughter. She smiled as she watched

Emilia clean the baby and wrap her up in a warm, fluffy towel. The tray was on the chest of drawers in the corner of the room, the knives still clean and unused.

Luisa went over to Bruna, who lay exhausted on the bed, and held the baby out to her. Bruna gently brushed her hand against its cheek.

'I can't, Mamma, I'm too tired.'

'Just hold her for a moment,' Luisa insisted.

'Later, please. Let me sleep for now.' Bruna turned her head away from her child and closed her eyes. Luisa frowned, but left her to sleep undisturbed.

'She'll pick up after a good rest,' Emilia tried to reassure her. Luisa wasn't so sure.

As she sat on the sofa with the baby sleeping in her arms, Luisa went over the events of the last few days in her mind. Seeing her daughter suffering so much pain had reignited the fury she'd tried to bury since witnessing the scene between Ernesto and Bruna. Now that it was all over, her mind started to wander, thinking about things she'd rather not. She remembered the look of anger on Bruna's face, the way she'd snatched her hand away from her father's touch, and Luisa knew the reason why.

She gazed down upon her granddaughter in her arms, trying to feel some love for her, but there was nothing there. Only a vast emptiness deep inside her that would slowly fill with hate for this child as she grew up, looking more and more like her grandfather every day. She could already see some similarities: the double crown in the middle of her already thick mop of hair that would be impossible to dominate and would drive her crazy as it spread in all directions. The little snub nose that would grow broader and longer. Those pale blue eyes that would probably turn into her grandfather's hazel brown eyes in a matter of weeks, eyes that would remind Bruna every day of what she'd been through. Luisa looked hastily away, a tear running down her cheek as she thought of the future and what it would hold for them. She brushed it away as Bruna came downstairs.

'Are you feeling better now?'

'A bit. I thought I'd get something to eat.'

'That's a good sign.' Luisa was impressed. Her daughter was recovering quickly from her traumatic labour, much more quickly than she had.

She watched as Bruna bent over to peer at her baby, and realised with a shock that her daughter was now a mother herself. The baby snuffled in its sleep, its mouth opening in search of food. Bruna gently took her daughter, then sat down in one of the armchairs and pulled open her nightgown. The baby hungrily latched on, making soft sucking noises, its eyes closed in contentment. Bruna lay her head against the back of the chair and sighed.

'She's a strong eater, isn't she?' Luisa said softly.

'She's going to wear me out.'

Luisa stood and ruffled her daughter's hair. 'Would you like a tea, or a coffee? And what would you like to eat?'

'A tea would be lovely, with some biscuits,' Bruna replied gratefully.

Luisa busied herself in the kitchen. As she placed everything on the tray, ready to take over to the coffee table, she caught the expression on Bruna's face as she looked down at her newborn daughter. There was love there, but also something else, an uncertainty; no, it was deeper than that, it was that pitying, contemptuous look people gave to the runt of the litter, knowing that it would never be accepted or loved by anyone. Luisa wasn't shocked. She knew exactly how Bruna felt.

31

'I don't *know* what I'm going to call her, Papà,' Bruna repeated. Luisa could see she was getting irritated. It was the fourth time that day her father had asked her the same question.

'She's two days old, she should have a name by now,' Ernesto grumbled. 'What about Gilda, after my grandmother?'

'Oh, Ernesto, really,' Luisa said. 'That's awful. Bruna will decide when she's ready, won't you, dear?'

Bruna smiled gratefully at her. 'There's plenty of time, the christening's not for a while. Actually, I was thinking maybe Tommaso could choose her name.'

'Me?' Tommaso exclaimed, jumping up. He already adored the baby, and kept saying how he couldn't wait until it was old enough to play with.

'Humph.' Teresa looked at him with disdain. 'I dread to think what the poor thing will be called then. You'll probably regret not calling her Gilda.'

Tommaso threw a cushion off the sofa at Teresa. 'I'll think of a great name for her,' he said, leaping out of the way as Teresa threw the cushion back at him. He poked his tongue at her and ran into the garden, laughing.

'He'll end up calling her Lizard or something stupid like that,' Teresa commented.

Bruna shrugged. 'I can't think of anything, so whatever he comes up with will be okay with me.' She jumped as she heard the baby's cries coming from upstairs. 'God, is it time to feed her again already? All right, all right, I'm coming.' She wearily stood and went to tend to her daughter.

Ernesto snorted. 'Can't see what's wrong with Gilda, it's a fine name that's been in my family for generations.'

'That's why it's time to have a change, maybe,' Luisa retorted. 'I'm going outside to check on Tommaso.' She closed the back door behind her, then paused. She was about to return indoors and apologise when she heard Teresa and Ernesto talking.

'I don't know what's up with your mother, she's been like that since the baby was born,' Ernesto said.

'Baby hormones,' Teresa replied, and they laughed.

'Be nice to everyone until things settle down,' Ernesto told her. 'Your mother and Bruna are like two bombs that are about to go off at any moment.'

Luisa clenched her fists and counted to ten before setting off to find Tommaso.

By the afternoon, everyone's nerves were frazzled. The baby had cried all day long, and they'd taken turns in trying to calm her down. Except Ernesto. He'd gone to the bar to 'cure his headache'. Luisa walked around the living room, singing softly, the tiny baby bawling in her arms.

Bruna threw herself down on the sofa. 'Will it ever stop? I'm starting to wish I was still in labour.'

Luisa laughed. 'All babies cry a lot at the beginning, she just needs to settle down. Give her a few days.'

'It's probably because she wants a name,' Teresa muttered.

She mimicked a little child's voice. 'All the other babies have a name, but I'm known as "it". All I want is a name.'

'That's enough, Teresa,' Luisa warned, seeing Bruna's expression. 'Your sister's exhausted, leave her be. She'll name her when she's ready.'

'Why do you always defend her? She can't even bear to look at her own daughter,' Teresa retorted.

'That's not true,' Bruna said, and burst into tears. 'And what do you care, anyway? Since when has naming the baby been so important to you?'

'Papà says–'

'Sod what Papà says,' Bruna snarled.

'Screw you,' Teresa yelled. She stormed out of the house.

'Teresa!' Luisa got up and followed her outside. 'Where are you going?'

'To Cosimo's, at least I don't get shouted at there,' she said, hurrying down the path towards the gate. 'And I won't be back until tomorrow,' she added, without turning.

Luisa stopped by the front door, watching her daughter until she disappeared down the road. Sighing, she went back indoors. 'I need to get dinner ready,' she said, feeling drained.

'Give her to me, Mamma.' Bruna held out her arms to take her daughter. 'It's not true, you know. What Teresa said. It's just...'

'I know,' Luisa reassured her. 'It takes time to adapt, for all of us but in particular for you. You'll be fine.'

That night Luisa lay in bed, listening to Bruna walking round and round her bedroom, trying to soothe her daughter's crying. Ernesto lay with his back to her, snoring softly in his sleep, his bulk barely visible in the dark room. Luisa listened to his rhythmic breathing, wondering how he could sleep so easily knowing what he'd done to his daughter. The familiar rage boiled up once more, and she clenched her fists tightly. She wanted to love her granddaughter, enjoy her first months of life, watch her develop and learn about the world around her; and yet, every time she looked at her, she could only see the image of her husband down some dark alleyway, his white backside pumping backwards and forwards, only this time it wasn't some floozy from the bar, but Bruna...

No! Luisa screamed inside her head, biting her tongue hard to stop the thoughts from coming. *No, no, no!* Her mouth filled with the taste of blood, the metallic flavour distracting her. She hated Ernesto; she was incapable of understanding the depravity he'd sunk to, unable to speak to anyone about it, and knew that she'd have to carry this terrible secret inside her until the day she died. But she also hated Bruna, as much as she tried not to. *How could she have allowed this to happen? Her own father?* Thoughts raced through Luisa's mind until she felt as if she would explode, and she sobbed quietly while the baby carried on crying in the next room.

Even Tommaso looked tired and tense the next morning. Fed up with the constant noise, he escaped into the garden straight after breakfast. Luisa couldn't blame him, even the sound of the church bells bouncing off the hills was more bearable than the baby's screams.

'I'm off to church, Tommaso, you comin'?' Ernesto called from the back door.

'No, Papà, I don't want to today,' Tommaso replied.

'This is the second week in a row, Don Luciano will have something to say.'

'Come on, Papà. I've hardly slept, I want to stay home,' Tommaso whined.

Ernesto grunted. 'All right. Your mother's not coming either, says she's got too much to do. Seems I'm the only God-fearing person here lately.'

'What about Bruna?' Tommaso asked.

'Bruna? Ha! She looks like she's going to have a nervous breakdown. And if she takes the girl into church, we'll be excommunicated. Never mind.' Ernesto went back indoors to get his jacket and hat, and set off to church.

Bruna was struggling to change her daughter's nappy, but she kept wriggling just as she was about to put the pin through the terry towelling cloth. 'Stay still,' she snapped, grabbing the baby's hips and trying to stop its legs moving. 'Damn.' The nappy fell off and the baby gleefully peed everywhere, chewing on her hands as if to stop herself from laughing.

'Give it here,' Luisa said, coming to her rescue. She deftly wiped the baby clean and put the nappy on, quickly snapping the pins into place before she could move again. 'There, all done.'

Bruna burst into tears.

'Oh, Bruna, don't,' Luisa said, taking her daughter into her arms while keeping one hand on the baby so she didn't fall off the kitchen table. Bruna sobbed tiredly on her shoulder, her whole body shaking.

'All right, it's all right,' Luisa crooned, alarmed. 'You're tired, you've been up all night.' As she spoke, she realised that the baby was silent. She turned to look. 'Bruna,' she whispered. 'She's sleeping.'

'Finally.' Bruna ran her hand tiredly through her unkempt hair, and Luisa noticed the dark shadows under her eyes.

'Go upstairs and have a lie-down, I'll call you when she wakes up.'

'No, you're tired too, and you've got work to do in the garden, I heard you telling Papà earlier,' Bruna replied. 'I'll take her with me. That way, you can do what you need to do, and I'll be there when she wakes.'

Luisa reluctantly agreed. Bruna took her daughter in her arms and went upstairs, gently rocking her and making hushing noises.

Luisa busied herself in the kitchen, tidying up and putting everything away. The downstairs was littered with baby things, and she put those away as well. She picked up a teddy bear that had belonged to Bruna, and with a sudden pang realised that it had been Antonio's favourite. What was Bruna doing, giving it to the new baby? Didn't she realise how precious it was? How could she bear to let that abomination touch something that had been a part of Antonio? Luisa had never allowed herself to grieve properly for Antonio, and now something inside her snapped. It was as if the pain had suddenly become a gigantic ball that was choking her, filling her with a poisonous gas, the fog in her head becoming more and more dense, dulling her mind.

Luisa made her way upstairs, clutching the teddy bear close to her chest, and stopped outside Bruna's room. She could hear her daughter's and granddaughter's rhythmic breathing, slow and steady. She turned the handle, trying not to make any noise. Stepping into the bedroom, she could see the two of them asleep in the bed, Bruna lying with one arm draped protectively over her daughter's body. Luisa heard the baby snuffling, those blocked-nose sounds newborns make. Her grip tightened on the teddy bear as she remembered Antonio when he was a baby, how she'd loved him with all her heart, how she'd loved all her children. She took a step towards them, then another, until she was next to the bed, her shadow covering the baby. As if in a drugged state, she dropped the teddy bear and picked up the pillow that Bruna had placed behind her daughter to stop her falling off the bed. She held it in her hands and looked at it, wondering what it was. A roaring noise filled her ears, and all she could see was Antonio, and Ernesto so proud of having a son at long last, Antonio, Ernesto, Antonio...

She bent over and placed the pillow on the baby's head, her eyes squeezed tight shut. Tears rolled down her cheeks as the pain flowed through her body, years of suffering and keeping quiet surging through her, until it burst out of her the only way it could. Leaving the pillow where it was, she gently moved Bruna's hand so that it rested on top of it. She picked up the teddy bear and looked at the scene before her, still crying silently. She felt nothing, just a cold numbness that seemed to spread through her, destroying any feelings she'd had up until that moment.

32

Tommaso noticed his mother coming out into the garden, and instantly forgot about the baby lizard he'd been playing with. He ran over to her and threw his arms around her legs, hugging her tight. She jumped, as if coming out of a trance, and looked down at him.

'Mamma, I did it, I chose a name,' he said, his face alight with joy.

'Good, good,' she said. He was puzzled by the vacant expression on her face.

'Don't you want to know what it is?'

'What, Tommaso?'

He gave up. 'Nothing, I'll tell you later.'

'That's probably best. Come and help me in the garden, there's some weeding you can do.'

They worked together, side by side, as Luisa explained the various plants to him and showed him how to clear the ground under their bases so they wouldn't get choked by weeds. Tommaso followed her instructions, happy to be alone with his mother and far away from the screaming baby. Much as

Tommaso adored her, the last three days had left him feeling irritable and the slightest noise got on his nerves.

As he dug, he thought over the name he'd chosen for his niece. Malva. Just like the plant his mother used to cure the villagers' colds and flu. He hoped Bruna would like it, but on the other hand, she'd told him that whatever he chose would be all right with her. A dragonfly suddenly appeared before him, hovering at eye level, and he marvelled at its lightly veined, transparent wings and beautiful, vibrant colours. As he watched, time seemed to stop, the dragonfly's wings moving in slow motion, up and down, hypnotising him with their steady movement. Its large, bulbous eyes gazed unblinkingly at him, as if it wanted to tell him something. Tommaso stared back, willing himself to stay still, afraid that the slightest movement would make it fly away. They remained suspended in their private bubble of time, oblivious to everything else around them. Then, all of a sudden, the dragonfly sped off towards the trees and disappeared from sight. Tommaso shook his head and blinked, as if waking from a long sleep.

A piercing scream rang out in the clear blue sky. Luisa sat frozen on the ground, trowel in hand, as the back door crashed open and Bruna's wails filled the air.

'Mamma!' Bruna screamed, running through the garden. She was cradling her daughter in her arms, tears pouring down her cheeks.

Tommaso jumped up. 'Mamma?' he said.

Luisa heard him, but couldn't move.

'Mamma,' he repeated, shaking her shoulders.

Luisa dropped the trowel and slowly stood. She stared at Tommaso, confused, then regained her composure. 'Wh-what is it, Bruna?' she called. 'I'm coming.'

'Oh, Mamma, the baby, when I woke up she was under the pillow. Sh-she's not breathing.'

'All right, stay calm,' Luisa said. 'Give her to me, I'll have a look.' She gently took the baby from Bruna's arms and removed the blanket she'd wrapped her in. Her sweet, angelic face looked like it had been carved from marble, and her skin was cold under Luisa's fingers. She touched the blue-tinged lips and stroked a pallid cheek.

'M-mamma?' Bruna said hesitantly.

'I'm sorry, but she's–'

'No,' Bruna screamed. 'No, she can't be. Not my baby!' She burst into deep, racking sobs, her whole body shaking.

'Come, let's go indoors,' Luisa said, putting her arm around Bruna's shoulders. She was barely aware of Tommaso trailing behind them, his feet dragging along the ground.

Once inside, she laid the baby in its cradle and guided Bruna to a chair at the table. 'Sit down, and tell me exactly what happened.'

Bruna sank heavily onto the wooden chair, her eyes staring wildly. Luisa saw Tommaso creep over to the cradle, where he stood looking down at his niece's tiny body, his eyes glistening with tears.

'I-I woke up. I'd slept so well, I remember thinking at long last she'd let me sleep a few hours, and, and I turned to her, and there was th-the p-pillow on top of her.' She burst into tears again.

'Sshh, it's all right,' Luisa said, stroking her daughter's hair, even though her own heart was breaking inside. She sat on the chair opposite Bruna and waited for her to speak.

'Th-then I picked up the pillow, and it looked l-like she was sleeping.' Bruna hiccupped. 'I touched her, and she was so cold, too cold, so I picked her up and, oh God, Mamma.'

Luisa hugged her daughter tightly, wishing she could undo

what she'd done. Steeling herself, she said, 'Bruna, I-I don't know how to tell you, but–'

'I know, Mamma,' Bruna replied miserably.

'Y-you do?' Luisa said, startled.

'I-I must have done it in my sleep. I-I was th-thinking horrible things when I went upstairs, but it was only because I was tired. I would never have done them, honestly.'

'What sort of things?'

'I only wanted to get some sleep, and she'd been crying so much, and I was so, so tired.' She looked at her mother, pleading with her to understand.

Luisa nodded. 'Go on.'

'I wanted her to stop crying and let me sleep, and I imagined how nice it would be if I could turn her off for a while,' she sobbed. 'Only for a couple of hours. I didn't mean to do... this. But I must have done it in my sleep, mustn't I?'

Luisa wanted to tell her the truth, but the words wouldn't come out. She thought about how much her daughter would hate her, and what the rest of the family would say. They wouldn't do anything to save her from a police investigation, she'd go to jail for a long time. Which would leave Ernesto free to carry on with his abhorrent behaviour.

But on the other hand, if she let Bruna think she'd done it by accident, maybe, just maybe, they could cover it up, and she would still be here to protect her children. She'd known the village doctor for a long time, and was sure she could persuade him it was a natural death. The police wouldn't even have to get involved. Bruna would get over it, the young bounced back so quickly.

Luisa's mind whirred as ideas spun around her head, desperately trying to think out a plan that would save everyone. And at the back of it all was the one constant whisper: Ernesto. If it hadn't been for him, none of them would be in this situation.

Ernesto. The whisper grew louder, coated in hate. She pushed it back down, she would deal with it later.

'I-I think you must have done,' she said, despising herself as she said it. But there was no other way.

Bruna burst into tears, and pulled wildly at her hair.

Tommaso ran over to her. 'Bruna, don't!' he shouted. 'Mamma, stop her, please stop her.'

Luisa wanted to but remained where she was, guilt overwhelming her, unable to comfort her daughter. Her heart broke at the sight of Bruna's tear-streaked face, bright red and swollen.

Tommaso stroked Bruna's hair, until she stopped screaming. 'Don't, Bruna,' he mumbled, trying to comfort her. 'I found a name for her, I was going to tell you later. I chose Malva, what do you think?' Bruna started to calm down as Tommaso talked continuously to her, reassuring her.

Luisa stood back, watching, her heart breaking as she witnessed her children's despair.

They decided to bury Malva in the Grove, as she hadn't yet been baptised and couldn't be buried in the village cemetery. It felt right to keep her there at the cottage with them, still part of the family she'd left too soon.

Ernesto and Tommaso had prepared the ground for the burial, and Bruna had chosen a headstone with a simple engraving. They stood with their heads bowed as Ernesto and Tommaso lowered the tiny coffin into the hole they'd dug. Tommaso's small arms struggled to hold its weight but he bravely carried on, determined not to drop it. Ernesto stood tall and straight as he said a few words, then they recited the Lord's Prayer together. Teresa took hold of Bruna's hand and squeezed it, quietly speaking to her. It was only the six of them at the funeral, they hadn't invited anyone else from the village. Bruna hadn't been able to bear the thought of making small talk with the other women, and Luisa hadn't wanted them nosing about their business.

As Ernesto started shovelling earth down onto the coffin, Luisa turned to her children and Emilia. 'Come, let's go indoors and leave your father to finish here.' They followed her quietly into the kitchen.

Luisa looked around, frowning. 'So many things have happened in here,' she said. 'Whatever crisis we have, we always seem to end up in the kitchen. It's the heart of our family, where we'll always be ready to help each other.'

Emilia sat down at the table, sighing. 'It's always been that way, ever since I can remember. Through the good times and bad.' Malva's death had hit her hard. Her skin was pallid and Luisa knew her mother wasn't sleeping.

Teresa cleared her throat. 'I-I have something to say, Mamma.'

Luisa stared at her. 'Well?' she asked, when her daughter didn't continue.

'I've spoken with Bruna already, she knows.' Teresa glanced over at her sister, who nodded in support. 'I've decided to move in with Cosimo's family,' she blurted. 'H-he's asked me to marry him in the spring, and I th-thought it would be best if I move out as soon as possible.'

'I see.' Luisa gazed thoughtfully at Teresa. 'Any particular reason why?'

Teresa blushed. 'We never could hide anything from you, Mamma, could we? I'm pregnant. That's why Cosimo wants to marry me, and that's why I have to move out.' She glared defiantly at her mother. 'And that's why I told Bruna. I don't want to hurt her; it will be bad enough when the baby's born. Please tell me you understand, Mamma.'

Luisa sighed. 'I forget you're grown up now. I think you're right, Teresa, it's probably for the best.'

'Really?' Teresa sounded surprised it had been that easy. 'You're sure?'

'Of course. Just come and visit us every now and then, maybe.' Luisa smiled, trying to hide the pain she felt inside. Her heart and her chest ached. Bit by bit, it seemed that her family was falling apart, destroyed by the one person who should have been their mainstay. Ernesto.

33

1962

'Tommaso, I've already told you, I don't want you coming to the village with me today,' Bruna said, starting to get irritated.

'But I haven't got anything to do. Mamma doesn't want me to help her in the garden and I don't feel like playing by myself.' He looked up at her with pleading eyes.

It was already a hot summer's day, and it was only ten in the morning. Even the insects fluttered half-heartedly around the garden. Luisa had disappeared to the Grove straight after breakfast, wanting to tend the plants before it got too unbearable. Tommaso had started doing some of his summer homework, but was already bored with it.

Bruna sighed. It was going to be one of those days. 'No, Tommaso,' she said sternly. 'Not today. I've got to meet someone.'

'Who?' he said, perking up immediately. When Bruna met up with her friends, they usually went to the bar or gelateria. Maybe he would get an ice cream.

'No one you know. Please, Tommaso, it's important. I'll tell you what. I'll bring back a tub of ice cream, we can share it later.'

He grumbled but finally relented, insisting that she got his favourite flavours. She kissed him on the forehead and ruffled his hair. 'Love you, shorty,' she said.

He frowned as she sauntered off down the road towards the village, her dress swinging around her legs, her freshly washed hair a golden halo in the sunlight. She'd become more distant lately, as if she was always thinking about something else, and he felt excluded. Ever since Malva had died, he'd sensed a hole in the family, and it seemed to be growing bigger and wider. Teresa had gone, and was now married to Cosimo, living in a village down in the valley with their daughter and another child on the way. They didn't see her very often, not that Tommaso missed her sniping comments and arrogant behaviour.

He thought his mother looked sad; she spent more and more time in the Grove, making medicines and testing new theories and ingredients. He often helped her, even though he knew he wasn't really meant to be there; it was a place for the mother and the eldest daughter of the family. But Bruna refused to help her mother, saying it was old-fashioned and they should rely on modern medicines nowadays, not herbal folklore. His mother had been hurt by her comments but hadn't said anything, she'd merely let Bruna do what she felt was right. Tommaso was a poor substitute, he knew that, but when his mother gave him one of her rare smiles, it made up for all the pain and sadness.

His father was the cause of their problems, this much Tommaso knew. When they sat down for dinner in the evenings, the atmosphere was so tense that eating was a torture. His parents ignored each other as much as possible. Bruna ate as fast as she could without earning a rebuke from her mother, then invented an excuse to avoid being in their company any longer. Tommaso usually helped his mother clear away the things and wash up, both working in total silence while his father listened to the radio. He wondered how much longer things could go on like this.

A few days later, Luisa's life was shattered when Bruna made an announcement. She arrived for dinner that evening with a guest.

'Mamma, Papà, this is George,' she announced. George held his hand out to Ernesto, who shook it, a bewildered look on his face.

'Pleased to meet you, signore,' he said, his English accent making his Italian sound bizarre. Luisa put her hand to her mouth, smothering a laugh.

'And you, signora,' he added, turning to Luisa. She shook his hand, looking at her daughter's flushed face, and wondered what was going on.

'And you must be Tommaso, Bruna's told me all about you.' George gave him a big grin. 'She never shuts up about you, it's always Tommaso this, Tommaso that. Maybe later you could show me that snakeskin she said you keep in your room?'

Bruna slapped his arm, blushing. 'I thought George could have dinner with us tonight, so you could get to know him. If that's all right with you, Mamma?' She deliberately avoided looking at Ernesto.

'Of course, there's plenty to go around,' Luisa replied. 'Tommaso, stop gawping and set another place at the table.'

Tommaso snapped his mouth shut and ran to prepare a place for George. In no time at all, they were sat together at the table.

'So, where are you from, George?' Ernesto asked, his mouth full of pasta.

'I'm from England.'

'Really? And what are you doing here then?'

'I came over on holiday last year with my parents, and loved it so much I had to come back. I've got a summer job working at the Tenuta Floreana.'

'And how did you meet Bruna?' Ernesto raised his eyebrows.

'Oh, we met last year down at the village,' George replied.

Luisa thought he looked nervous behind his apparently cheerful exterior.

'Last year, hmm?' Ernesto muttered. 'Couldn't you have stayed in England this year?'

'Ernesto!' Luisa snapped. 'Take no notice, George, he's always grumpy. I think it's lovely you met up with Bruna again. How long are you staying for?'

Bruna and George glanced at each other. 'Mamma, George came back again this year for me,' Bruna began.

George interrupted her. 'When I met Bruna last year, I fell in love with her. We've been writing to each other all year long, and I came here again to confirm what I already knew.'

'All year?' Luisa looked at Bruna and raised an eyebrow.

'I gave him Teresa's address.' Bruna pursed her lips, defiant.

Luisa had to hold back the tears at the thought of Bruna hiding this from her. All she'd ever wanted was her daughter's happiness.

George leaned forward. 'I want to marry Bruna. Signore, I'd like to ask you for your daughter's hand in marriage.'

There was an uncomfortable silence. Ernesto cleared his throat, swallowed hard, then coughed again. 'I-I don't know what to say.' He wiped some sweat off his brow. 'This is such a surprise.' His voice trailed away as he halted, embarrassed. 'What do you think?' he asked Luisa.

She frowned, irritated at his hesitation, then smiled at the two young people sat in front of her. 'I think it's wonderful. I wish you'd told us sooner, Bruna, but I'm very happy for the pair of you. Where will you look for work?' she asked George. 'There are probably more opportunities down in the valley. You could ask Teresa and Cosimo if there's anything going.'

Bruna shifted in her chair. She leaned forward to speak, but George took hold of her arm and stopped her. 'That's the other thing we need to talk about.' Two red dots appeared on his cheeks. 'You see, I already have a job in England, a good job. They let me take a couple of months off, but I will have to go back soon. And I would like to take Bruna with me, as my bride.'

Luisa stared at them, stunned.

'But you don't speak English, Bruna,' Tommaso said. 'How can you go to England if you can't speak the language?'

'I've been learning it, Sister Nunzia has been teaching me over the last year,' Bruna said gently. Her eyes glistened with tears. 'I don't want to leave you, Tommaso, but–' She glanced over at her father briefly. 'I must. I love George, and his job is in England. My future is there. You can always come and visit us.' She looked at Tommaso pleadingly, as if willing him to understand.

'It's your fault,' Tommaso yelled at his father, making everyone jump. 'Everything's been your fault, ever since...' He stopped, panting heavily, visibly trembling with rage. 'I hate you, and I hate what you've done to this family.' He ran out of the house, slamming the back door behind him.

'That could have gone better,' Luisa said, clearing away the plates. 'Does anyone want anything else?'

'I think we've all lost our appetites,' Bruna remarked.

George got to his feet. 'I'm going to have a talk with Tommaso.'

'Are you sure that's wise?' Bruna asked.

'No harm in trying.' He glanced at Luisa. 'Would you mind accompanying me? He might listen if you're there as well.'

'Of course.' Luisa put the dirty dishes in the sink and rinsed her hands. 'But you're doing all the talking.'

34

They went into the garden in search of Tommaso and found him sitting underneath a shady apple tree, bees buzzing above his head in search of the sweet nectar in the fruit. Luisa stood to one side, arms crossed, ready to step in if needed.

'Hey, you,' George said, crouching so he was on the same level.

Tommaso looked up, his face tense. 'What do you want?'

George ignored his hostile tone. 'I thought maybe we could talk. I think I owe you an explanation.'

'What's there to say? You're going to marry Bruna and take her away from me.' Tommaso scowled at him. 'End of discussion, right?'

'Yes, but I'd like you to be happy for Bruna. She told me about the baby, and what happened. It destroyed her, Tommaso, she never thought she'd be happy again. She's just been existing, living day to day. Surely you want her to be happy?'

Tommaso nodded. 'But what about me?' he asked miserably. 'I loved Malva too. I wanted to teach her about nature. We could have gone fishing together, or hunting rabbits. I was happy when Teresa left, she didn't like me anyway. But if Bruna goes, there's nothing left here. Papà always comes home drunk and that upsets Mamma.' He glanced guiltily at Luisa. She gestured to him to continue. He rubbed his nose, and sighed. 'What will I have if Bruna goes?'

Luisa's heart ached for Tommaso, it seemed he was carrying the weight of the world on his shoulders.

'Things will get better,' George said. 'How old are you now, eleven?'

'Ten,' Tommaso corrected him.

'All right, ten. In five or six years you'll be able to get a job, maybe meet a pretty girl and get married too. You'll make your own family and your own future. This won't be forever, Tommaso. And Bruna deserves a future. Don't make her feel guilty about being happy. By the sound of it, your mother needs you too.'

Tommaso sat in silence. 'I guess you're right,' he said eventually. 'It's going to take some getting used to, that's all.'

Luisa clutched her hands together, relief flooding through her.

'Good man,' George said, beaming at him. 'Now, how about you show me that snakeskin?'

George and Bruna got married a month later in the village church with only a few people present. Bruna wore a simple pale blue dress she'd made herself, and George was wearing an elegant suit he'd brought over from England.

During the quick lunch after the ceremony, Bruna took Luisa to one side. 'I wanted to thank you for everything you've done. Letting me marry George, it's given me back my dignity, and my hope for the future. I couldn't have done any of this without you.'

Luisa hugged her, tears rolling down her cheeks. 'Oh, what

am I going to do without you?' she sobbed. 'I'm going to miss you so much. But you'll come back, won't you, and let me see my grandchildren?'

Bruna shook her head. 'I'm never coming back, Mamma.'

'What? Never?' Luisa exclaimed.

'I can't. Please try to understand, there's too much pain here. The cottage, the baby, and everything that's happened. I have to get away from all that, otherwise it will drive me crazy.'

Luisa felt her temper rise. 'But the family, our tradition... the first-born daughter has to carry on, become the healer. You can't deny your heritage. I'm only asking you to come and visit us occasionally.'

'I'm sorry, Mamma, but I won't be the next healer,' Bruna said firmly. 'I'm going to England to start a new life with George and I don't want to ever come back. You could always ask Teresa.'

'Teresa? You've got to be joking.'

'Break the tradition then, get Tommaso to do it. He loves helping you in the Grove, he knows all about the plants and how to make the remedies. He'd love to learn.'

Luisa shook her head. 'It has to be a girl, and it has to be the first born,' she said sadly. 'I can't make you change your mind, can I?'

'No, Mamma, I'm afraid not.'

'Does it have anything to do with your father?'

'Papà?'

Luisa saw a shadow pass over her daughter's face, and felt a knife twisting in her heart. 'Yes, Papà.'

Bruna frowned. 'Don't get involved in things you don't understand, Mamma.'

'You owe me that much, at least. Just tell me the truth. Is he the reason why you won't come back? I can't believe you would give up the cottage, your birthright, your baby's grave forever, for the reasons you've told me. There has to be more to it.'

Bruna sighed. 'You always did know me better than anyone else, Mamma. Yes, you're right. It will break my heart to leave Malva in her grave here, and the cottage and the village will always be a part of me. But there's something evil in this place, something that gets under people's skin if they let it. I don't know what it is, but I've always felt it, and it got into Papà somehow. Don't you feel it, Mamma?'

'My mother talked about it, but I never believed her,' Luisa said slowly. 'How can there be anything like that at the cottage? We are a family of healers, we care for people, we help them when they are dying, we do nothing but good. How can evil come from that?'

'I don't know,' Bruna said, 'but something happens to certain people. Look how Teresa became, spoilt and whining all the time. Poor Antonio died when no one else in the village did. And Papà–' She stopped, biting her lip.

'Go on,' Luisa said, her heart in her mouth.

'I heard the gossip in the village, those horrible women thought I wasn't listening, but it was hard to ignore their stupid giggling voices. I know what your life has been like, what he's done to you. Don't cry, Mamma,' she said, as fresh tears welled up in Luisa's eyes. 'Oh, come here!'

As the two women hugged, Luisa let the tears flow freely. Bruna knew some of the things Ernesto had done to her, but Luisa knew exactly what he had done to Bruna. And she was going to make him pay for it, for everything he'd done to her and her family.

35

The cottage was eerily empty after Bruna left. Tommaso felt lost without his sister, and the cottage seemed twice as large as before. He felt abandoned by everyone and became quiet and withdrawn. His father's temper grew worse and Tommaso soon learned to keep out of his way. Ernesto would often lash out at him for no reason, hitting him around the side of his head as he walked past. Mealtimes were a torture, as Ernesto criticised the way Tommaso ate, what he ate, how he drank, the way he held his cutlery, putting his arms on the table, hiding his hands in his lap... Tommaso would bite his lip and say nothing, forcing food down his throat and into his tensed-up stomach.

His mother tried to defend him at the beginning, but soon stopped as Ernesto turned his attention to her, shouting and thumping his fists on the table. She would glance at Tommaso, an apologetic expression on her face, and the two of them would carry on eating in silence. Even so, Tommaso's arms and back were covered in bruises, which he tried to hide from his mother.

One day, Tommaso returned home from school, happy that the weather was good enough for him to stay out in the garden all afternoon. It had been raining a lot lately, and he was fed up with being cooped up inside. There was a particularly interesting spider he'd found; its unusual markings and incredibly intricate web needed further investigation. He ran into the cottage, threw his bag on the floor and dashed across to the kitchen for a glass of water.

'So you're home then,' came a voice from behind him as he was filling up a glass from the tap. He jumped, spilling most of the water into the sink.

'P-papà,' Tommaso said, turning round.

Ernesto sat in his armchair, holding a leather belt taut in his hands. A glass of wine was perched dangerously on the arm. 'Surprised to see me?' he slurred.

'A-a bit,' Tommaso replied. 'Did they close the factory again?' Just lately, his father had been coming home early from work, saying there was a problem with the machinery.

'Yeah, again,' he said gloomily, closing his eyes. 'Permanently, this time.'

'What do you mean?' Tommaso didn't want to continue the conversation but was unable to stop himself. 'They're shutting down the factory? That'll be a disaster for everyone in the village.' He thought of the men who worked there, and how they relied on the factory for their livelihood.

His father opened his eyes and glared at him. 'They're not shutting it down, they've only closed it permanently for me.' He grinned, and raised his glass to Tommaso. 'Cheers, son, looks like you've got to be the man of the house now. Apparently, I'm not up to the job; neither at work nor at home.'

'Does Mamma know?' Tommaso asked, confused. What was Papà talking about?

'No, and you're not going to tell her,' Ernesto said, narrowing his eyes. 'D'you hear me, boy? She's not to know about this.'

HELEN PRYKE

'Wh-where is she?' Tommaso asked, looking around frantically. He glanced at the belt resting across his father's legs.

'Where she always is. Out tending her damned garden. If only she looked after me half as well as those damn plants, we'd never be in this mess.' He finished off the wine in one big gulp. 'Fetch me another bottle,' he bellowed at Tommaso.

'D-don't you think you've had enough?' Tommaso realised his mistake as soon as he'd spoken the words.

His father glared at him. 'Who the hell do you think you are, telling me whether I can drink or not?' He slowly raised himself out of his chair and walked over to the kitchen, the belt dangling from his right hand. 'I asked you, who the hell do you think you are?'

Tommaso cowered before his father, a small, frightened boy in front of this huge, angry man. He recoiled as Ernesto slapped the belt against his leg, the noise deadened by the thick material of his jeans. He bent over Tommaso, his eyes empty and staring, as if he didn't know what he was doing. Then he raised his arm and brought the belt down on Tommaso's back. Again and again he hit out, anger distorting his features as the leather made dull thudding sounds on the boy's body.

Tommaso screamed the first few times, then his cries turned into whimpers as his body became numb to the pain. He had no idea how long it lasted, it seemed as if his father had been hitting him forever. But eventually the blows lessened, and Ernesto stopped. He moved backwards, looking disdainfully at Tommaso, curled up on the ground in front of him.

'Not a word to your mother, boy, or I'll do the same to her,' he snarled. Tommaso whimpered, shaking his head.

'Let that teach you never to question my drinking. Get out of my sight, before you make me start all over again.'

Tommaso dragged himself up onto his feet. His back felt as if it was on fire, the stinging welts making him wince with every

204

movement he made. He was sure that if he lifted his shirt and looked in the mirror, he would see a mass of cuts and bruises.

He shuffled over to the back door and went outside, glad to get away from his father, and carefully made his way down to the bottom of the garden, to the chicken coop. He sat down under the apple tree, tears springing to his eyes as his shirt touched his bruised back. He watched the chickens scratching around in the dirt, beaks pecking at microscopic crumbs or insects, and wished he could be in there with them, without a care in the world. He tried lying on his stomach, and that seemed to relieve some of the pain. He rested his head on his hands and fell asleep.

'Tommaso?' His mother's hand touched his shoulder as she gently shook him awake. He started as pain shot through him, and tried to wriggle away.

'Is everything all right?' she asked him, looking worried.

He sat up, every muscle in his body protesting against the movement. 'I-I'm fine, Mamma, just give me a moment. I must have fallen asleep,' he said, rubbing his eyes.

'Come here, you've got dust all over your shirt,' she said, brushing it off his shoulders. She jumped as he screamed and pulled away from her. 'What? What's wrong?'

'Nothing, it's nothing, Mamma.' Tommaso struggled to stand up but his body wouldn't obey, and his legs collapsed beneath him.

'Tommaso!' Luisa held him close to her, and he yelped as she touched his body. She lowered him to the ground, then pulled his shirt up. The blood drained from her face as she saw the mass of bruises covering his entire back. 'Who did this?' she whispered.

'Don't, Mamma,' Tommaso mumbled.

'Was it your father?'

He pulled away from her, avoiding her gaze.

'Tommaso?'

'H-he said he'd do it to you too, if I told you.'

'Let me see,' she insisted. Tommaso turned around. 'Oh, dear Lord,' she said when she saw his battered body. 'Come, we'll get some ointment for it, that will take some of the pain away.'

'No, he's indoors, he'll see us.'

Luisa pursed her lips. 'What's he doing home? It's too early for him to have finished work.' She gripped Tommaso's shoulders, making him wince. 'What's going on? Do you know something?'

'He's finished work, Mamma, for good.' Seeing her puzzled expression, he explained. 'He lost his job, I don't know why. He was sitting in his armchair, drunk, when I got home. He wanted me to get him another bottle of wine, and when I didn't... he did this.' Tommaso looked down at the ground, ashamed.

'Sacked.' She said it as if she'd been expecting it. 'You're right. It's better we don't go indoors. I've got a pot of salve in the garage, I keep it there in case I hurt myself when I'm gardening. I'll go and get it. You stay here out of the way.'

She lowered him gently to the ground, her face grim. He wanted to tell her he was sorry, that he shouldn't have made his father so angry, but he was too numb to say anything. He knew that later the anger would come, along with the tears.

36

Luisa found the ointment for Tommaso's wounds at the back of the garage and picked it up. Then she hesitated, and glanced at the other bottles on the shelf. She saw the small one there, hidden behind the others. Hidden for a reason. Almost without realising it, her hand reached out and took the bottle. She placed it in the pocket of her apron, and returned to Tommaso.

The bottle seemed to get heavier as the day wore on. She could feel it bumping against her leg as she worked, and she was so tense that she was sure her face would give her emotions away. Anger filled her whole body, a deep burning sensation that threatened to consume every particle of her being. An image of Tommaso's back flashed in her mind, and she remembered how he'd bravely stood still while she applied the soothing balm. He was only ten, how could anyone do that to a child? How could Ernesto do that to his own son? Her stomach clenched as she thought what Ernesto had done to his own daughter. Was Bruna right? Was there something evil here that worked its way into weak people? What if it wasn't Ernesto's fault?

The doubt that Ernesto could be innocent stayed with her all evening, and she kept glancing at him as he sat sprawled in his armchair. She couldn't help remembering how handsome he'd been all those years before on their wedding day, and how she'd looked forward to their future. What had happened? Had something at the cottage changed him? Or would he have become this monster regardless? She reached down and touched the outline of the bottle, taking comfort from its presence. She had to decide: let Ernesto live and make her life miserable until the day she died, and risk losing Tommaso as she'd lost Bruna and Teresa, or... The bottle seemed to pulse beneath her fingers, heat flowing up her hand and along her arm, all the way to her heart.

'I'm going to bed,' Ernesto announced, making her jump. 'You comin'?'

'In a moment, I'd like to finish this.' She gestured at the open book on her lap she'd been pretending to read.

Ernesto grunted and went upstairs. Luisa breathed a sigh of relief, and went to retrieve the ancient recipe book from the cupboard. Sitting at the table, she opened it and found the page she needed. The parchment here was worn thin and she was almost afraid to touch it, in case it crumbled to dust beneath her fingers. There were recipes written in different hands, and Luisa marvelled once again at the way the healers had left their mark on the paper over the centuries. Her eyes moved to the recipe at the top of the page. The ancient calligraphy was faded and smudged, the lettering difficult to make out.

She slowly read through the recipes, smiling at the various names her ancestors had given the plant over the centuries. Banewort, devil's berries, death cherries, devil's herb, dwayberry, belladonna, and deadly nightshade. But none of them mentioned what she was searching for. She needed the right dose: too little and it wouldn't work, too much and it could leave evidence that would cause suspicion, making everyone point their fingers at her.

Nothing. Only innocent recipes with the very small doses necessary for relieving pain, particularly for women's monthly problems or for elderly men with gout. She rubbed her eyes. Absentmindedly, she turned the page, expecting more of the same. To her surprise, it was blank, except for a few lines of text right at the bottom. They seemed written almost as an afterthought, so small that she had to lean close to the parchment. She read the words: *Used in higher doses, the berries of the banewort plant will cause a quick, painless death. Firstly, steep the leaves...*

Luisa gasped, putting her hand to her mouth. This was it. She turned to the previous page and checked the handwriting; it was the same as that of the first entry. Luisa wondered under what circumstances her ancestor had had to write it, and why it was hidden on the back of the parchment. Shaking her head, she flipped the page to the recipe once more.

After reading it through several times, she leaned back in her chair, pressing her fingers against her temples. Now she had to make her choice. Images flashed through her mind: her wedding day, holding each of her babies in her arms for the first time, Ernesto's look of joy when Antonio was born, the women in the village whispering about her, Antonio in the darkened bedroom, fighting so hard against the disease that would kill him. An image of Bruna appeared, her face contorted with hate as her father tried to touch her when she passed, her belly round and taut as the baby grew within her, holding Bruna's hand during those long hours of labour. And then, that moment when she placed the pillow over the baby and pressed down, her heart breaking as she destroyed the one thing that would have kept Bruna there at the cottage. She felt a tight band around her head, so tight she thought it would crush her skull, her brains oozing out onto the kitchen table. Still she allowed the images to come. Ernesto with that floozy in the alley, Ernesto drinking and lashing out at both her and Tommaso, poor Tommaso after his father had beaten him with his belt. Everything that had happened came back to Ernesto. He was the pivotal point of all their pain and heartbreak.

Luisa placed her hand in her pocket and took out the bottle, holding it in front of her face. The berries had lost their shine and were wrinkled, the leaves were dry and brown at the edges. She placed it on the table and went to get a bowl from a cupboard. She removed the stopper from the bottle and shook its contents into the bowl, counting out the exact amount. She knew how toxic this plant was, and was careful not to touch anything as she poured warm water over it. The berries and leaves needed to steep for a few hours, so she covered the bowl and hid it at the back of the pantry.

As she crept into bed a little while later, she couldn't help giving a small sigh of relief. Very soon, their problems would be over.

37

'No arguments, Tommaso, you're going to Nonna Emilia's for the day,' Luisa said, as her son protested for the hundredth time.

'But, Mamma, I told you I need to study those hornets that have built a nest near the coop.' He hopped from one foot to the other impatiently.

'It can wait until tomorrow, one day won't hurt. Nonna needs you today, she said she's got a lot of work to do in the garden, and she isn't up to it.'

Tommaso sighed theatrically. 'I s'pose, if I really have to.'

'Yes, you do,' Luisa said. 'Now shoo, you've got a long day ahead of you.'

Ernesto made an appearance later that morning, his blood-shot eyes and three-day stubble making him look ten years older. Luisa had got up early and gone straight to the pantry to check on the mixture in the bowl. Satisfied it was just right, she'd strained off the juice and thrown away the swollen berries and leaves, careful that no one could accidentally touch them. The tainted bottle of wine stood on the counter in the kitchen, waiting.

'Ugh, I feel terrible this morning,' he groaned. 'How much did I drink yesterday?'

'I don't know, but it was probably too much. You're getting through bottles like there's no tomorrow, Ernesto.'

He grunted. 'Only thing I've got left.'

Luisa privately agreed. Her once-handsome husband had become so flabby and aged that the women in the village probably didn't even look at him anymore, let alone open their legs for him. And she hadn't let him touch her since the night he went to the bar after Tommaso's birth. *Let him drown his sorrows in alcohol*, she thought, the rage building up once again. *Let's see how that solves everything.*

She gestured to the bottle on the side. 'Why don't you see if another glass makes you feel better? You know, hair of the dog and all that.'

'Maybe later,' he said, belching loudly. 'Right now, I need a really strong coffee.'

Luisa cursed inwardly, but made him his coffee. 'I'm going out to the Grove,' she said, handing him the cup. 'Signora Paoli asked me to make some more cordial for little Vittorio, it seems it's the only thing that stops those fits of his. Call me if you need me.'

She sauntered out into the garden, humming under her breath, her mouth dry as she made her way to the Grove. She was certain that Ernesto wouldn't be able to resist the bottle of wine. It was only a matter of time.

The morning passed quickly. The sound of the church bell ringing at midday reminded Luisa she had to prepare lunch. She put away her things and returned to the cottage. Holding her breath, she opened the door with trepidation. She could see the back of Ernesto's head over the edge of the armchair, unmoving. She silently moved forward, ready for what she would find. Her foot caught the edge of the coffee table, which scraped across the tiled floor and echoed loudly through the room.

'Jesus, Luisa, what are you sneaking about for?' Ernesto grunted, turning towards her.

Luisa screamed.

'What the hell, woman? I dropped off for a moment, there's no need to make so much fuss.'

Luisa put her hand to her chest, willing her heart to stop jumping about. She glanced over to the kitchen counter; the bottle was still there, untouched.

'I'm going to make some lunch. What would you like?' she asked, trying to sound normal.

Ernesto glared at her. 'Nothin', I'm not hungry.' He sounded like a sulking child. 'Why'd you wake me up?' He walked over to her, a little unsteady on his feet. She backed away from him, until she felt the edge of the sink behind her. He raised his hand and she flinched, expecting him to hit her.

'Only getting my wine, woman. Jesus, you're a bag of nerves.' He reached past her to grab the bottle and leaned in close, leering, then turned and went back to his armchair. Luisa busied herself in the kitchen, trying to ignore her shaking hands.

She ate some cold meat and bread, she didn't have the energy to cook herself something. She could see Ernesto's profile through the kitchen door, and almost choked when she saw him pour a generous glass of wine. Suddenly the meat tasted like cardboard, and she could hardly swallow the piece of bread she was eating. She hurriedly gathered up her plate and fork, threw the remains in the bin, and put everything in the sink. She couldn't stay there any longer, she thought she might be sick.

'I'm going upstairs for a lie-down,' she said to Ernesto, trying to plaster a cheerful smile on her face. 'I overdid it in the garden, I'm afraid.'

'Just as long as you leave me in peace,' he snarled. 'My head's thumpin', I can't be putting up with you yapping on at me.'

She noticed that his face was covered in a film of sweat. She glanced at his glass, it was already half-empty. 'I-I'll leave you to it then,' she said, hoping he wouldn't hear the tremor in her voice. He merely grunted in reply, and took another gulp of wine.

Luisa escaped upstairs to the bedroom and closed the door. She took a deep breath and sat on the edge of the bed, her head in her hands. Her whole body shook, her mind a whirlwind of thoughts. She couldn't stay still, so she started to walk around the bedroom, careful not to make too much noise. The last thing she needed was Ernesto coming upstairs to shout at her. She picked up the book on her bedside table and opened it, her eyes skimming over the pages without seeing anything. She continued to pace, backwards and forwards, the book in her hands but her mind buzzing.

'Damn it,' she cried out, and threw the book against the wall, where it landed with a thud on the floor, pages askew. What she was doing went against everything she'd ever been taught. She was a healer, the last in a long line of women who had fought against death all their lives. She felt tainted, an abomination to her family; she could almost hear the faint, ghostly cries of the women who had come before her, pleading with her to stop what she was doing. She grabbed her hair with both hands and pulled hard, desperate to make the voices go away. Her scalp stung but they were still there, louder now, clamouring to know why she was doing this. She squeezed her eyes tight shut and put her hands over her ears, trying to block them out.

Suddenly there was a crash from downstairs. The voices in her head shut up instantly. Luisa slowly took her hands away from her ears and opened her eyes. She listened carefully but there was no other sound from below. She felt strangely calm, as if this moment in her life was meant to be. She went and picked up the discarded book, smoothing the pages, and put it back on her bedside table. She ran her hands over her hair, patting it back into place, and straightened her dress.

'Now hush,' Luisa said to the voices, putting her finger to her lips. 'It's over. You know it had to be done.' There was a hum of protest, then she sensed a strong presence she'd never felt before and the voices faded. She felt a calm come over her, as if she'd received a blessing, and she knew she'd done the right thing.

Walking down the stairs, the first thing she noticed was the strong smell of fruit and alcohol. It permeated the whole cottage with its nauseating odour. Then she saw the bottle, lying smashed on the floor, the puddle of wine still spreading across the tiles, soaking Ernesto's slippered feet. His *immobile* slippered feet. This time she didn't try to be silent, but made her way over to the armchair, careful not to step in the spilled wine. His hand drooped over the armrest, fingers splayed, the wine glass smashed on the floor below. She forced herself to raise her head and look at her husband's face. His expression was fixed in a painful snarl, and his glassy eyes seemed to bore right through her as though he were searching for her soul. His whole body was locked in a rigid caricature of a statue, the veins standing out as if a sculptor had chiselled them into a block of marble. She stood and stared at her dead husband, numb, unable to move.

She didn't know how long she stood there, but she realised that she had to go for help if she was to keep up the charade. She pulled her shoes on and grabbed her coat, then ran out of the cottage to her mother's house down in the village.

38

She thought there would be an investigation, considering the mysterious circumstances in which Ernesto had died, but she was wrong. The doctor, well acquainted with her husband's habits, diagnosed death from a stroke, brought on by drinking and eating too much. The police, satisfied with the doctor's verdict, closed the case. To them it was yet another drink-related incident, all too common in the area since the work had dried up; they had more important things to do.

The village gossips weren't as lenient, however. Luisa knew they were talking about her, whispering together in the shops and doorways, nudging each other as she passed by. As always, she held her head up high and ignored them, but each comment she overheard cut into her soul. Before, she had been better than them, innocent while they had been guilty, and she had felt no shame. This time it was different. This time their barbed observations were horribly accurate, and she carried the weight of her guilt inside her.

The day of the funeral the church was packed. The villagers turned up to pay their last respects to Ernesto. Luisa sat stiffly in the front pew next to Tommaso, her mother, Teresa and her family. She concentrated on the priest's sermon, barely audible over the sounds of women sniffing and sobbing, trying to find solace in his words.

Luisa threw a single white rose onto Ernesto's coffin before they covered it with earth; only she knew that it was entwined with a cutting of belladonna, its purple flower nestled among the leaves of the rose. Her face grim, she watched as other women from the village threw flowers into the grave, trying to maintain her dignity as the grieving widow in the face of their effrontery.

'Now it's just you and me, Tommaso,' Luisa said when the ordeal was finally over, hugging her son tightly. He wriggled, trying to get away. 'You won't leave me, will you?' she pleaded.

'Of course not, Mamma. But can you stop hugging me in front of all these people?' he whispered, his face reddening.

She let go of him. 'I forgot you're the man of the house now,' she whispered back, winking.

Tommaso did his best for her, but wondered why he often heard her pacing around her room late at night, muttering to herself, or sobbing her heart out when she thought he was asleep. He noticed that she looked exhausted, and he was sure she was losing weight. He tried talking to her, but she reassured him that everything was all right, she was just missing Ernesto and the girls. He wasn't convinced.

He knew he had to do something to help her and had an idea that could work. He waited until she went down to the village to do some shopping one afternoon as he knew she would be gone for a couple of hours at least. He knew where she kept the recipe book, he'd seen her take it out of the cupboard hundreds of times. He took it out and sat down at the kitchen table to carefully open it. He was rarely allowed to look at the book, his mother had never let him touch it, and he had to stifle his sense of wrongdoing as he gently turned the pages.

There were recipes for every kind of ailment, from simple complaints to more serious diseases, written over the years by women in the family and amended or added to as they perfected the concoctions. The old parchment was worn in places and tissue-paper thin, and his eyes opened in wonder as he imagined his great-great-great-great-grandmother bent over a rough wooden table, scratching her notes with a feathered quill. Centuries of history were contained in that one leather-bound book, and it made him feel dizzy to think how many women had contributed to it, including his mother. He occasionally found notes she had written, her slanted handwriting easily recognisable.

He searched each page for something that would help his mother sleep, and calm her during the day, but couldn't find anything suitable. Then he turned a page and saw some pencilled notes underneath some old-fashioned writing. He flicked the page back over and looked at the heading. Belladonna. He frowned, and returned to the pencilled notes. He knew what belladonna was; his mother had drummed it into him from an early age that he was never to touch the plant at the bottom of the Grove; just touching its leaves with his bare hands could make him sick. No one but his mother tended the plant, and she was always careful to cover her skin before getting close to it. Once he'd asked why she kept it, if it was so dangerous.

'Because, in very small doses, it can actually be beneficial,' she'd explained. 'It is essential for some of the medicines, but I must always weigh it out precisely. That's not for you to worry about, Tommaso. Bruna will learn how to use it, as I did from my mother.'

But Bruna's no longer here, Tommaso thought. *And these notes were written by Mamma.* He bent closer, trying to see what was written. He bit his lip as he read the first sentence: *Used in higher doses, the berries of the banewort plant will cause a quick, painless death.* He skimmed over the recipe, not wanting to read it but feeling himself drawn to it against his will. Then he arrived at his mother's pencilled notes. At first, he couldn't make sense of them; a series of numbers, some calculations, times... He took a deep breath and tried to clear his head and understand what she had written.

He rose from the table and stared out of the window, racking his brain for an answer to the puzzle. Something was nagging at him, hidden away in some dark corner of his mind. He paced backwards and forwards, glancing at the book every time he walked past the table, willing it to speak to him and reveal its secret. Then something clicked in his mind and he found the answer. He wished he hadn't.

He ran over to the sink and vomited, shaking as his stomach spasmed, over and over again until he had nothing left. His legs were weak and trembling as he gripped the edge of the counter, his knees barely supporting him. He used all his strength to pull himself up. Coughing, he cleaned the sink thoroughly and opened the window to get rid of the smell.

Tommaso was still shaking as he went back to the table and sat down, staring at the book. He didn't want to touch it, his whole body trembled as the shock of what his mother had done hit him. Why? Why had she killed his father? He hadn't been the nicest person in the world, but he had worked hard for his family and had given them everything they needed. An unpleasant thought tried to push its way out, reminding him of the beatings he'd suffered at the hands of his father, and a flashing image of Bruna, heavily pregnant, crossed his mind, but he pushed them back down. Out of sight, out of mind.

With trembling hands, he closed the book. He stumbled over to the cupboard and put it back where he'd found it, vowing never to touch it again. Crying bitterly, he knew it was a secret he would have to take to his grave if he wanted to protect his mother. No one must know, not ever; he could never trust anyone with a secret like this.

39

2014

W orking in the garden was harder for her these days. Luisa felt her bones creak and muscles complain every time she bent down to pull out a weed or cut off a shoot. She stood, stretching her back, and looked around, taking in the Grove and the plants she'd lovingly tended over the years. Her glance passed over the grave; poor Malva had been dead fifty-four years and Luisa had been reminded of what she'd done every day since then.

She'd never seen Bruna again, although she'd met her daughter, Rita, when she had come over for a holiday. Snorting, Luisa took off her gardening gloves and threw them in the basket next to her. Bruna was dead now, she would never come back. Rita and her daughter Jennifer were settled in England and there was no hope of either of them taking over the healer's duties. That left Teresa's daughter, Liliana. She was all right in her own way, but showed no healing abilities whatsoever. The few times she'd helped Luisa in the Grove many years before had been a disaster; she'd had to stop her digging up precious plants, until she'd shouted at her in frustration. The poor girl had never helped her again. Liliana's daughter Agnese showed promise, but Luisa was too old to teach her. Lately she felt every one of her ninety-four years in her creaking bones.

Thank goodness for Tommaso, she thought. He'd been her mainstay for all these years, standing by her side when everyone else had left her. He'd loyally stuck by her, even during those months after Ernesto's death when certain people in the village had spread malicious lies about her.

Mopping her brow, she sat down in the chair Tommaso had placed underneath the plum tree for her, sinking thankfully into the padded fabric, and leaned her head back. She stared tiredly into the distance, her heart fluttering every now and then as she recovered her breath. She couldn't tolerate the sun so much nowadays and was thankful for the shade the branches of the plum tree offered.

She must have fallen asleep as she had the strangest dream. A dragonfly appeared before her, hovering a few inches from her nose. She jumped, startled, but it continued to flutter in front of her. Mesmerised, she watched the whirr of its brightly coloured wings, beating so fast they were a blur of colour. Then it suddenly flitted up into the branches of the plum tree and landed on a ripe plum. Her eyes followed its path as it flew to a raspberry bush, and settled on top of a raspberry. It repeated this over and over again, flying from one plant to the next, going faster and faster, its wings shimmering in the bright afternoon sun, hypnotising her with their silvery flashes, until it came back to the plum tree. This time, when it rested on the plum, the fruit fell off and landed in Luisa's lap with a soft plop. She picked it up and rolled it around in her bony hand, wondering what it could mean. The dragonfly hovered in the air, then flew to the ancient bush and circled over it. Luisa frowned; she usually used the leaves in her remedies as the bush yielded little fruit each year. But she opened her eyes in wonder when she saw that the delicate plant was now filled with tiny berries, so many that its branches drooped towards the earth.

The dragonfly returned, and she slowly held out her free hand, palm up. It seemed to scrutinise her, its black, bulbous eyes staring deep into hers. If she concentrated a little harder, she believed she'd be able to hear its voice telling her what it wanted her to do. The dragonfly settled on her outstretched palm, its legs tickling her, its wings finally at rest.

'What do I have to do?' she whispered, looking at the plum in her other hand. 'Tell me, please.'

She saw the tiny veins in its transparent wings and the different sections of its body in minute detail, and those black eyes dragged her into its mind, calling her. She felt as if she were drowning, floundering in a sea of red liquid, gasping as it entered her mouth, filling her lungs. Juice, it was juice, the sweet nectar of her fruit trees, the ones she had tended all her life. After all these years, she understood...

She suddenly jerked, her eyes wide open, as the dragonfly flew away. There was a strange mist surrounding her, but that was impossible, it was midday. She almost screamed as three figures stepped out of the mist towards her. The shadowy figures began to take shape, and she saw that they were her children. Bruna, young and rosy skinned, as she'd been before Ernesto had started molesting her, before the pregnancy had taken its toll on her body and mind; Teresa, once more with her long, dark hair flowing in the breeze, full of vitality, not the skeletal shell ravaged by cancer, lying in a hospital bed as Luisa had last seen her; and Antonio, no longer pallid and covered in red spots, his face once again tanned brown from the summer sun, and his curly hair as unruly as ever.

She covered her mouth with her hand as they moved forwards, smiling at her, forgiveness in their eyes. Tears streamed down her face as she gazed upon them, knowing that her time was almost over, and she would be reunited with them soon. They forgave her; she could feel their love emanating from them, washing over her like a calming breeze, reassuring her that she'd done nothing wrong. Then the mist stirred; they glanced over their shoulders and when they turned back to her, she saw terror in their eyes.

'What?' she whispered. They started to fade, and she struggled to get up out of the chair. 'No,' she called as they disappeared. Her legs suddenly collapsed beneath her as she saw the reason why.

Ernesto stood before her, his black shape unmistakable even in the swirling mist, and she noticed that he was holding something. She sank back in her chair and peered through the mist. He held out the bundle in his arms, grinning at her, and she saw that it was a baby. Its pale, lifeless body hung limply in his huge hands, and she screamed hysterically as she realised it was her granddaughter.

'Mamma, are you all right?' Tommaso stood over her, shaking her shoulder, his voice full of concern.

She struggled to get up, but she was too weak to stand.

'Mamma? Do I need to call the doctor?'

'No, no, I'm all right,' she gasped, her breath rasping in her throat. 'I-I had a nasty dream. Teach me to work too hard, won't it?' She looked up at Tommaso's worried face. 'Honestly, I'm feeling better already.'

'If you're sure.'

'Positive,' she replied. 'See, much better now. What about you go and put some coffee on?'

'All right. If you're not up at the cottage in five minutes, I'll come and get you,' he said, squeezing her hand.

Luisa watched him walk up the garden, noticing he was limping. Time hadn't been kind to Tommaso; he'd aged so much, and she knew his arthritis caused him a lot of pain. She wished things could have been different for him, that he'd found a wife who could take care of him when she was gone. The rest of the family said he was strange and avoided him. She could hardly blame them; he'd taken to muttering to himself as he went about his business, and didn't care what people thought. A tear rolled down her cheek. She knew that she had little time left in this world, and she didn't want to leave him all alone.

Getting to her feet with some difficulty, she thought about the dream she'd had. A shiver ran through her body as she remembered the last part, of Ernesto holding Malva, lifeless. She tried to decipher the message she knew her children had tried to send her, but her brain was too tired. She would go indoors and think about it afterwards.

Tommaso was waiting for her in the kitchen, the wonderful aroma of coffee hitting her senses and making her feel more alive.

'I need you to help me, Tommaso,' she said as she sipped her espresso.

'Anything, Mamma. Tell me what you need.'

'Tomorrow, I want you to collect all the fruit off the trees and bushes,' she said. 'Plums, apples, all the berries, grapes.'

He looked at her questioningly.

'We're going to make fruit juice, Tommaso, bottles and bottles of juice. But not just any old juice. Grove juice. And call Agnese, she can help us. Otherwise we'll never get it done in time.'

She knew he wouldn't try to get any more information out of her when she was in one of her moods, and she was grateful for his silence.

That night, Luisa jolted awake as the church bell struck midnight. She knew what she had to do, she could almost hear the other healers voicing their approval. She went downstairs to the kitchen and took a notepad and pen out of the drawer.

'I will confess everything,' she murmured, smoothing the paper beneath her hands. 'Purge my sins, cleanse my soul, prepare myself for the next step by unburdening my heart here and now.' She grasped the pen in her twisted, rheumatic fingers, and started to write.

In the early hours of the morning, she lay down her pen and reread what she'd written. She blew gently across the paper to dry the ink, then carefully folded it in four. She took the recipe book out of the cupboard and slipped the paper inside the back cover.

'If there should ever be another healer in the family, I hope she will understand,' she whispered, closing the book and pressing it against her lips. She groaned as she got up, her whole body aching, and put the book back in its usual place, then made her way upstairs to her bedroom.

She slipped gratefully under the covers, her mind at peace once more, and fell into a deep sleep where she dreamed of ghosts and dragonflies.

JENNIFER

40

I slowly came to, feeling confused, as though I'd slept for hours. I couldn't understand what had happened; had I watched my great-grandmother's life as if at the cinema, or had I actually been there, a part of the story? I glanced down at my hands, trembling, as I realised they still held the letter. I hadn't got past the first paragraph.

Turning towards the wine bottle on the coffee table, I was startled to find it was empty. I didn't remember having poured any out, but the evidence said otherwise. Surprisingly, I didn't feel the slightest bit drunk. Then I remembered Luisa telling Tommaso they were going to make fruit juice. It was only fruit juice, not wine? Baffled, I went back to reading the letter.

August 2014

As I near the end of my life, I realise that I cannot carry this burden to the grave. I must write everything down, in the form of a confession, in the hope that whoever reads it will understand my motives and find it in their heart to forgive me.

The day I found out that Ernesto was abusing Bruna, I wanted to die. Not from shame, but to prevent me from doing him harm. I cannot believe I was so blind, that I didn't realise what he was doing to his own daughter. I could put up with him sleeping with the women in the village, it was preferable to him touching me, but not that, not Bruna.

I never spoke about it with Bruna – how could I? How do you ask your daughter if her own father is abusing her? But the fact that she never told me, that hurts. I thought we were close, that she could trust me, talk to me about anything, but it seems I was wrong. And when I found out, it was too late. She was already too far along, there was nothing I could do. If she'd told me in the first couple of months, I could have given her an infusion, it would have been over so quickly and painlessly.

I told myself I would love the child anyway, I would look at it as Bruna's baby and not think about the father. But when she was born, she had his features, his temper – straight away, you could tell she was of his blood. When I looked upon her, I couldn't see my granddaughter, I could only see Ernesto, grinning at me, sneering at me, mocking me as he taunted me with his conquests in the village. Raising his fist, lashing out at me because I refused to give my body to him, telling me it was all my fault.

I wanted to save Bruna from him, and hurt Ernesto for everything he'd done to us. Mamma told me from a young age that I was a healer, I was put on this earth to help people, cure them. And if I couldn't save them, then I would help them live their last days as comfortably as possible. How could I save Malva? She was contaminated by his evil seed, perhaps she had that part of him inside her, and would have become just like him, or worse. But I could save Bruna, save her from all that heartache, that constant daily reminder of what he'd done to her. So I suffocated Malva with a pillow, to put an end to everything.

There, I've written it down at long last. I have waited so long to confess. Too many years. I was a coward back then; I allowed Bruna to think she'd done it in her sleep, that it had been a terrible accident.

I wanted to tell her – I almost did, but the thought of losing my children as well as my granddaughter stopped me. And who would have protected them from Ernesto? When Bruna said it was her fault, I kept quiet. I had to make sure I would be around for them.

To what cost? Bruna never forgave herself. I know she carried that pain inside her for many, many years. She never forgave me either – for what, I don't know, whether it was for her father, or Malva, or both. I don't blame her, I can't even forgive myself for what I did.

Bruna was the future, the next healer. Without her, the tradition will end and the cottage will leave the family. What will happen to the Grove? My heart breaks at the thought of it finishing like this – how can I be the last healer? That's why, when she left, I hated Ernesto. I hated him as I've never hated anyone before. I wanted to destroy him, my every waking thought was on how to get my revenge. And then he beat Tommaso. When I saw my son's back covered in those red welts, the bruises already forming, I knew what I had to do, for my sake and for Tommaso's. I couldn't let that monster live anymore, breathe the same air that we breathed, eat the food I prepared every day.

I found the recipe. Belladonna. It's an ingredient for some of our remedies, used in small quantities, but in high doses it's lethal. I carefully calculated the right amounts, and then slipped it into the bottle of wine. People in the village wondered if I'd killed him, but there was never any proof. Until now. I freely confess that I put enough belladonna in that bottle to kill him, and I would gladly do it again if it meant we could be free of that evil man. I only wish I'd done it years earlier.

Whoever reads this letter, I hope you can find it in your heart to forgive me. I am not a bad person, I would never have done any of this had the circumstances been different. I have suffered for what I've done and paid my penance.

Luisa Innocenti

'I understand, I truly understand,' I whispered, tears pouring down my cheeks. 'You must have been so strong, you went through so much.' I thought back to how I'd drowned my sorrows in booze instead of facing them head-on, and felt like kicking myself. It was true that I'd lost my babies, and the chance to be a mother, but I couldn't even begin to imagine what Luisa must have been through. Wife battering may have been the norm back in those days, but she'd had to deal with so much more. And she'd lost her children too. I'd been weak in the past, but that didn't mean I couldn't change now.

It was still dark outside. Glancing at the clock on the mantelpiece, I was amazed to see that it was only midnight. I didn't want to go to bed. My head was whirling with everything I'd learned, and I felt restless.

I went outside in the garden and breathed in the cool night air. The sky was so clear up here in the mountains, and looking up I could see a myriad of stars above me. Bella followed, quietly padding about, sniffing at invisible trails along the ground.

'Mum was wrong, the magic isn't in the cottage. It's in the Grove, in the plants that grow there. Somehow, I've no idea how, it all comes from there. The wine – hah, the fruit juice – it came from the Grove, there's something in it that...' I paused, searching for the right word. 'That heals you.' I gasped; since I'd started drinking it, I'd felt more at peace with myself, stronger, more able to carry on with my life without fear of where it would take me. I imagined leaving this place, going back to England, and realised that I didn't want to. The cottage, the Grove, the mountains, it was all a part of me, as much as the blood flowing through my veins. Tommaso had written that I was destined to be the next healer. Could I really do it? I had a lot to think about over the next few days. I wanted to get my ideas straight before Mum arrived, so that I could tell her I'd finally got my life in order, that I had a future ahead of me.

. . .

I spent the night reading through the recipe book, making my own notes in a separate jotter, trying to decide which recipes I would make first. I wanted to start with something easy and work my way up to the more difficult ones. I hoped the family would be willing to help, as I would need some guinea pigs.

When the book lay open at the page about belladonna again and I found Luisa's notes on the back, I understood what Tommaso had meant by thanking his mother for helping him find a way out. I remembered him telling me not to touch the plant with my bare hands, that it was extremely toxic. Had he already known what he was going to do? I hoped it had been quick and painless, after everything he'd been through.

As the sun rose, I slowly stretched and got up to put on the coffee. I planned to go down to the Grove straight after breakfast and start picking the berries and leaves I needed. I'd decided I would try a few headache remedies, but first I needed to identify and label all the plants to make sure I got the right ones. I groaned – it was going to be a long morning.

I had just finished my coffee when I heard a hesitant tap at the back door. I quickly shoved the book in a nearby drawer.

'It's open,' I called.

Agnese popped her head round the door. 'Is it too early? I was afraid you'd still be in bed.' Bella ran over to greet her, wagging her tail.

'No, it's fine, come in. I'm glad you came. Do you want a coffee?'

'Uh, no thanks,' she said, looking a bit queasy. 'I'd love a glass of water, though. You look tired,' she added.

'I haven't slept all night. Is it that obvious?'

'I'm afraid so. Nothing wrong, I hope?'

'No, nothing another coffee won't solve.' I busied myself at the stove, and pulled some biscuits from the cupboard. 'Some sugar might help as well.'

I got the feeling that Agnese wanted to tell me something; she kept opening her mouth and taking a deep breath, then closing it again as if she'd changed her mind. After a few minutes of this, I decided to help her out.

'Agnese, is something bothering you?'

'No, of course not,' she replied, but she avoided looking at me. She sat down at the kitchen table.

'Come on, you can tell me,' I said.

'No, honestly, it's nothing.'

'You didn't come here at the crack of dawn because nothing's wrong,' I insisted. 'Come on, we're friends, you can tell me anything.'

'I-I came to see you because I need to talk to you.'

'Okay. I'm listening.' I reached over and held her hand.

'No, I shouldn't be here,' she said, getting up from her chair. 'You don't want to hear this.'

'Agnese, sit down. You came here to talk to me, so talk.'

She sat, sighing. 'But I don't want to upset you. It's not fair to burden you.'

'I can take it, I'm a big girl.'

'It-it's a secret and you can't tell anyone,' she said urgently.

'Don't worry, my lips are sealed.'

'Seriously, Jen, you can't tell my family. If they find out... I need help in deciding what to do, I'm so confused.'

'I'll do everything I can to help you, Agnese. Talk to me.' I sipped my coffee to give her some time to gather herself, wondering what on earth she had to tell me.

41

Agnese took a deep breath. 'I-I'm pregnant.'

Of all things, I hadn't expected that. 'Oh my God.'

'I'm so sorry, I didn't want to tell you after everything you've been through, but I didn't know who to turn to. I can't tell Mum or my family, they'll kill me.'

Thoughts whizzed around my head. I felt sick, light-headed. I told myself to get a grip and concentrate on Agnese.

'Who's the father?' I asked. It felt like I was reliving Luisa's story all over again.

'S-someone in the village,' she replied.

After everything I'd seen, I had to ask. 'Not someone in your family?'

'My family?' She looked at me incredulously. 'Why on earth would you think that?'

'I know, stupid question, sorry. But can he help you? Will he marry you? Do you want to marry him?' I added as an afterthought.

'I don't know. I don't think so,' she said, crying. I presumed that was her answer to all three questions. 'What am I going to do, Jen? I want to keep it, but my family, what will they say?'

'They won't be that bad, will they? Aunt Liliana loves you all so much, and we're no longer in the 1950s; the world has changed, people have changed.'

'Not here they haven't. Everyone knows everything in the village, they'll be talking about me as soon as news gets out.'

'How far along are you?'

'About three months.'

'Have you been to the doctor?'

'How can I? He'll tell Mamma right away.'

I groaned inwardly. Three months. I'd never got further along than four, but I still remembered that giddy excitement on finding out that I was going to be a mum, those first weeks of making plans, wondering whether it would be a boy or a girl, thinking about names and how to decorate the nursery, only to have my dreams destroyed a couple of months later.

'Jen?'

'Sorry. I'm glad you told me, and I'll do whatever I can to help you, whether that means telling your family or...' I hesitated.

'Or if I decide to get rid of it,' she finished for me.

'It's your body, your future, and only you can make that decision.'

'I don't know what to do, I'm so confused,' she sobbed. 'I have to decide soon, before it's too late and I don't have a choice anymore. Please help me.'

My heart broke for Agnese, for the choice she had to make. I knew it wasn't going to be easy, either way. 'First of all, you need to tell me who the father is,' I said.

She pursed her lips. 'He's not a part of this.'

'Actually he is. And if you're going to make such an important choice, it's vital to have all the facts.'

'Okay.' She smiled weakly at me. 'It's an Englishman who lives in the village. Mark.'

My head spun as I stared at her in shock. I'd had my doubts about him from the beginning, my instinct had told me there was something about him that didn't seem quite right. *That snake.* I clenched my fists as I imagined exactly what I'd do to him if he was in front of me at this moment.

'Jen?' Agnese's voice interrupted my thoughts. 'Is everything okay?'

I shook my head. 'Well, I guess we can rule the father out of any decision you make.'

'Why?'

'Because he's a low-down, two-timing rat,' I snapped. 'All those sob stories about his ex-wife and her family. I bet it was his fault she left him, not her mother's.' I paused for breath, then saw the stunned expression on Agnese's face. 'I'm sorry,' I said, more gently. 'I shouldn't have told you like that, it's just that it was such a shock.'

'I understand,' she said, and burst into tears.

'Oh, don't, Agnese.' I handed her a tissue.

'I feel so stupid. H-he told me he loved me, he wanted me to go and live with him, after you'd gone back to England. He wanted to wait so I could spend as much time as possible with you, he said, because I'd probably never see you again. Christ, he was playing me the whole time.' She slammed her fist down on the table, making the cups rattle. I knew exactly how she felt.

'If I'd known you were together, I'd never have gone out with him, Agnese. You have to believe me. I might have been a drunken mess over the last few years, but I've never hurt anyone in that way.' I smiled sadly at her. 'I was a drunken mess, but I was a faithful drunken mess.'

Agnese blew her nose. 'I believe you. So, now what do I do?'

I sighed. 'Now you've got the biggest decision of your life to make.'

She glanced down at her stomach and rubbed it with her

hand. 'A-at three months it's still early enough to, you know... isn't it?'

'Have an abortion?' I asked, then mentally kicked myself for being so blunt.

'Yes.' She was silent for a moment. 'Would you do it, if it was you in this situation?'

'I think you know the answer to that. Even if the father legged it, I'd keep the baby. But my story's different. This is you we're talking about.'

'What if my family disowns me?'

'Do you really think they will?' I pictured Aunt Liliana, always so open and welcoming, and knew she wouldn't abandon her daughter, whatever happened.

'Who knows?' Agnese looked downcast.

'I don't think they will. And even if they do, I'll be here.'

It took a few seconds for my words to sink in. 'Really? You're staying?'

I nodded.

'Why? I mean, how? Oh, I'm so pleased.' She stood and threw her arms around me, enveloping me in a tight hug. 'What made you change your mind?'

'Mainly you and our friendship, then this place, and the fact that Tommaso left me the recipe book.'

'The book? You've got it?' Her face lit up. 'Can I see it?'

I took it out of the drawer and placed it on the table. 'I've been up all night reading it. It's very... interesting, shall we say.'

'Can I look at it?'

'Of course.' I pushed it over to her.

She opened it almost reverently, her hand trembling as she slowly turned the pages. 'It's beautiful,' she said. 'I've heard so much about it, but I've never seen it before. Luisa was so secretive about it, no one knew where she kept it.'

'Except Tommaso. I found it hidden among his things at his house.'

'Really? So, what are you going to do with it?'

'I don't know.' I took a deep breath. 'I found a letter at the back, it sort of slipped out. Luisa wrote it.'

'And?' Agnese looked at me eagerly.

'She wrote down some things she did, that she felt she had to do.' I stopped, unable to carry on. Agnese had grown up with Luisa, had loved her. Did I want to destroy her memories of her great-grandmother?

'Bad things?' Agnese whispered.

I nodded again.

'She kept saying weird things towards the end,' Agnese said. 'I remember Mamma getting upset. About Ernesto, and how he'd ruined their lives. Her mind was going by then, so we put it down to the dementia. What does the letter say?'

'Do you really want to know?' I asked. She looked miserable but held out her hand for the letter. I passed it to her and watched her eyes grow bigger as she read.

'I can't believe it,' she said, giving it back to me.

'There's something else I have to tell you,' I said, 'and you're going to find it even more incredible.'

42

I n the end, we decided to go out to the garden. It was a beautiful morning in late August, the air was cool on our faces and a faint mist still hugged the ground. We walked into the Grove and slowly wandered around as I told Agnese what had happened to me the night before. We stopped in front of the belladonna bush. Uncle Tommaso had taught me how to handle its branches carefully, making sure I wore protective gloves and trimmed only what was absolutely necessary. The harmless-looking black berries shone in the sunlight. It was difficult to believe they could be so deadly.

'So, you saw everything, as if it were a film playing in front of you?' Agnese asked, glancing at me.

I couldn't blame her for being sceptical. 'I know it sounds weird, I'm sure it was the juice I drank. Maybe Luisa put something in it that makes you hallucinate. I don't know.' I was tired and couldn't think straight. 'All I do know is that everything I saw ties in with the letter, which I didn't finish reading until afterwards.'

'She was a strong woman, wasn't she?' Agnese said.

'The strongest,' I agreed. 'I felt a bit pathetic after seeing what she'd been through. You know, getting drunk all the time, not facing my problems.'

'We deal with our problems in our own way, whether that way is right or wrong.'

'I guess.'

'Don't be so hard on yourself, Jen.' Agnese gave my hand a reassuring squeeze.

We walked over to Malva's grave and stood in front of the tombstone. I read the inscription one more time.

'She never had a chance to live, yet it wasn't her fault,' Agnese whispered. She bent over, kissed the palm of her hand, and placed it on top of the inscription. 'I've decided.' She turned to me with tears pouring down her cheeks. 'I'm going to keep the baby.'

I hugged her tightly, almost crying myself. 'You won't regret it, and you won't be alone,' I promised.

We left the Grove, still holding on to each other as we made our way back up to the cottage. The familiar aroma of coffee greeted us as we entered the kitchen. I smiled. It felt like coming home.

Agnese picked up the recipe book once more. 'So, are you going to make any of these?'

'Of course. I was trying to decide which one when you arrived. I thought I'd start with something simple to begin with.'

'Hmm, there are lots in here. Maybe you could try this one.' She showed me a short recipe for a cream that would alleviate acne.

'That looks easy. Why not?'

She flicked back through the pages. 'Have you seen this? Look at these names written in the front, all the healers throughout the centuries.'

'Yes, I noticed but haven't had time to read them yet. I was more interested in the recipes. Is Luisa's name there?'

'It's the last one. Just think, now you're going to add yours.'

I was thrilled at the thought. Her excitement was contagious and I felt happy all of a sudden, glad to become a part of this incredible family.

'Ooh, look here,' she cried out. 'The first name, it's Agnes. Do you think I was named after her?'

'It's possible. I wonder who she was.' A thought occurred to me. 'Tommaso said it all started with an English girl, centuries ago. I wonder if this is her?'

'No idea, nobody's ever mentioned it,' Agnese replied.

'I'm sure that's what Tommaso said.' Another idea suddenly popped into my head, pushing aside all thoughts of our ancient ancestor. 'Agnese, you've helped Luisa over the years, haven't you?'

'Yes, she often let me help prepare the plants for the medicines.'

'Great. How would you like to help me? I don't have a clue what I'm doing. You could teach me what you know, and we'll figure out the rest together.'

'Really? I'd love to,' she exclaimed, then looked downcast. 'But I can't. I'm not meant to be a healer.'

I grabbed a biro off the sideboard, bent over the book, and carefully wrote my name underneath Luisa's. I handed the pen to Agnese. 'Your turn.'

'Are you sure?' she asked, her voice trembling with emotion. 'I don't think those are the rules.'

'I'm the healer now, and I'm sure,' I said.

Agnese held the pen above the page, as if trying to decide, then wrote her name below mine.

'Now we're both healers,' I said. 'Shall we get to work?'

Even though I was exhausted, it was pleasantly relaxing trying out the recipe. We chatted together while we worked, and came up with a plan to tell Aunt Liliana about the baby. I would go to lunch the next day and Agnese would mention it to her mother.

'With any luck, my mum will be here the day after and they'll be so excited about seeing her that they'll stop going on at you.'

'Crafty, but it could work.' Agnese laughed. 'The old distraction technique.'

'Maybe I'll bring some of Luisa's "wine". It might take the edge off things.'

Agnese frowned. 'Can I see it?'

I fetched a bottle from the hallway cupboard and handed it to her.

'Hmm, interesting,' she said. 'I helped Luisa and Tommaso make this. The whole family thought we'd gone mad. Tommaso and I spent all day picking the fruit off the trees in the Grove, and Luisa had loads of large glass bowls lined up. God only knows where she got them from, someone in the village, I imagine. I helped her wash the fruit while she boiled saucepans of water. We put the fruit in separate bowls, poured over the water and left it to steep. She brought out a jar full of the dried leaves of some plant from the pantry – I don't know which one, she wouldn't say – and she added a few leaves to each bowl. She kept saying we had to work faster, as she wanted to be sure to finish. That's when she started to go downhill, saying all those weird things that didn't make any sense.'

'But she did it, didn't she?' I said, gesturing at the bottle.

'Oh yes. We worked for days, and every night we went to bed shattered. Our hands were permanently stained purple from the juices. Once the fruit began steeping, we knew we had to wait at least ten days for it to ferment. Tommaso phoned me a couple of days later, saying Luisa wanted to bottle it right away. We did everything we could to persuade her to wait, we told her it hadn't had time, but she was adamant. She insisted the moon was in the right phase and it had to be done immediately. So we strained it off – that was backbreaking work, I'll tell you – and put it in the bottles. She died about a week later.' Agnese sighed. 'I'm glad I spent that time with her during her last weeks, it made it easier when she died.'

'I thought it was wine when I first drank it because it had such a strange effect on me. It was like getting drunk, but without the hangover the next morning.' I paused. 'I wonder if that was due to those leaves she put in it?'

Agnese shrugged. 'I've no idea.'

'That first weekend, after we'd cleaned the cottage, I went crazy; I desperately needed a drink and searched everywhere, until I found those bottles in the garage.'

'It was that bad?' Agnese looked concerned.

'Yes,' I said, embarrassed. 'I only drank one glass, though, and that's when the dragonfly appeared.'

'Dragonfly?'

'I thought it was the wine, making me see an insect that wanted me to follow it.'

Agnese giggled.

'Huh, you can laugh. I thought I was going out of my mind! Anyway, this dragonfly was insistent; it led me down to the Grove. And to Malva's grave.'

'That must have been a shock,' Agnese said.

'I screamed and ran back to the house. The wine didn't exactly give me Dutch courage that evening.'

'But you went back the next day.'

'I felt calmer, more able to deal with things. It was odd, I hadn't felt that way for ages.'

'There's got to be more in that juice than just fruit. I wonder if we'll find the recipe in the book,' Agnese mused.

'I've looked but I didn't find it. She must have had a secret ingredient, but we'll never know.'

'Maybe I should drink some, it might give me strength for tomorrow,' Agnese said, laughing.

'You know, that's not such a bad idea.' She looked at me. 'I'm definitely going to bring a bottle with me,' I said, winking.

'Luisa saves the day again,' Agnese exclaimed, and we both burst out laughing.

43

I stood outside my aunt's front door, bottle in hand, feeling as nervous as a child outside the headmaster's room. I rang the bell, and chuckled at the sound of commotion inside.

'Oh, Jennifer, it's you. There was no need to ring, you could have come right in.' My aunt scuttled down the hallway before me, rushing back into the kitchen. The house was filled with the wonderful aroma of various things cooking and bubbling away on the stove. Bea ran out of the living room and threw herself at me. I managed to catch her, holding the bottle up in the air as she hugged my legs.

'Here, let me take that,' Piero said, plucking the bottle from my hands.

'Thanks.' I turned my attention to Beatrice. 'What's that you're saying? Slow down a bit, otherwise I can't understand you.'

She breathlessly told me about a school project she'd been working on, the words pouring out of her so fast that I had trouble keeping up. I finally understood that it was about the cottage and Luisa, and that she'd got top marks for it.

'Well done,' I praised, infected by her childish excitement.

'Let Jen come and sit down,' Giulia said, coming out into the hallway. 'She was so excited you were coming to lunch, she wanted to tell you all about her project.'

'It sounds like she worked hard on it.'

'Oh, she did. And she used some of the photos you gave to Liliana. We got some copies made, there are some for you as well. She used them as the starting point and wrote her project about the people and images.'

'Clever girl,' I said. She jumped up and down, proud of her achievement.

'And how are you?' I asked Giulia, glancing at her ever-expanding stomach.

'Tired. It's been a long summer, luckily it's getting cooler now. I can't wait till it's over.'

'How much longer?' I asked sympathetically. She looked enormous, and I could imagine how fed up she was.

'About another month. But Bea arrived two weeks early, so I'm expecting this one to make its appearance at any moment.'

'Come on, Bea, let's go and sit down so your mum can take the weight off her feet.'

'She can't wait, she keeps on about her new little brother or sister,' Giulia said as we made our way into the living room. She sank down onto the sofa, sighing in relief.

'I'll bet.' I sat next to her. 'I always wished I wasn't an only child, I'd have loved someone to get into mischief with.'

We chatted while Bea ran from the living room to the kitchen, helping put things on the dining table and passing messages between us and Aunt Liliana. Piero went out in the garden with Dante, and we could see them through the window, talking.

Lunch finally ready, we gathered around the table and tucked in, passing plates to one another, reaching in front of someone to grab a piece of bread, holding our glasses up to be refilled with Luisa's juice. Amidst the laughter and chatter, I watched Agnese, sitting quietly at one end of the table, her body tense, unable to join in. Bea said something to her and she smiled back, a brief stretch of her lips that quickly faded.

As I mopped up the last of the juices from the delicious roast with a thick piece of crusty bread, there was silence at long last. Pleasantly full, everyone started to relax under the effect of the juice. I glanced at Agnese and raised my eyebrows. This was her chance.

Agnese cleared her throat. Everyone turned and stared at her. 'Er, um,' she began, twisting her hands together. I nodded encouragingly at her. 'I have something to say.' We all waited. 'I, er, oh... I'm pregnant, Mamma, Papà.'

There was a moment's stunned silence, then everyone started talking at once. Poor Agnese was close to tears as she was bombarded with questions from all directions. Then Dante stood and slammed his hand down hard on the table, making us all jump.

'Shut up,' he ordered, and everyone obeyed. He looked at Agnese. 'I presume this isn't some terrible joke. Who's the father?'

'I wouldn't joke about something like this,' she said quietly, her voice trembling. 'I-I can't tell you who the father is, he's not interested.'

'My God. Have you thought this through?'

'I've done nothing but think about it, ever since I found out.' She glanced at me, then lifted her chin. 'And I've decided to keep it.'

'And what about your family?' Dante said, raising his voice. 'Your mother already has enough to do, running around after everyone, and now you spring this surprise on us. You'll be a single mother. And where will we put it? Your room is barely big enough for you, let alone a baby and all its bits and pieces.' He paused for breath. 'And who do you think is going to help you, when the time comes?'

'I will,' I said. Dante turned and concentrated his gaze on me. 'I've decided to stay at the cottage, I'm not going back to England. I'd already decided before Agnese told me–'

'You knew?' he interrupted.

'She told me yesterday. She wanted some moral support, she knew it wouldn't be easy telling you. Like I said, I'm staying and I'm going to learn about healing. I want to take over from Luisa. And I want Agnese to help me, she already knows something about it.'

They stared at me in shock. I started to feel sorry for them. Aunt Liliana touched her husband's arm and gestured to him to sit back down. He glowered at me, but did as he was told.

'This is a big surprise, obviously,' she said, her eyes flitting at everyone around the table. 'We're very happy that you're staying, and that you want to become a healer, the village has sorely missed having one since Luisa died. And I thank you for offering to help Agnese, although I'm sure that once the shock has worn off, we will support her. We're no longer in the Middle Ages.' She glared at her husband. He lowered his eyes, looking abashed. 'Our biggest worry is space, as Dante said. Our house is not as big as we'd like.'

'That's not a problem,' I said, the idea dawning on me as I spoke. 'Agnese can come and live at the cottage.'

Agnese looked startled. 'I can? Are you sure?'

'Of course. I'm going to need you around anyway, to help me learn. Maybe I can even get to grips with that bloody stove. And once the baby's born, I'll be on hand to help you.'

'I think it's a brilliant idea,' Giulia said. 'And of course we'll all pitch in, won't we?'

'Absolutely,' Piero said, and Lorenzo nodded in agreement.

'I'm going to have another baby to play with!' Beatrice

screamed in excitement, jumping up and down behind her mother's chair. Agnese seemed relieved at her family's acceptance of her news and even managed a weak smile.

'This doesn't mean you're off the hook, young lady,' Dante told her, helping himself to another glass of Luisa's juice. 'Your mother and I are going to want to have a very long talk with you.' But his expression mellowed as he drank, and I knew that everything would be all right.

'If you're going to stay, you have to get that work done on the cottage,' Piero said. 'You said the roof leaked sometimes and I know the tiles in the bathroom need replacing.'

I thought back to the storm and shuddered. 'Yes, and I'd like to turn the garage into a work area, a kind of laboratory,' I said. 'So we can keep everything away from the children.'

'Good idea,' Giulia said. 'Who can we get to do the work?'

'I've already asked a friend who does that sort of thing, he did say he was available after the summer,' Lorenzo said. 'I'll give him a call, get him to come out and have a look, tell you how much it would cost.'

'Thanks, that's really appreciated.' I looked at everyone, suddenly proud to be a part of this wonderful family. All reprimands forgotten, they were talking about the future as though it had been planned that way all along. I realised that I loved Italians; such volatile people, quick to anger but also quick to forgive and rally round in times of need. It explained a lot about my own character, the part of me I couldn't control at times and that scared me so much. It was that part of me, I now realised, that had given me the strength to get through the bad times; and in trying to suppress it, I had turned to drink as a way of restraining the monster inside me. But in reality, I had only succeeded in making myself weaker, unable to face my problems head-on, destroying the only part of me that could have helped me get through it all. It had taken the cottage, Luisa's juice, and my Italian family to show me that I had the strength to change my life for the better.

I stayed with the others while Agnese and her parents had their 'long talk'. It was early evening when we eventually managed to say our goodbyes. They'd agreed that Agnese could come back to the cottage with me, and we'd move her things gradually during the week. Aunt Liliana hugged her daughter tightly as they kissed each other's cheeks.

'I'm not leaving forever, Mamma,' Agnese said, but I could see that her eyes glistened with tears. It was the first time she'd left home, and it was a wrench for all of them.

As Agnese and I made our way back to the cottage, the first heavy drops of rain began to fall. By the time we reached the front door, gasping as we ran, it was pelting down. I closed the door. We looked at each other and burst out laughing.

'We look like two drowned rats.' I giggled. Agnese's hair hung limply, her clothes plastered to her body as she dripped over the floor. I imagined I was no better. Bella came trotting along the corridor and looked at us as if we were mad.

'I guess you need to go outside, Bella.' She glanced at me in disdain, turned around and went back to her cosy spot on the rug in the living room. 'Can't say I blame you. But you're going to need a pee sooner or later.'

I turned to Agnese. 'I'll go and get us some towels to dry off, and some clean clothes.'

'Okay. I'll make a hot drink to warm us up.'

I ran upstairs and picked up a few things, taking my time. The cottage seemed strangely silent, and there was no aroma of coffee in the air. I glanced down the stairs and noticed that Bella was no longer on her rug.

'Agnese?' I called.

'Down here,' came her voice, slightly muffled. Frowning, I went downstairs.

Agnese was sat at the kitchen table, her back rigid. She glanced up at me as I entered the room, and I saw she was crying. She was holding tightly on to Bella, who was growling, her hackles raised.

'What's–?' I began, and then I saw him. Standing by the sink was Mark.

44

'What the hell are you doing here?' I snapped. Mark looked shocked. 'Well?'

'I popped round to see you.'

'And you let yourself in?' I could feel the anger building up inside me.

'The back door was unlocked,' he said, glaring at me. 'I wasn't expecting to find *her* here, though.' He jerked his head towards Agnese.

'Funny, that. The last thing *I* expected was finding you in my kitchen. I told you I never wanted to see you again.'

Bella started barking, straining against Agnese's hand.

'Bloody dog!' Mark shouted, and lunged forward. He grabbed Bella by the scruff of her neck, dragged her to the back door and swung it open. She snapped and snarled, managing to catch his arm with her teeth as he threw her outside. Bella landed on her feet and turned, leaping towards him, only to crash against the door as he slammed it in her face.

'That's better,' he said, looking at his arm. His jumper was ripped; I hoped she'd managed to break the skin underneath too.

'I wanted to see if you'd changed your mind, and we could try again,' he said, rubbing his arm. 'I didn't think I'd find this welcoming party. What's she doing here?'

I passed the towel to Agnese, realising she was still soaking wet. She took it from me without speaking. The storm was directly overhead now, evidenced by the low rumble of thunder. Rain pattered against the windows, driven by the wind, and a flash of lightning lit up the sky briefly. I hoped Bella would find shelter, she would be terrified.

'Agnese lives here with me.'

'What, best of friends already? That was quick.'

'We have something in common. We're attracted to dickheads like you. It helped us bond.' I clenched my fists, and wondered how to get rid of him. What the hell did he want?

'Is she a drunk too?'

'I want you to leave. Now.'

He smirked. 'That's not very hospitable of you, Jen. I thought we were friends.'

'You thought wrong. Go. Or I'll call the police.' My mobile was in my handbag by the front door, but he didn't know that.

He stopped smirking. 'Look, Jen, you threw me out the last time I was here. I think I have a right to know why. You've avoided me since then, and you don't answer my messages.'

He leaned against the kitchen counter, arms folded, watching me. I was amazed by his attitude; the bastard was calmly turning everything around, knowing full well he was the guilty party. I noticed Agnese twisting the corner of the towel in her hands, almost snarling as her anger took over. A loud clash of thunder made us jump, and sent rattling vibrations throughout the cottage. I heard Bella barking outside, and thought about running over to open the back door.

Agnese threw the towel down on the table, and turned to face Mark. 'Why?'

HELEN PRYKE

'What?'

'Why did you betray me?'

'Betray you?' He looked confused, then laughed. 'Oh, you mean with Jen?'

'Who else?' she snapped.

'We were over, remember?'

I could see Agnese shaking. 'We were not over. The day Jen arrived, you called me and said you needed a break, time to think. A couple of days later you apologised, and we were together again.' Her chest heaved with emotion. 'I didn't know you were seeing Jen as well, otherwise I'd have told you to drop dead.'

'Nice. We weren't really together, though, were we? You wouldn't let me anywhere near you.' He shifted his weight on his feet, fists clenched by his sides, and two red dots appeared on his cheeks.

I frantically tried to think of some way to defuse the situation.

'Because you were acting weird,' Agnese blurted, standing up and facing him. 'You kept texting and phoning me, demanding to know where I was, what I was doing, who I was with. I couldn't deal with it. First you dumped me, then you wanted to know my every movement. I was so naïve. You told me that we would leave Gallicano, get away from everything here, and make a new start. How stupid I was to fall for all that.' Her face was white, her body rigid as she spoke.

'I wasn't to know I was dating the ice maiden,' he snapped. 'Leading me on, then pushing me away after we slept together a couple of times. I'm not used to women turning me down.'

'No, you just get them drunk if they refuse you,' I said, my voice bitter. 'You really think you're God's gift to women, don't you? Instead, you're a sad divorced bloke who blames women for all his problems. You need to get a life.'

His cheeks flushed red. 'Why don't you go and drown yourself in a vat of wine?' he hissed. He turned to Agnese. 'I suppose I could give you a second chance. I know I came here for Jen, but you're the one I really want.'

'Go to hell. I wouldn't touch you with a barge pole. Especially not now.'

'What does that mean?'

I touched Agnese's arm. 'Nothing,' I said firmly. 'You're leaving.'

'I'm pregnant,' Agnese said, her head held high as she glared at him.

'Pregnant? You're joking.' His face drained of all colour.

'Yes, she is, and no, she's not joking,' I snapped. I'd have preferred she said nothing, but the damage was done. 'And she doesn't want you involved. For the last time, leave.'

He raised his arms and strode across the kitchen. He shoved me with all his might, and I fell sprawling to the floor. I hit my head hard on a cupboard and remained there, stunned, for a moment. Unable to move, I saw him grab Agnese by the hair and drag her across the room to the hallway.

'You bitch! No one treats me like that,' he snarled. Agnese screamed in pain as she tried to pull away from him. He slapped her face. 'Shut up, or I'll slap you again,' he said, his face centimetres from hers. I saw her recoil in disgust as flecks of spit hit her. My head thumping, I tried to get up, but my legs wouldn't obey.

'Agnese,' I called, scared for her. I could hear noises as they went along the hallway and Agnese whimpered, either from pain or fear, or probably both. I struggled to haul myself up, and grabbed a bread knife from a drawer. Staggering into the hallway, I could see that they were almost at the front door. Bella barked incessantly, her claws scraping at the back door. The thunder was almost constant, booming and crashing around the cottage, the mountain storm frighteningly powerful in its fury. I could hear the rain bouncing off the ground, the roof, the walls, adding to the cacophony of noise all about us.

'Let her go, Mark,' I shouted. He turned, and raised his eyebrows in surprise at the sight of me leaning against the wall, panting, a long knife in my hand.

'You're not going to use that,' he sneered. 'You haven't got the guts.'

'Try me,' I replied, but my head throbbed again and I felt sick. I bit down hard on my lip, trying to stay upright.

'Nice try,' he said, and reached for the door handle. Agnese kicked and screamed, twisting her body in her desperation to escape. He shouted at her, but I couldn't understand what he was saying, everything was spinning and my ears were buzzing. He pulled open the front door, with Agnese still yelling, and as I sank once more to the floor I saw a black figure silhouetted against the night sky, rain bouncing off the umbrella it held above its head.

'What the hell is going on here?' Mum exclaimed in her so very British accent. The world faded around me as I fell to the floor.

45

I drifted in and out of consciousness, the sounds of shouting and screaming mingling with the storm raging outdoors and within my head. I had no idea how long I was out, but I eventually opened my eyes to the sight of Agnese, Mum and Bella hovering over me, identical worried expressions on their faces.

I tried to move and groaned in pain, pinpricks of light flashing in my vision. Bella shoved her cold nose against my face, making me wince.

'Lie still, Jen,' Mum said, pushing Bella away. 'You've had a nasty bump, it should pass.'

'M-Mum? Wh-what are you doing here?' I asked, confused.

'I took an earlier flight. I was supposed to get here tomorrow, but I decided to come sooner. Good job too, by the looks of it.'

'Agnese?' I mumbled.

'I'm okay,' she said, her voice trembling slightly. 'More shocked than anything.'

I grimaced. 'And M-Mark?'

'I've given him an hour's head start, then I'm calling the police,' Mum said grimly. 'I couldn't believe it when I arrived, it was like all hell had broken loose. I could hear the screaming and yelling, and

I was about to break the door down! And when that, that piece of *shit* opened it, dragging poor Agnese by the hair, I saw red.'

Mum rarely swore in front of me. I couldn't help but giggle.

'I hit him with my umbrella and demanded to know who the hell he was and what he was doing,' Mum said. 'I had no idea what was going on.'

I smiled. 'Poor Mum. What a welcome.'

'He ran out of the house pretty quick, I can tell you. I shouted that he had an hour to get out of town, but I don't know if he heard me over the rain.'

'Just like a sheriff from the Wild West.' I laughed, then clutched at my head. 'Do you think I could get an aspirin or something? My head's killing me.'

'Let's get you into the kitchen and we'll make a nice cup of tea,' Mum said. The two of them helped me up, and we walked to the kitchen with Bella quietly padding down the hall after us. I sat down, grateful that the room had stopped spinning. Agnese busied herself putting a saucepan of water on to boil and prepared the teacups. Mum glanced at the clock.

'I guess it's time to call the police,' she said.

'Is that really nec–?' I began, but Agnese interrupted me.

'I'll do it.'

'Are you sure? I don't mind doing it,' Mum said.

'It'll be my pleasure,' Agnese stated.

'My mobile's out in the hallway, in my bag,' I told her. She nodded and left the kitchen.

'So,' Mum said, breaking the silence. 'Want to tell me who that slimeball is?'

I lowered my gaze, embarrassed. 'He's... we had a thing, then I found out he's the father of Agnese's baby.'

'She's pregnant?'

'He found out tonight, and didn't take it too well.'

'I saw.'

'I guess you didn't expect to find all this when you arrived.'

'You can say that again. When I saw you lying there in the hallway, I wanted to kill him, but then he ran off.'

'I-I'm sorry, Mum.'

'What are you sorry for? It wasn't your fault, was it?' I shook my head. 'I'm glad I arrived when I did.' She reached over and squeezed my hand. 'Agnese seems nice, she was as worried about you as I was.'

'I can't believe that,' I said, knowing what a worrier Mum was. 'Yes, she's great. We get on really well. Mum...' I hesitated, not knowing how to tell her. We could hear Agnese talking in the hallway, a soft murmur interspersed with pauses as she listened to the voice on the other end.

'Go on,' Mum urged.

'I've decided to stay,' I blurted. 'Take over from Great-grandmother Luisa and become a healer. I feel like I've found my calling.' I waited for the explosion. But it didn't come.

'I'm so proud of you,' she said instead, brushing a tear away from her eye. 'You've changed so much since I last saw you. You've become the woman I knew was always there, hidden beneath the alcohol and problems. I told you there was magic in this cottage, didn't I?'

I started to cry too. 'Being here has given me time to think, to get rid of all the baggage I had in England. The family has helped a lot too, especially Uncle Tommaso and Bella.' I glanced down at the mongrel, head on my feet as always, ready to protect me with her life. 'And yes, there is magic here, you've no idea how much.' Mum looked quizzically at me. 'I'll tell you everything, I promise. You're right, I have changed. For the better. I found the recipe book,' I added.

She gasped. 'The book. Liliana told me about it when I came

over, it was all very hush-hush and mysterious. Really, you've got it?'

Agnese came back into the room before I could reply. 'The police are on their way over to take statements,' she said. 'And they've sent a patrol to go and find Mark. I hope they arrest him and throw away the key. Now, what about that cup of tea?'

It was obvious we weren't going to get much sleep that night. Two *carabinieri* arrived twenty minutes later and questioned each of us in turn, then told us to go to the station the next morning and make a formal statement. They said other *carabinieri* had been to Mark's house but there was no sign of him. We were glad when they left, but as exhausted as I was, I couldn't face going to bed. I knew I'd stay awake going over the whole evening in my head until it drove me crazy.

'I reckon we're all going to have trouble sleeping,' Mum said, as if reading my mind. 'I think we should stay together tonight. How about we use Luisa's room?'

As I lay down between Mum and Agnese, I thought how lucky I was to have them there with me. Our breathing slowed to a deep, regular rhythm, finally relaxing as we took comfort in each other's presence. I heard nails clicking on the tiled floor and Bella nudged the door open with her nose. I patted the bed and felt it sag slightly as she jumped up. Agnese groaned and moved a little, then everything was still once more. I let myself fall into unconsciousness as Bella lay across our legs, as much in need of us as we were of her.

46

Mum, Agnese and I went to Aunt Liliana's after going to the police station to give our statements. We agreed beforehand not to say anything about Agnese's pregnancy, as she didn't want anyone else in the village to know. Instead, we told them that Mark had been unable to accept that I didn't want to see him anymore and had gone crazy, threatening the two of us. The police reassured us that they'd do everything in their power to find him, and said that he'd probably never show his face again. But we knew we'd find the strength to deal with it, if or when necessary.

Aunt Liliana burst into tears when she saw Mum and hugged her as if she'd never let go. Then she took one look at my bruised head and ushered us into the house, demanding to know what had happened.

'Get the family here and we'll tell you,' Agnese said with a sigh.

Aunt Liliana muttered something, but made a tremendous effort not to question us right away. She phoned everyone and ordered them over for lunch, accepting no excuses.

'I haven't told them you're here,' she said to Mum, beaming

through her tears. 'They'll love the surprise.' She glanced at us and frowned. 'You'll explain everything when they get here.' We nodded.

She took Mum by the arm and led her away, chattering non-stop, and I smiled at the bemused look on Mum's face.

'I bet she'd forgotten how overwhelming Italians can be,' I remarked.

'Especially Mamma,' Agnese said.

Lunch was a riotous affair, with the whole family around the large dining table. Mum, Agnese and I told them what had happened the previous evening, using the same story we'd told the police. After their initial shock, they accepted the facts once we told them the *carabinieri* had everything in hand.

I knew I would never reveal what I had found out about Great-grandmother Luisa either. As open and loving as my Italian relatives were, there were some things they would never be able to comprehend, and I instinctively knew that it was better to keep her secrets to myself.

We left the house in good spirits after dinner that evening, and slowly made our way back through the village to the cottage. Bella greeted us with raucous barking as we opened the front door, throwing herself on us and covering us in doggy kisses.

'Yeah, we missed you too, Bella. I'm sorry you couldn't come with us, but Aunt Liliana doesn't like animals in her house.' I buried my hands and face in her fur. 'Come on, I bet you want some food, don't you? And probably a run in the garden too.'

'I'm going to bed, Jen,' Agnese said. 'I'm done in, it's been a long day. My family can be very... tiring.' She winked, and Mum laughed.

'Yes, it's been lovely seeing them again after all this time, but it's like they don't have an off button,' she said, and giggled.

'Tell me about it,' Agnese replied dryly. 'Well, goodnight, both of you. I'll see you in the morning.'

''Night,' we both called.

'Cup of tea?' Mum said, raising her eyebrows.

'I've got something even better,' I replied. I grabbed a bottle from the cupboard in the hallway and went into the kitchen.

'Jennifer,' Mum said.

'It's not wine, Mum.' She gave me the look. 'Honestly. I thought it was...' I paused, embarrassed as I remembered how I'd turned the cottage upside down looking for anything alcoholic when I first arrived. 'I only drank one glass and had the most peculiar experience, but I didn't have the usual hangover the day after. I thought it was really strong home-made wine, then Agnese told me she'd helped make it, and that it was only juice. Luisa hadn't let it steep enough time to ferment and become alcoholic.'

'Really?' Mum looked relieved, and I couldn't blame her.

'Agnese promised me it's only fruit juice. We couldn't find the recipe in the book, though. It was just before Luisa died, she probably didn't have time to write it down.'

'The book.' Mum seemed in awe of it. I almost laughed but managed to stop myself in time.

'Here.' I got the recipe book from the cupboard and put it on the table. Mum looked at it as if she were afraid to touch it.

I poured us a glass of juice while Mum leaned over, holding her hand to her mouth. I knew how she must have felt, finally setting eyes on this ancient heirloom. 'Can I?' she said breathlessly.

'Of course.'

She slowly turned the pages with the same reverence Agnese had shown.

'Look here,' I said, pointing to the list of names at the front of the book.

'Wow, the first one was written in the 1300s,' Mum exclaimed. 'Agnes. Do you know anything about her?'

'No, unfortunately, but I'd like to find out who she was.'

'And here's you,' she said, sniffing loudly.

'Mum?'

'No, it's okay. I'm so proud of you, I knew you'd find your way sooner or later. And at least I can go back to England knowing you're in good hands.' She winked at me. 'I'm pretty sure Liliana is going to be keeping an eye on you.'

'And you'll be the first to know everything. She'll be straight on the phone to you.' I handed Mum her glass. 'Here, taste it. It's pretty good.'

She sipped carefully. 'Incredible, it tastes exactly like wine. You even get that warm feeling in your tummy as it goes down.' She drank again.

'See, Mum, this is the magic I was telling you about,' I said, sipping from my own glass. 'The wine – juice – it opens you up to certain... things. I don't know what they are, maybe they're memories, imprints left behind by the others, but I saw...' I stopped, not knowing how to explain what had happened to me.

'Tell me,' Mum said.

'Shall we go out into the garden?' I suggested. She picked up her glass and stood. I whistled to Bella, who obediently trotted behind us.

Outside, the leaves of the trees rustled in the cool breeze. The full moon lit up the night sky, bathing the garden in its silvery glow. As we made our way through the garden, the dragonfly appeared and flitted around our heads, flying in a figure of eight, its wings humming. We stopped and watched as it settled on the rim of my glass, its streamlined body outlined in the moonlight. Neither of us said anything and even Bella remained immobile.

The familiar dreamlike sensation filled me once again. Even

my breathing seemed to slow down, as if an eternity passed between one breath and another, the Earth changing as eons flowed by, mountains rising and falling, oceans covering the land and receding once more; and then the dragonfly fluttered its wings and sped off into the night. Time returned to normal, but I felt different somehow, as if I'd really lived for all those millennia instead of my brief thirty-one years. I turned to Mum and saw that she was affected as well.

'Jen,' she whispered, her eyes glistening with tears.

'It's okay, Mum. I felt it too. It was so...' I couldn't find the words.

'Magical,' she finished for me, finding the perfect description.

'Come, I want to show you something,' I said, taking hold of her arm. I led her down to the Grove and opened the gate. It looked different in the moonlight; the bushes and trees stood out in stark contrast to the darkness around them as the cold light reflected off their leaves. Everything seemed to be carved out of marble, a black and white representation of this garden that was normally a riot of colours during the daytime. I thought back to how it had looked when I first arrived, the fruit trees covered in pretty blossom that blew about my head.

Mum stopped just inside the gate. 'I remember helping Luisa here. She had a huge wicker basket, and would point out exactly what she needed. I'd pick the berries and leaves she needed for her remedies. The only plant I wasn't allowed to touch was...' She turned around, searching until she found it. 'That one.'

'Ah, good old belladonna,' I said. 'That's deadly nightshade to you and me,' I added.

'Yes, I remember her saying it was poisonous. She used it in her potions?'

'Oh yes, it's got quite a few uses, in tiny doses, though. Come, do you remember this?' I led her to the grave in the middle of the garden.

'Vaguely. Wasn't someone from the family buried here? I did ask Luisa about it, but she changed the subject.'

I took a deep breath. 'There's a three-day-old baby buried here. Malva. She was Gran's daughter.'

Mum gasped. 'Daughter? She had another daughter?'

'Yes. A couple of years before she moved to England. They said she killed her. Except she didn't.'

'What?' Mum whispered, her face pale.

I sat down on the ground next to the grave and patted the space beside me. Mum lowered herself down, gingerly touching the ground to see if it was damp. Feeling it was dry, she sat down with a groan. Bella ran over and lay down behind us, head on her paws.

'Okay, tell me everything,' Mum said.

So I told her the healer's secret.

47

Incredibly, Mum believed me. Never once did she make a face, or try to interrupt me, or say anything. She listened. And when I finished, she cried. We sat there together, beside Malva's grave, hugging each other while Mum wept on my shoulder. Then it was my turn to listen while Mum spoke.

'What Luisa did may seem unforgiveable to someone from my generation, and in particular yours. But we must remember how hard things were back then for women. It was practically impossible to get out of a bad marriage. "You've made your bed, now you lie in it",' she said, mimicking an old woman's voice. 'I can't even imagine how hard it must have been for her, especially when she discovered what Ernesto was doing to Bruna. It must have been bad enough knowing he was sleeping with other women from the village and having to endure their taunts, but sleeping with his own daughter?' She shuddered. 'That would have driven anyone crazy, even a strong woman like Luisa. And losing Antonio to measles, when she was able to cure every other child in the village. That must have broken her heart. Losing a child is so...' She stopped and looked at me.

There was something in the way Mum was looking at me;

with pity, yes, and understanding, but with something else, something deeper. With pain. She was looking at me with a profound pain in her eyes. I gasped.

'Y-you never wanted to talk about my babies–'

'Because I lost my own,' she finished, tears pouring down her cheeks once more. 'Three. One before you, and two after. At three months.'

'Like me.'

'Like you. I didn't know if they were boys or girls. I never saw them, I couldn't say goodbye. One minute I was pregnant, the next I wasn't. They were gone, as if they'd never existed. There was just me in my hospital gown, waiting for the doctors to say I could go home and try again. After the third one, I gave up. I couldn't face it anymore, I didn't want to feel that pain ever again.'

I started crying too. All the hurt, all those times she'd stopped me from talking about my miscarriages, I'd thought it was because she didn't care. Now I realised that it was because she cared too much.

'I'm so sorry, Jen,' Mum said, as if reading my mind. 'I couldn't bear it, seeing you suffer like that, but I couldn't comfort you because the pain was too raw. I never got over my own losses. Your grandmother, she wasn't able to help me. I guess it brought back too many memories for her as well. I had to carry on, regardless, and I did the same to you. Can you forgive me?'

'I-I think so,' I stammered, overcome with emotions at this point. I felt the old anger resurfacing, and I tried to stop it, but it was too late. 'Why did you push me away that first time, Mum? My heart was breaking and I needed you to tell me it would be all right. Instead you told me to go home and have a hot bath, and try to forget about it.' My voice got louder as I spoke, and I could feel my blood surging through my veins, threatening to burst out in a fountain of hate and pain. 'Do you know what I did when I left your house?'

She shook her head, looking utterly miserable.

'I went to the nearest pub and drowned my sorrows. I forget what I drank that night, a bit of everything, I think. I remember the men crowding around me, egging me on, laughing and pointing at me. And I kept on drinking, swearing at them and even hitting a couple of them. Paul found me, I don't know how, and dragged me out of there. I was still screeching like a madwoman and grabbing at people's drinks, trying to get a last few sips. I don't remember any of this, he kindly told me everything later. The day after, I felt so ill, my head was pounding, and I kept vomiting. I couldn't face eating anything, but I discovered that it stopped me thinking about the baby. So I carried on, and each time I lost another baby, it got worse. I found ways to hide the bottles, hide the effects, carry on as if I was completely normal, but the only time I didn't drink were the few hours I slept every night.'

'Oh, Jen, I didn't know,' Mum exclaimed, trying to take hold of my hands. I pulled away from her, the pain still pouring out of me. I was like a wounded animal, afraid that her touch would hurt me even more. I wanted to keep my pain to myself but hurt her at the same time, make her feel exactly how she'd made me feel.

'I thought drinking was the answer,' I shouted, half-crazy with all the emotions running through me that had been trapped through years of angst. 'I didn't want to feel any more pain, I just wanted to escape from the world. Paul had his important job that kept him busy, so he didn't have to think about our babies. What did I have? A mind-numbingly boring secretarial job that I could do with my eyes closed, that's what. There was no escape for me, nothing to distract me. After the last time, I had to type up a report for Mr Pennington. He burst out of his office, asked what the hell I was playing at, and threw it back on my desk. I'd written the names we'd given to each baby, over and over again, instead of writing up his precious report.' I stopped, breathing heavily as I relived the scene once more in my mind.

'Jen, I am so, so sorry,' Mum said, her voice heavy with emotion. 'I will have to live with what I did to you for the rest of my life. I can't change the past, but I want you to know that I'm here for you now. I'm ready to listen to you, and to cry with you, for everything you've lost.'

And just like that the anger left my body, leaving me feeling like a deflated balloon. 'Oh, Mum, I feel so tired.' She took me in her arms and this time I didn't resist. Her love washed over me and began to heal some of the wounds I'd thought were too deep to ever be reached.

We stayed for a while like that, enveloped in each other's arms, truly mother and daughter for perhaps the first time in our lives. I reluctantly let go, the pins and needles in my legs too painful to remain in that position. I sat back, leaning on my elbows, and smiled weakly at her.

'Sorry, Mum. I didn't mean to explode like that.'

'It was about time you did. Feel better now?'

I nodded. I searched for something to say, not wanting to finish like this. 'What about Dad? Did he help you?'

She brushed the hair out of my eyes, smoothing it against my head. 'Your dad was fantastic. He gave me all the time I needed to get over each one. He took over looking after you without complaining, and he let me cry in his arms. I presumed you were getting the same support from Paul. And by the time I realised you weren't, it was too late. You'd already turned to drink, and he was divorcing you. If only I'd known how bad it was.' She squeezed my hand.

'Mum, it's okay, honestly. I could have come to you for help, but I was too proud. I wanted to show you that I could do it by myself. Only I couldn't.'

'This wine – juice – is pretty good.' Mum held up her empty glass. 'How about we go back inside and have another?'

'Good idea. Although I'd prefer a cup of tea right now.'

We stood, and Mum ran her hand over the headstone, then kissed her fingertips and touched the inscription. 'Rest in peace, Malva,' she whispered.

48

I woke up the next morning feeling a sense of peace that I'd been missing for so long. I stretched lazily, smiling as I caught the aroma of coffee drifting up the stairs. My mouth watering, I quickly got dressed and made my way downstairs, meeting Agnese on the landing.

'Hmm, smell that coffee,' she said, yawning widely. Then her face turned pale. 'Uh oh, I don't think little one likes coffee too much!' She ran to the bathroom.

I carried on downstairs and found Mum in the kitchen, standing over the bubbling percolator. There was a plate of croissants in the middle of the table, and three places were set.

'Ooh, how posh,' I said, giggling. 'You're spoiling us, Mum.'

'Oh, it's nothing. I was awake at the crack of dawn, so I went down to the village. Luckily the bakery was already open, and those croissants looked so inviting... et voila.'

I reached over to grab one, but she smacked my hand. 'Let's wait for Agnese, at least,' she scolded.

'I don't think Agnese is going to want anything this morning.' I winked. 'The smell of coffee didn't go down too well.'

Mum grimaced. 'Ah, the joys of early pregnancy. Now *that* I did experience. It was garlic for me, though. I'd start to feel queasy even standing next to someone who'd been eating it.'

'I couldn't stand certain washing powders, soaps or perfumes. I drove Paul mad. I kept sending him out to buy new ones until I found one that didn't make me feel sick.' We looked at each other for a moment, lost in our pasts.

'I think you should probably turn that off, otherwise it'll boil dry.' I pointed at the percolator that was still gurgling away. It was our usual tactic whenever we talked about babies: change the subject before it got too deep and painful. But this time it was different, this time we had both acknowledged our memories, and our losses. It would take time, but I was positive we would get through this and come out stronger.

Agnese joined us a few minutes later, looking a bit pasty but otherwise in good spirits. Mum patted her hand.

'I've made you a herbal tea. Do you think you can manage a croissant?'

Agnese looked at me as I brushed away the powdery icing sugar residue around my mouth, and sighed. 'No thanks. I think I'll stick with the tea for now.'

'We'll save you one for later.' Mum picked up a croissant and put it in a paper bag. 'Before greedy guts here eats them all.'

'Oi!' I tried to say, but my mouth was full. We burst out laughing.

'Speaking of later,' Mum said. 'I bumped into Liliana at the bakery. I've invited everyone over for lunch on Saturday. Hope that's okay with you.'

'Yes, that's fine,' I replied, finally swallowing my mouthful of croissant. 'It's about time I paid them back for their hospitality.'

Mum and I spent the next few days together, precious time that we would hold in our hearts forever. Agnese refused to join us on our walks in the surrounding countryside, saying she wanted to try out some recipes for salves that Giulia could use after the birth. I was grateful to her for giving us those days. We walked for miles, leaving early in the morning with the autumn mist still hanging low over the ground, slowly dissipating as the sun's rays warmed the earth. And we talked about everything. Mum told me about her life, from growing up with Bruna to being married to Dad, and her grief at losing him when I was little. I could hardly remember either of them, so it was like getting to know them all over again. We also talked about the babies we'd lost, bringing up emotions we thought we'd buried years ago. We cried, we hugged, we even managed to laugh every now and then; but most of all, we listened to each other.

Saturday there was a hive of activity in the cottage. Mum and I spent the morning cooking and preparing, while Agnese tidied the cottage and sorted out the seating arrangements. I imagined it had been a long time since the old place had seen so much going on. When everything was well under way, I took a five-minute break and walked down to the Grove.

Some of the bushes had already finished their productivity and were starting to slow down in preparation for their long winter sleep. Others still had the last of their berries on the branches, and I made a mental note to pick them all before the first frosts set in. I stopped in front of the belladonna plant I'd trimmed back a few days earlier, and tried to imagine how Luisa must have felt the day she'd planned to kill Ernesto. I shuddered and turned away. The garden looked pretty, the sun-baked earth softer after the first autumn rains, the bushes and trees a healthy green. The tomb shone in the morning sun. I cleaned the white marble regularly every week, and kept the invading ivy at bay.

I felt proud of everything I'd achieved in the few months I'd been at the cottage. I would miss England, but my heart belonged in this place. My family was here – both present and past. It was my destiny to become a healer, I couldn't fight it even if I wanted to. As if to confirm my thoughts, the dragonfly appeared from nowhere and hovered above Malva's tomb. I held out my hand and it flew over to settle on my fingertips, its tiny legs tickling as its wings vibrated.

'Are you real?' I whispered, feeling the dreamlike state come over me once more. But before I could immerse myself in that other in-between world, it flitted off and disappeared into the sky. As I came to, I could hear a voice calling my name. For a moment, I thought it was Luisa.

'Jen! Where are you? I bet she's in the Grove, she's always going there.' It was Agnese, and there was someone else with her. I could hear a man's voice.

'Yes, I'm in the Grove,' I called back. Agnese came towards me with a stranger. I barely glanced at him, then did a double-take and looked more carefully. Tall and rugged, with light brown hair and a tanned face with weathered lines that suggested he worked outdoors, a faint outline of stubble on his chin and piercing blue eyes that glittered in the sunlight. I immediately named him Rugged Cowboy, then gave myself a mental slap and tried to act normally.

'Jen, this is Francesco,' Agnese said, oblivious to my state of confusion. 'Francesco, this is my cousin, Jennifer.'

'Ah, hi, Francesco,' I said, holding out my hand. He shook it, his grip firm and steady. I looked into his eyes and was lost.

'Lorenzo told me to come round, he said you had some work needed doing.'

'Oh, yes, of course, you're his friend he was talking about,' I replied. 'There's the garage, I'd like to refurbish that, and the roof leaks a bit in one of the bedrooms, so that'll need sorting.'

Francesco raised his hand to stop me. 'Why don't we take a look around? You can tell me what you'd like to do, I'll tell you if

I see anything else that needs fixing, and we'll start from there,' he suggested.

'Fine, great idea.' I could see Agnese's puzzled face, and felt the beginning of a blush on my cheeks.

'The rest of the family has arrived,' she said. I was suddenly aware of the sound of many voices, all talking at once.

'Have I come at a bad time?' Francesco asked. 'I can pass again tomorrow, if you like.'

'No, no, that's fine,' I said quickly. 'Why don't you stay for lunch? There's plenty of food, we must have cooked enough for fifty people.' I smiled at him.

He smiled back. 'If you're sure. It smells great. My mouth's watering already.'

'I'll set another place,' Agnese said, winking at me.

49

Lunch was riotous fun, and the cottage walls echoed with talk and laughter. Even Bella loved being the centre of attention, and patiently allowed Beatrice to put little ribbons in her fur. Giulia kept rubbing her stomach and grimacing; in her last days of pregnancy, even breathing was a lot of effort for her. I saw Piero glance at her worriedly every now and then, and whisper in her ear; she would pat his hand and reassure him that everything was all right.

Mum and Aunt Liliana talked non-stop, making Dante remark on how his ears would have to get used to the silence once Mum returned to England. Aunt Liliana slapped his arm, and went back to her conversation.

This time we served real wine, wanting to keep Luisa's bottles for other occasions. I politely refused each time they offered me a glass, and stuck to water. Agnese had placed Francesco opposite me, and I had plenty of opportunity to check him out without him noticing. He obviously knew the family well, and joined in with the banter, appearing at ease in their company. I guessed he was about my age, maybe a little older.

While we were waiting for coffee at the end of the long meal,

I stepped outside in the garden. Bella followed me, relieved to be away from the chaos for a while. We both stood under the horse chestnut tree, its wide leaves shading us. I leaned back against its trunk, enjoying the quiet.

'Am I disturbing you?' Francesco appeared in front of us.

'No, not at all. Are you escaping as well?'

'I love that family,' he said with a grin, 'but sometimes you need a break.'

We burst out laughing.

'I hear you're going to stay here at the cottage, instead of going back to England. Why's that? Won't your friends miss you?' He hesitated. 'Your husband?'

'I don't have that many friends back there, I lost them when I became an alcoholic,' I said. I thought it better to be honest straight away, to give him a chance to run.

'I see. And the husband?'

'Ex-husband. He left me, we're getting divorced.'

'Oh.'

'It's okay, I've moved on. Actually, I've moved away.' I gave a nervous laugh and mentally kicked myself. I sounded like an idiot.

'I'm glad you ended up here,' he said, then blushed.

I was amused, I'd never have thought he was as nervous as me.

'Thanks. And you? Wife, girlfriend?' Better to get everything out in the open from the beginning. I blinked as I saw the image of the dragonfly on my hand. The mist started to descend around me, and I wondered if it only ever appeared when something momentous was about to happen.

'Neither. I've never found the right person, you know, the one you click with right away,' he said, and paused.

'Of course. I've decided I've had it with men for the time being, I don't have the energy for all that anymore.' I spoke without thinking, but realised that it was true. Friends would do me just fine for the time being.

He coughed, and bent down to stroke Bella. 'So, do you want to show me what work you need doing?' he asked after a while.

'Okay. We should have time for a quick look, then we'll go back for coffee before they start talking about us.'

'Probably too late for that. They'll have us married by now!'

I was really starting to like this man.

As we turned to go inside, we heard loud shouting coming from the cottage. Mum flew out of the back door.

'Jen, Jen, where are you?' she called, not seeing us in her agitation.

'Here, Mum. What's wrong?' I said, making her jump.

'Oh, Christ, you almost gave me a heart attack. It's Giulia, she's gone into labour. She'd been having pains for a while. She's on the living room floor, about to give birth.'

'Oh my God, what do we do?' I started to panic.

Francesco placed his hand on my arm. 'First, you take a deep breath and count to ten.'

I did as I was told, and felt calmer. 'Now what?'

Mum smiled at me. 'You go and get clean sheets and towels, then you tell everyone to give you some space. You're the healer, remember. In the meantime, Francesco can take the men outside and call the doctor or an ambulance.'

'All right,' I said, grateful they were there with me. I gave Bella a pat and told her to stay outside, then followed Mum indoors.

In a matter of minutes, we had everyone sorted. Mum and Aunt Liliana went to collect some sheets and towels from upstairs, mainly to stop my aunt getting agitated. The men wandered outside, taking Beatrice with them, and I could hear Francesco talking calmly on the phone. Piero made to follow them, but Giulia stopped him.

'And where do you think you're going?' she asked, glowering at him.

'I was only...'

'You started all this, you can stay here until it's finished.'

'But surely you'll be better off without me?' he said, then noticed Mum shaking her head at him. He meekly went over to Giulia and sat down on the floor beside her. 'Comfortable?'

'Oh yes, never felt better,' she wailed, then grimaced as another contraction pulsed through her body. She groaned as we lifted her up and placed towels and sheets underneath her. I looked up at Mum and Aunt Liliana.

'Seems like this baby's in a hurry to come out,' I said, my voice trembling slightly. 'I don't know if the ambulance will arrive in time. What do we do?'

Aunt Liliana took a deep breath. 'It's not the first time I've had to do this,' she said, rolling up the sleeves on her blouse, 'but it's completely different when it's your own daughter-in-law. However, this is an emergency, we'll do what's got to be done.' She went to the kitchen sink and washed her hands under hot water until they were bright red. Without turning, she called to me and Agnese. 'You two had better scrub up as well. You might not get another chance to assist at a birth. Your great-grandmother delivered many babies in her time, but that was all part of a healer's chores in those days.' Glancing at each other nervously, we joined her at the sink. Finally, looking at our lobster-red hands with a satisfied air, she knelt down by Giulia's side and took charge.

Just as we heard the wail of sirens in the distance, Giulia's son made his appearance. Sliding out onto the fluffy towel, he blinked twice and tried to focus on this mysterious world he found himself in, then started bawling.

Aunt Liliana sat back, a tired, soppy grin on her face. 'Well done, Giulia,' she said, tears pouring down her cheeks. 'You've got a healthy-looking boy there.'

Giulia began sobbing as well, her body shaking after everything it had been through. Piero bent over and kissed her forehead, hugging her.

'You're a star,' he whispered, 'and I wouldn't have missed this for the world.'

We stood back as the ambulance crew burst through the back door and took over. In a matter of minutes, everything was cleaned up, mother, father and baby were on their way to the hospital, and the rest of us sat quietly in the living room.

'So, healers, are you still convinced this is what you want to do for the rest of your lives?' Aunt Liliana asked.

I nodded vigorously, and could see Agnese doing the same. 'Absolutely,' we said together. She hugged us, an expression of pride and joy on her face.

'I wish Luisa could be here to see this,' my aunt said, kissing my cheek. 'She would be so happy to know there are healers once again in the cottage.'

'Oh, she knows, Aunt Liliana. Believe me, she knows.'

50

The day before Mum was due to fly home, I showed her the wooden box I'd found in Tommaso's desk. She was intrigued by the dragonfly carved on the lid, and by Tommaso's drawings.

'It would seem that dragonflies have some significance for our family, but I don't know why,' she said. 'That night in the garden, there was a dragonfly.'

'It's not the first time I've seen it,' I told her. 'It led me to Malva's grave the evening I sat outside drinking Luisa's wine. There's some connection, but I have no idea what. I've even looked through the book for clues, but there's nothing.'

'I guess it's up to you to discover the mystery. Let me know if you do.'

'Of course. Do you really have to leave tomorrow? I'm going to miss you.'

'I'm going to miss you too. But your life is here now, and mine's back in England.' She hesitated. 'I might as well tell you. I've met someone.'

'Really?' I leaped out of my chair and hugged her tightly. 'That's wonderful, Mum.'

'Seriously, you're pleased for me?' There was doubt written all over her face. 'I thought, you know, your father...'

'Mum, you've been on your own for years. I think you deserve a bit of happiness at long last. I'm so happy for you. Tell me all about him.'

As we chatted, the years of bitterness and discord melted away, leaving space for growth and nurturing.

After she left, I wrote down Luisa's story in a notebook, in as much detail as I could remember. I got the wooden box out of my wardrobe, and took out Tommaso's dragonfly drawings. I put one at the back of the notebook, then tied it with a pretty blue ribbon I'd found. I went to place the notebook in the box, then stopped, frowning. There was something odd about it, but I couldn't quite place my finger on it. I stared at it for a few minutes, and then I saw it. The bottom of the box was a few centimetres higher on the inside than on the outside. Was something hidden in there?

I ran my fingertips along the edge, trying to find a catch that would release the bottom, but there was nothing there. I grabbed a knife from a kitchen drawer and tried to force it between the edges but there wasn't enough space to do it. Frustrated, I threw the knife down and sat back, thinking. I put my hands inside once more, pressing down gently, and suddenly heard a click. Hardly daring to breathe, I looked inside. The bottom was slightly askew. I took the knife again, and this time it was easy to wedge it underneath and lift up the piece of wood. Inside the secret compartment, I saw an oiled silk bag. I took it out and carefully pulled the drawstrings. I opened it and a rolled-up piece of material fell out, together with some dry, brittle leaves. I rubbed one between my fingers and recognised the scent from the unnamed plant in the Grove.

When I unrolled the material, I gasped.

It was a beautiful tapestry, similar to the ones that are usually hung on walls, only this one was about the size of a large sheet of paper. It was finely stitched with brightly coloured threads, and in the top left corner there was a banner with the words 'Famiglia Innocenti'. Underneath it was a coat of arms. I drew in a sharp breath as I recognised the scene depicted below: the cottage with its garden and the Grove, the village, the surrounding mountains; the whole valley was shown, the threads still with their original vibrant colours. On the right side of the tapestry, there was another scene of a typical manor house, village green, and surrounding forest. It looked to me like an English village with a maypole set up in the middle of the green, small figures dancing around it.

I stared at the tapestry, mesmerised by this incredible piece of artwork, and ran my fingertips lightly across its surface. For a moment, it was as if I was actually there. A soft breeze ruffled my hair, and I could hear children's voices shouting with joy as the figures started moving, performing their complicated dance, weaving in and out and between one another with the brightly coloured ribbons.

Startled, I dropped the tapestry, panting heavily. The voices continued to sing out, gradually fading away into nothingness as I returned to the real world. I took several deep breaths to calm down.

'I can't do this today,' I whispered. 'Sometime soon maybe, but not today.' I rolled the tapestry up, taking care to only touch the back of it, and returned it to the silk bag with the leaves. My hands trembled as I put the bag in the wooden box and placed the false bottom on top of it. I heard it click once more into place. I lay my notebook on top and closed the lid of the box, vowing not to speak about this with anyone. I put it back inside my wardrobe, and went downstairs to Agnese.

. . .

We spent our days learning how to become healers. Our first attempts were complete disasters; our creams were a lumpy mess that turned a horrible grey colour after a few hours, and our cordials were a cloudy, murky liquid with residue at the bottom of the bottle. But we learned from our mistakes, thanks to the detailed notes the previous healers had written next to each recipe, and our products gradually took on a more professional appearance. After testing them on ourselves, we then moved on to the family, where they had a surprising success. Giulia swore by our postnatal creams and recommended them to her pregnant friends. The villagers once more began beating a path to the cottage door to buy remedies for every ailment I'd ever heard of, and quite a few I hadn't.

We mastered the art of keeping a straight face while the villagers told us about their most intimate problems. The women were the worst, they had no qualms talking about their various bodily functions, but some of the men were pretty open too. For an Englishwoman who'd only ever heard the answer, 'Fine, thanks' to the question, 'How are you today?', it was quite an eye-opener.

Francesco started working on the repairs around the cottage, arriving early in the morning and usually staying until after dinner in the evening. Bella became his shadow, following him everywhere.

'You two seem to be getting on very well,' Agnese remarked one morning, noticing my flushed face. I'd been out in the garden explaining to Francesco how I wanted to turn the garage into a laboratory, and we'd ended up having a heated discussion about whether to get planning permission from the council.

'Huh,' I grunted, still feeling het up. '*He* says we can turn the garage into a lab without bothering the council. But I'd like to make it official, to save any problems in the future.'

Agnese giggled. 'Oh, Jen, you're so British when you talk like that. Try to remember you're in Italy now, things work differently here.'

'Really?' I said haughtily. 'Maybe you'd like to enlighten me.'

As she explained to me how Italian bureaucracy worked, I realised that I still had a lot to learn about this country. With all the rules and regulations that Italians worked so hard to break and get around as much as possible, it was completely different from England, and I felt a sudden pang of nostalgia.

'I guess I owe Francesco an apology then,' I commented when she'd finished.

'You can start by making me a coffee,' he said, as he came in the back door, shaking water off his coat. 'It's started pouring down so I doubt I'll be able to get much more done today. But if you like, we can start drawing up some plans for your laboratory.'

I snorted, still sore about being wrong. 'I guess. And I suppose you'd like lunch as well?'

'Thought you'd never ask,' he replied with a grin.

51

I had to admit that I liked having Francesco at the cottage. The leaky roof was fixed before winter truly set in, and he repainted the bedroom ceiling that had become discoloured with damp over the years. He slowly worked through the rooms, fixing every little thing, and just as slowly worked his way into my heart. Agnese and I had long discussions about him, but I was adamant that she, the baby, the cottage, and our work would come before everything else. I'd already been burned twice, I wasn't about to jump back in the fire again.

Agnese's pregnancy progressed, her stomach swelling as the baby inside her grew strong and healthy. Everything was all right with her routine check-ups, and we talked excitedly about the day the baby would be a part of our family. Whenever we saw Giulia with Antonio, it would only make us yearn even more for the future.

Winter in the mountains was very different from anything I'd experienced in England. It was unbearably cold; Agnese and Francesco burst out laughing the first time they saw me wrapped up in layers and layers of jumpers. After the long, hot summer, I hadn't been expecting this drop in temperature.

'You'll learn to adapt,' Francesco said, trying to hide his amusement. 'Wait till it snows.'

'Oh, something else to look forward to,' I said, shivering. 'Make sure the central heating's working by then, please.'

The best moment of the day was the evening, after dinner. We'd light the fire in the living room and collapse on the sofa, reading a book, watching TV, or talking. Bella would curl up on the rug, her snout hidden under her tail, and fall asleep, twitching occasionally.

'It'll be Christmas in a couple of weeks,' Agnese said one evening.

'Already?' Time seemed to pass so quickly here. I looked at her lying down on the sofa, one hand on top of her belly, the other holding a magazine.

'Uh huh. And look, there are some ideas here for decorating the cottage.' She pulled herself up into a sitting position with some difficulty and passed me the magazine. 'Maybe we can make some biscuits and cakes. We'll have to go to Mamma's for lunch, but we can make something to take with us. What do you think?'

'Great idea. Are you sure you're up to it?' She'd been getting tired lately, and often had to take a nap in the afternoon to get through the day.

'I'll be fine,' she said, patting her stomach. 'There's more than a month to go, I'm not ready for bed rest yet.'

For the next week or so, the cottage was filled with the sweet aroma of biscuits and cakes baking in the oven as we made our preparations for Christmas. Francesco brought us branches of pine that we wove around the banister and over the fireplace. We made a wreath out of holly and ivy, and hung it on the front door.

By Christmas Eve, everything was ready. Francesco turned up with an enormous bunch of mistletoe just before dinner.

'Here,' he grunted as he came through the door. 'I read somewhere that Americans use mistletoe at Christmas, so I presume the British do too.'

'Where on earth did you find so much?' I squealed in delight.

'It grows on the trees round here, there's loads of it. I'm glad you like it. What *do* you use it for?'

'You mean, you don't know?' I grinned wickedly at him.

'Obviously not, otherwise I wouldn't have asked.'

I broke off a small sprig and twirled it in my hands. Glancing at Agnese's inquisitive face, I decided to go for it. I moved close to Francesco, raised myself up on my toes, and held the mistletoe above our heads.

'And?' But I saw a twinkle in his eyes, and knew he already understood. I gently leaned over and kissed him on his cheek. He closed his eyes for a moment, as if expecting more, then opened them again with a disappointed expression.

'Later,' I whispered, feeling a thrill run through me.

'Jen,' Agnese said from behind us.

'I know, I know,' I said without turning.

'No, Jen, I-I think–'

I whipped around to face her and saw liquid pouring from between her legs onto the floor. 'Oh my God. It can't be, it's too early.' I saw her terrified expression and made myself relax, for her sake.

'Phone the hospital and let them know we're coming,' I said to Francesco. 'We'll take her in your car, the ambulance will take too long. Everything will be okay,' I reassured Agnese, feeling a strange sense of calm come over me.

The moment we had been preparing for during the last few

months had finally arrived; a little bit early, that was true, but I was ready.

I ran upstairs and got her hospital bag, which we'd only packed a week earlier. I could hear Francesco talking on the phone, and Agnese moaning softly as the first contractions started. Going back down, I nodded to Francesco.

'We're good to go,' I said. He squeezed my shoulder, then we put our arms around Agnese and gently helped her walk to the car. Bella stood at the gate, watching us forlornly as we sped down the road.

52

'You're coming in with me, right?' Agnese's anxious face stared at me from the stretcher, her brow furrowed as another contraction flooded through her.

I glanced at Francesco. 'Go,' he urged. 'I'll wait out here.'

Agnese held out her hand and I took it, wincing as she squeezed it tightly. 'Sorry,' she gasped.

I bent over and kissed her forehead. 'You can squeeze as much as you like, anything that helps. Let's get this done.'

Francesco touched my arm. 'Good luck, all three of you.'

I smiled weakly at him and followed Agnese into the delivery room.

I heard the nearby church clock strike two as Agnese gave one final push and her baby was born.

'Thank goodness she came early,' a nurse remarked. 'She must weigh at least three and a half kilos. Imagine if she'd gone full term!'

'Sh-she?' Agnese panted. 'It's a girl?'

I looked down at the squirming newborn. 'You've got a beautiful daughter, Agnese,' I said, stroking her hair off her sweaty brow.

'With a right pair of lungs too,' the midwife exclaimed. 'Listen to her yell.' The baby was crying her little heart out, so loud I was sure she'd wake the entire hospital.

'Do you have a name yet?' the nurse asked Agnese.

She closed her eyes and rested her head back on the pillow, exhausted. 'Yes.'

I raised my eyebrows; we'd often spoken about possible names, but Agnese had refused to choose one before the birth.

'She's going to be called Malva,' she said.

I clasped my hands in delight and felt like dancing. 'Oh, Agnese, that's perfect.'

'I knew you'd like it,' she whispered. 'Malva Luisa Innocenti.'

The nurses shooed me out of the room while they cleaned everything up and made Agnese and Malva presentable. I found Francesco sitting on a plastic chair, head in his hands. He looked up as I approached.

'Everything okay?' he asked. 'I heard a baby crying, was it...?'

I nodded and burst into tears.

'What's happened?' he asked, worried.

'Nothing,' I sobbed. 'It was so incredible, you should have seen how wonderful Agnese was.'

'And?'

I stared at him, not understanding.

'Is it a boy or a girl?' he prodded.

'Ah. A girl, a beautiful baby girl, and Agnese's called her Malva.' I burst into tears again, my emotions finally finding release.

'That's great,' he said, and I saw that he was welling up too. I'd shown him the grave some months before and told him about my miscarriages, so he knew how much this moment meant to me. I promised myself that I would tell him the rest of the story as soon as I could.

'Just wait till I call Mum, she'll be on the first plane over.' I grinned, imagining Mum screaming down the phone.

Francesco checked his watch. 'Give it a couple more hours, it's only one in the morning over there.'

'Really?' It felt like we'd been up for days, not mere hours.

'Signora?' The nurse poked her head out of the delivery room. 'We're about to move Agnese to the ward and take Malva to the nursery. Would you like to come?'

'Do you mind?' I said to Francesco.

'Don't be silly. I've already phoned the family, I'll wait here till they come.'

'You're a wonderful man,' I said softly.

He grinned at me. 'And don't you forget it.'

I poked my tongue out at him and followed the nurse into the room. The baby was wrapped up and lying in a cradle, and Agnese was almost asleep. She came to as I stood beside her, and yawned.

'I need a good sleep,' she said. 'They've told me Malva's fine, even though she's a bit early. You can go with her if you like, I want to rest now.'

'All right. I'll keep an eye on her for you. Get a good night's sleep and I'll see you in the morning. Oh, and Agnese.' I kissed her on the cheek. 'Happy Christmas!'

I followed the nurse pushing the cradle down to the nursery. She wheeled it in between the others, four or five babies who had been born earlier that day. I watched as she fussed over the baby and made sure she was comfortable, tucking the covers firmly around her.

She smiled at me as she left. 'You can stay as long as you like, just don't disturb the others,' she whispered.

'Thank you,' I mouthed and sat down in a nearby armchair.

The events of the night had left me drained of all energy and emotion, although I knew it wouldn't take much to start me crying again. I gazed upon the tiny bundles in front of me, full of wonder for these miracles. *If things had been different, how many would I have had by now?* I thought. *One? Two?* Paul had never mentioned how many kids he wanted; he'd never mentioned wanting to have kids at all. With a sudden pang, I realised that I had been the only one who had wanted a child. My marriage had been based on that desire and that alone. It had been destined to fail, right from the start.

I hoped it would be different with Francesco. Over the last few months I'd told him a lot of things about my past. He knew about my inability to have children, and how it had destroyed my marriage and my faith in men, and he knew about my disastrous experience with Mark. If there was to be any chance of us getting together, I wanted to have everything out in the open right away. I suddenly realised that I was seriously considering a relationship with the man. Malva, only a few feet away from me, symbolised a new start for my family, a way to put our past behind us. Anything seemed possible.

I jumped as she started to cry, a weak mewl that quickly turned into a loud, demanding wail. I picked her up, still swaddled in blankets, and looked down as she settled in my arms, falling back to sleep again. I'd had my doubts about whether I would feel jealous of Agnese being able to carry a child to full term, or whether I'd resent its presence and intrusion on our daily routine that would completely turn our lives upside down. But those doubts dissipated as I held Malva in my arms, her trust in me absolute, her innocence protecting her from all the hurt in the world. Malva was destined to be a healer, this I knew as certainly as if it had been written in stone. I bent over and breathed in her scent, my heart filled with unconditional love.

'Welcome home, Malva,' I whispered, delighting in the

baby's soft snuffling sounds as she moved blindly, searching for her mother.

Francesco found me in the nursery still holding Malva in my arms, tears pouring down my cheeks. He wrapped his arms around us, silent, transmitting his strength to me. I looked up into his face, and knew that I was where I belonged. Finally.

In the distance, we could hear the voices of the Innocenti, and I smiled as their footsteps echoed along the deserted corridor. I had everything I'd ever wanted: a family, a baby, and a good man. My life was complete at long last. I turned to greet them: my family, the people who had healed me.

THE END

ACKNOWLEDGEMENTS

I first got the idea for *The Healer's Secret* about ten years ago, which slowly evolved into the book you've just read. The story spans the centuries from medieval times to present day, but was too long for one book, so you can read the rest of Jennifer's story in *The Healer's Curse*. I will also write the stories of other healers from the Innocenti family, starting with Sara in *The Healer's Awakening*.

Since I published my first novel, *Walls of Silence*, in 2016, I have been on quite a journey, culminating in a publishing contract with Bloodhound Books. I've met authors and readers online, and have made some very good friends from all over the world, who I would love to meet in real life one day. Thank you to everyone who has given me their support and encouragement over the years, it's very much appreciated.

As part of my research for the Healer's series, I spent a few days in Gallicano with my husband and son a couple of years ago. We explored the area thoroughly, and took a guided tour through the Grotta del Vento. It was a wonderful experience, and they did actually turn the lights out at one point!

A big thank you goes to my editor, Morgen Bailey, for all her hard work on the manuscript, and to Bloodhound for the gorgeous cover. Thank you also to the rest of the team, Heather, Tara, the proofreaders, cover designers, and everyone else involved in creating our books, and to my fellow Bloodhound authors.

I'd like to thank the wonderful members of my street team, Sarah, Kayleigh, Monika, Kim, Krissy, Annette, John, and Abby for their support over the last couple of years. I also want to thank the wonderful members of the Facebook group Skye's Mum and Books for brightening up each day!

The last thank you goes to my husband, Ivan, for believing in me and giving me the strength to write this story. Your support and love mean everything to me, and every day I fall in love with you a little bit more. *Ti amo, amore mio.*

You can follow me on my Facebook page:
https://www.facebook.com/helenprykeauthor

On Twitter:
https://twitter.com/helen_pryke

On my blog:
https://pinkquillbooks.wordpress.com

On Instagram:
https://www.instagram.com/helenpryke

You can sign up for my newsletter at https://sendfox. com/lp/1knl41
for up-to-date information on my books, behind the scenes details, chat about life in Italy, and freebies/promos of other authors' books I think you may like.
I only send my newsletter out once a month or so, unless I have any exciting news to share with you!

Printed in Great Britain
by Amazon